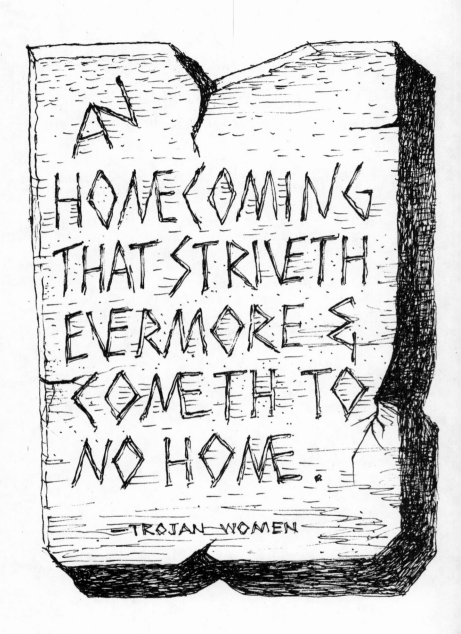

A HOMECOMING THAT STRIVETH EVERMORE & COMETH TO NO HOME.

—TROJAN WOMEN

PAUL GOODMAN

Parents' Day

Illustrations by Percival Goodman
Afterword by Taylor Stoehr

Black Sparrow Press/Santa Barbara/1985

PARENTS' DAY. Copyright © 1951 by Paul Goodman.
Copyright © 1985 by Sally Goodman.

AFTERWORD. Copyright © 1985 by Taylor Stoehr.

LIBRARY OF CONGRESS CATALOGING IN PUBLICATION DATA

Goodman, Paul, 1911-1972.
    Parents' day.

    Reprint. Originally published: Saugatuck, Conn. :
5 x 8 Press, 1951.
    I. Title,
PS3513.O527P3   1985   813'.52   85-9218
    ISBN 0-87685-635-0
    ISBN 0-87685-634-2 (pbk.)
    ISBN 0-87685-636-9 (deluxe)

TEXTUAL NOTE AND ACKNOWLEDGEMENTS

With the exception of typographical errors, and the modernization of the punctuation (omitting commas, etc., where a dash is also used), the text is that of the first edition, published by the 5 X 8 Press, Saugatuck, Connecticut, in 1951. The author's brother Percival Goodman has drawn a new set of illustrations to replace those he did for the first edition. I wish to thank him, and also to thank my friend Geoffrey Gardner for his help with the afterword.

T.S.

Parents' Day

CHAPTER I

one

The interview took place in the bedroom of the little apartment that the Director kept in the city. His wife was packing a trunk in the other room. Where was *she* going? I asked myself.

"Do you sing?" Dixon asked. "Tenor? Could you *support* a tenor?"

To have a place to live with my child, I was ready to tell any lies to get the job at this school. But this irrelevant question confused me.

He sat arched violently backward with his grinning head thrust forward. The poor fellow—was he deformed? He changed his posture but at once began to crack his knuckles. I felt that if he let go all parts at once, he would pounce.

I felt guilty before male persons in authority, and I held onto myself, held myself stiff, to preserve my dignity. "I like to sing, but I can't sing," I said.

He rubbed his palms in glee. "Good! Mark Anders sings bass . . ."

He himself was the tenor that needed reenforcing; but he was not truly a tenor, but forced his voice thru his nose.

"Is your wife going on a trip? . . ."

I used, at that time, to have a kind of catch-as-catch-can intuition for the right stroke that would make me very intimate and necessary—until the inevitable reaction; and even while I was dealing the stroke I lived in fear of the future reaction. What I feared was to accept my warm intuition, that was the best part of me.

I said, with difficulty, "I have to have a place, right away, to live with my boy, because my wife and I have separated."

The frank avowal made me tingle. I breathed deep and relaxed. But I did not tell him that I was homosexual.

"Fine, fine," he said sympathetically. "Everybody's got some problem. I'll phone Mark right now and arrange an interview. He must decide."

"Can't it be decided *now*?" I wailed in despair. I took a grip on myself. "Who is Mark Anders?"

"He's acting director this year. I teach only the top group because I come to town for analysis. You're supposed to fill in for me when I'm away."

"It's none of my business," I said cuttingly, reacting to my despair at the delay of a day, so that I would have said anything to get the solace of a little victory—but I was at my wit's end—"that seems to me to be a bad arrangement for Mark, for you to be around if he's the director."

"Michael deVries—he's the one you'll love!" said Dixon, rubbing his hands, "he reads everything. But his problem is a reading-reversal. Do you know about reading-reversals?" He started on rhapsodic technicalities about adolescents I did not know; that I would have listened to with interest, because I was a good teacher; but in my situation they were grating.

"Who is your analyst?" I asked, to cut him short.

"Oh?" He named a well known woman.

He went into the other room and spoke to his wife, and Mae Dixon, a small brunette, came in to discourage me from taking the job; but I saw this was a ritual procedure. She explained, with a certain vehemence, that the living was rough, there was no privacy, some of the people were hard to get on with. The doglike look in my eyes told her that these things were beside the point.

I was glad, I found it hopeful, that the interview took place in a neighborhood of the city where artists lived. This was the environment of my friends. This was where our school came from; and I knew that I'd be happy at our school.

Dixon came back. "The cook is a pupil of Busoni!" he cried. "She'll give you lessons. Do you play?"

Parents' Day

While I stood at the door he made the telephone-call, explaining that I was exactly the right sort, that I could teach Latin, French and History and had an *insight* into Mathematics and Physics; and all of this was true enough.

two

Usually on a train-trip I could enjoy a moment's pause, a pause to display a happier character, because it was a period in-between. But this trip was too brief, the towns came pell-mell. I could hardly plan what face to put on when I arrived.

The name of a town we passed stirred an old meaning: my family used to vacation there before I could remember. A State hospital for the insane was now located in this region. The rolling farmland, not too far from the city, was the reasonable location for hospitals and schools; just as in my mother's time it was the place for vacations. As the city spread, the place for vacations became the place for these institutions. These were unnerving thoughts.

I got off the train and 'phoned the school. They told me to look for the truck unloading vegetables and driven by Dorothea who was wearing blue jeans, I could not mistake her.

— She stared at me with toothful amiability and hungry curiosity; I thought that it was a girl of fifteen, mentally defective, ravaged by troubles till she looked nearly middle-aged. They had sent me, I thought, to a school for deficient children. I wanted to run away but I did not. With pounding heart I helped her unload baskets of beets.

She was a gentle, cultivated Dane, of about forty, and spoke English rather better than mine, but a little careful. "Won't you have a cup of coffee after your trip?" she invited me and led me into a place.

"Where is your little boy? Tony—his name is Tony?"

"He'll come later. I don't have the job yet."

"Oh you'll do. I'll say that you unloaded the beets without being asked."

"That's just why I did it! to establish myself here—with

11

'Oh you'll do. I'll say you unloaded
the beets without being asked."

you—concrete act—" that is, in order to keep myself from running away because I thought she was a mentally deficient adolescent.

"I am to take care of Tony; I get all the odds and ends. I have three of my own. Teddy will hate Tony and will try to murder him, but he's not quite strong enough—he's five too."

"I take it," I fished, "that *Mrs.* Dixon is going away on a trip?" I fished in troubled waters. I gave the impression that I knew more than I knew. I longed to be accepted.

Dolly did not become reticent, but expatiated; and I learned many valuable things, that solidified my sense of belonging in this place. That Dolly Homers herself was in full flight from the war, and one of her warring impulses was never to return to her husband.

The war was raging everywhere in the world and we were trying, in retreat, to get a little quiet and one flash of happiness while we lived.

The school was some untidy houses down a back road, and a larger dark red building of peculiar mien, of a plan that you could not read off from the facade, a building that would serve as a symbol for the insides-of-mother in a bad dream. Whatever I saw seemed untidy and out of the way, like myself. As we drove up the road, I did not notice the lovely brook and the contour of the hills.

The doctor, in an open white robe, was examining each of a long line of children as they passed before him into dinner. He examined the eyes, the glands, the respiration, and he asked a question.

And there was a new child, who was hanging back. She would not talk to the doctor, nor to the children, nor to anybody. She was wearing baggy trousers that came up to her armpits; she sank her head between her shoulders and peered above the waistline like a turtle trying to withdraw. But she was trapped in awareness and could not withdraw further.

three

Mark Anders, acting director, took me to his apartment in the dark red building. We were not sympathetic to each other. He was tall and had a pleasantly homely face, but he held his back and neck stiff. He was younger than I but looked older, and I looked younger than I was. Because we were cold to each other, he tried to be more than kind. He played the professional and questioned me on methods of teaching, and this annoyed me, for I felt that it must be taken for granted that I was a good teacher.

As for me, I was haunted by the need to explain what I was doing *here*, as if the prima facie explanation that I had to make a living and had no home for my boy did not suffice. I elaborated a long lame lie about wanting to spend a year at a country-school in order to learn some details of community-living, because I was preparing a book on communities. This lie, except in intention, was of course a deeper truth than my truths. And indeed, as I spun it, fortified by my need to make a living and find a home for the boy, I understood the reason for the coldness between Mark Anders and myself.

It was that some of us, most of us here — like myself, or Dolly Homers, or the refugee doctor, or Sophie Nordau whose husband was overseas in the war, or Lawrence Dixon who was committed to take his father's place in his father's school — we could not get another job; our job was bound to a place that we could sink into or vanish into, and this was the place. It was ours. But Mark wore a presentable tie and collar; at other times he changed into proper work-clothes to lead my big boys in some manual work that he enjoyed because it released what was pent-up in him, that he could not release otherwise. What was *he* doing here, at our school? He could always find another job. (If one of us had to leave, it would be he!)

I waved aside his questions and began to question him, as befitted my greater age and experience.

He said that he was working toward a degree in education, and he moved about the apartment to show me his notes. "I'm afraid I disagree with your thesis," I said firmly.

14

"We'll have time to talk about it later."

He had met his wife at our school; their baby was born at our school. His wife passed thru the room; she was drawn and somewhat over-gay. He gasped with asthma and my heart went out to him.

In the dark strange building they had set themselves up a little apartment, carefully furnished and finished. The sun shone in brightly. The books and files were orderly on new shelves that must have taken him considerable labor to make. They were wrong to put so much of themselves in an environment where they would not be happy. I felt warmly toward him and put my hand on his arm.

"This crazy building," I said, "just coming up here now — I never saw such a stupid plan."

"Is it? Maybe it is. I never thought about it."

"Kids aren't kept in here, are they? It seems to be offices and assembly."

"We keep the smallest ones here, in the other end. There's good hot water." He turned on a tap and the steam rushed out, with snorts and gurgles.

"Not my boy! won't be kept here! . . . I'd rather have him with me . . . Well? When do you decide if I am to teach here?"

"Why, I think we can try you out. We can try each other out."

"That's not very satisfactory," I said bitterly. "If I have to bring my child all the way out here. He can't have too many changes."

four

The question was often asked amongst us: How did *he* come here? — that is, from what kind of difficult or broken home the child was sent to our school.

The question also: And how did *you* come to come here? — from Frankfort or Baden, or perhaps sent as an ambulatory patient from the State institution nearby, or being a war-widow, or that it was convenient for a person having a child and no home to come to a school to teach.

Sophie's children showed signs of their father's absence,

especially the little boy, as if he had been assuming his father's traits and had suddenly been stopped short, with half a character.

In principle it was an ideal arrangement for parents and children, far better than a private home. We were a community. Our children had the presence of a parent, to love and console them and be individually concerned for them; but the authority over them was shared by many, by all the teachers. The authority was less tyrannical, more avoidable, and did not have to be faced alone, for all the children were brothers and sisters. No parent would intervene directly for his or her child; yet the child would come freely to our rooms. The voices of love and of authority were not the same voice.

The misfortune was that we did not adopt this better arrangement as free choosers, but we brought into it our old disasters.

How did *he* come to come here? And how did *you* come to come here? To this question there were not many gentle or happy answers.

I came there, I think, because of my unfinished childhood. It is said, "Those who cannot do it, teach it"—and what if the subject is the art of being happy? The teacher will come where the children, the other children, are even now repeating the disaster for him. I used to have a recurring dream, of being called on to recite and being unable to find the text in the book, or being again and again asked the incomprehensible question. I came here to review those primary operations in arithmetic and the simple Latin verbs: that are really simple problems: what are the genitals for, and where are mama's and why are there two sexes, and where do the babies come from, and what is the meaning of zero?

five

Thru the autumn twilight I used to walk the half mile to Lawrence Dixon's young people. From a house on the way sounded a melody of a recorder. The brook was lovely and there was a contour of the hills. I improvised a wordless song. By the time I arrived it would be the allegro of a sonata: I would keen it, cry it, growl and shout the climaxes, something frightful (I was ashamed to be overheard and yet I sang it out), as if the stretto trill would vibrate and snap the strings of the world. I came breathing softer and deeper.

On the columned porch, or cycling in figures on the road, or playing an unlikely ball-game among the trees on the lawn, were the beauties I wanted to embrace. (I refrained from doing so.) Mae Dixon had prophetically enrolled them in the city, selecting those who would grow up at our school to be as beautiful as could be.

I looked at the boys but averted my eyes from the girls. For long ago, when I was that very age, threats and punishment, and ineptitude and hurt pride, made me turn from the girls to the boys for easy love; and this habit persisted by attaching to itself some earlier desire that I no longer remember; and this desire persisted by warding off some still more forgotten terror. I chose during my adolescence to avoid guiltiness by means of what eventually, when I was adult, roused much greater guiltiness. Surely it was in the guilty fear itself that I breathed softer and deeper, and in livelier pain.

Davy Drood was searching angrily for a ball in the brush, muttering "Bungler!" as if he were cursing the one who had lost it, but it was himself. The brush was dry and beginning to be leafless.

I walked to the spot and easily picked up the ball. I had at this moment a more than normal ability.

"How did you do that?" said Davy Drood.

"I did it because I wanted to very much."

"Hm."

"What kind of Welshman are you if *you* don't believe in magic?"

—Altho (because) for many reasons I held myself back, I knew how to attach these beauties to me personally by particular references and particular emphases.

I longed to move in an atmosphere of guiltless simplicity and ease. My behavior created at once an atmosphere of complicity and particular understanding. Later, Mark

17

Anders accused me of conspiring with the boys against the order of the school; justly, in that there was a conspiracy, tho I used my influence to preserve the order of the school. But was not the conspiracy, the sense of personal complicity between them and me, itself against the order of the school? Well, I preferred this relationship to a more lifeless one.

The more living it was, the more able to release love, the greater the anxiety. The fault was that we could not love without anxiety, but this was not our fault.

I came for the first time to see Lawrence Dixon's boys to bed. I was the "new man" and they threw water and pillows and barricaded the doors with chairs. Lucy, the housekeeper, kept the girls in good order, but they poked their heads out their doors to watch the rumpus. I allowed myself ten minutes of commands and idle threats and then composed myself placidly on the stairs with a pad and pencil.

"What's the matter? Are you mad?" said Michael, who was the roommate of Davy Drood.

"No. Obviously I can't handle the situation."

"That's right," said Lucy. "Lawrence Dixon will fix them tomorrow."

"What are you writing?" said Michael, "are you taking notes?"

"No. I'm writing a poem about war and peace."

It was important to me that these children should know that I wrote poems, and admire me.

"Why aren't you in the army?"

"I'm not in the army because I told them I wouldn't. I'd rather not discuss it tonight."

"Oh. Should I ask you again?"

"Yes, do."

"Are you going to tell Lawrence Dixon about the rumpus?"

"No. I don't see any reason why you shouldn't make a rumpus. Only, the rule is that I'm supposed to stop you, and since I'm new here I still obey all the rules."

"Oh," he said. "I like you."

"Naturally you like me, because you let off steam and the pleasure of it attaches to me."

"No, that's not it," he said. "It's because you said, 'Obviously I can't handle the situation'—and obviously you can't.

18

Nobody could handle twenty unless you're willing to beat somebody."

"Why couldn't twenty, or even two of you, beat me?"

"We wouldn't. If you hit somebody it shows you're really angry, and then there's no telling."

"Well, I'm not angry."

"Are you afraid to be angry?" He had hit it.

I finally looked up at him. He was leaning solicitously over the balustrade, as if he were my protector; and there were a few others.

"I'm not afraid of anything," I said coldly.

—Is it what I said? If I said it, I meant it truly, for I would not tell a lie or a half-truth to the boys, tho I would to Lawrence Dixon or Mark Anders. My image to the boys was my image to myself and one cannot intentionally lie to himself. Then if I said it, I meant that I was not afraid of blows, jail, or death, for I would clamp my teeth, hold my breath, and beat them. I was not afraid of disgrace or to say my say back, for I would inhibit my shame and stuttering and blurt it out. I was not afraid of poverty, I would do without. Yet if I said it, it was a lie; it was a lie in the sense that I could equally truthfully have said, "Yes, I am afraid of everything, of blows, and disgrace, and poverty."

Yet just this dual meaning was obvious to them! the meaning that answered to both the fright and the iron that was in most of them (except a few of the more cunning sort). These boys loved me, as I loved them, with a guilt and complicity reverberating from the earliest black hell. The tears came into my eyes because we could not love without anxiety. Davy was hanging over the balustrade.

"Tell me, Michael—you're Michael, ain't you?—Dixon spoke of you—and that's Davy Drood—I'm not going to say anything to Lawrence Dixon, but how the devil could he punish you in a place like this?"

"Lecture."

"Is that bad?"

"No. But with him there's no telling—what he'll do."

"What do you mean?"

They looked at me uneasily.

19

"He's a baby," said Davy. "He has tantrums. He might expel somebody."

"He's bad papa, but he expels you," said Michael, "instead of running away with an actress."

"Expel?" I said sadly. "Would he expel somebody?"

"Are you a good writer?" asked Michael.

"I am the best writer in America," I said.

"No no, he means it!" cried Davy Drood.

"Listen, you kids," I said angrily. "You'll find I never say anything to you I don't mean. I seem to joke, but I'm never really joking."

six

When thru the autumnal twilight I started out, to go to my girls and boys half a mile up the road, and several recorders were sounding, my little boy stood screaming after me in the road, "Daddy! Daddy! Come back."

He ran after me.

"No. You go back. You mustn't follow me. It's time for Dolly to put you to bed."

"No! No!" he screamed. "Daddy!"

I angrily carried him into the house. He did not stop wailing, but I fled away. My pleasure was spoiled.

The young people sensed an ambiguity, or incongruity, in my attitude, which they expressed by saying, "It's hard to think of you as a married man" or "as a father"; or "you look to be about eighteen years old, sometimes."

I avoided questions about my relations with Tony's mother, because I longed for the image that there were nowhere in the world difficulties of any kind whatever.

It was important for me to prove to these young persons that there was in myself no ambiguity, but a simple continuity between their friend whose erotic interest in them was evident, and the father of the little boy, and the teacher who taught them the same propositions that he had once taught to candidates for the doctorate at a great university. I had to *prove* the continuity, which in fact existed just when I was not trying to prove it but was acting it. But when I was proving it, and the more I tried to prove it, the deeper the ambiguity infected my own heart. I lost confidence in myself.

When I started out in the autumnal twilight, and my little boy stood screaming after me in the road, I returned and picked him up and said, "Don't cry, little Tony. I won't go tonight. Tomorrow morning you come with me and see what's to see there. Now let's go for a walk together."

We crossed the bridge and went a way up Shepherd's Hill. There were bursting milkweed pods, and the floating threads shone in the dry air in the rising moon. We turned.

"I don't want to go to sleep yet," said Tony.

"No sleep. Late sleep tonight. And no Latin. We'll build blocks."

In the big block-room, we built a bridge together, and each built a building of his own. My character was to build a structure of unbalanced cantilevers, kept firm by adding always more weight on the shorter arm, and so the whole grew more intricate and inter-dependent. Before I could see what he had made, Tony demolished his building with loud joy; but I did not want to knock down mine, and we left it.

Upstairs, Dolly and I sang the children to sleep. I could sing the American songs like "I Wonder as I Wander" or "Tenting Tonight," but Dorothea could sing songs in Danish and German.

In the doorway stood a little girl who had stolen out of the dormitory of the Second Group. It was Harriet, the turtle. She reached out her head to hear, but she would not talk.

The children slept. Dolly was quieted, and the more deeply disturbed, by the renewed presence of a man in her domestic scene. In an illusory way, the circumstances seemed to her better, almost as if she had chosen them, and an ocean away from the old ones. I did not find her physically attractive, tho she was dear in every way. I felt that I was falling down in my duty to be serviceable.

seven

At the Staff Meeting, the principal discussion turned on whether or not Donald Torgesson should be permitted to go home during the weekend to visit his mother. He was in the Second Group, and their teacher was Caroline Brandy-wine, a plain colorless young woman.

In meticulous detail Caroline explained the situation in the Second Group. When somebody went home, the little clique, the two Jimmies and Steve, began masturbating, and they tortured the children in Group I. Just this week she had finally got them all "in good shape." The new girl Harriet spoiled breakfast for them all by soiling her pants. Donald had a good relationship with his mother, but then he himself was thrown off when he returned, and boasted; this hurt, but if she would put it up to him not to boast because it hurt the others' feelings, he would be sensitive and intelligent enough to cooperate. This would have the effect of deepening his understanding of the social group. But it was too much to ask of him to sacrifice the trip altogether. On the other hand, some, especially Shirley, brightened up when Donny came back and boasted. Altogether, out of 18, whether he went or not was indifferent to about 9. If she could lay down a general rule, "no visits for anybody," probably there would be no protests. Donny still would not take down the picture.

Donald's mother was a dancer usually on tour; that was why he was at our school. Above his bed he had pinned up a nude photograph of his mother.

Caroline's explanations were interminable not because anything was petty or irrelevant, but because taken as a whole they did not add up to a conclusion nor even to a dilemma. They had the ring of primary experience, either the infinity of creative possibility or the impassive morass of the facts of life (one could not tell which). Her own disposition seemed to be "permissive," but one felt it was a learned permissiveness. In any case her behavior was punctuated by pointed fits of anger.

I sat on the edge of my chair, enthralled by the concern of so many, more or less wise and expert, for an individual child, an individual act of an individual child. Being new, I had resolved to say nothing. I was sensitive of my importance and sensitive of my immodesty. The result of deciding to hold my peace in any eventuality was that the room buzzed about me and, sitting on the edge of my chair, I had a painful crick in the neck.

Mark Anders kept feeding the fire and banging the logs with a poker so that the sparks cascaded upwards. He neatly chose a momentary pause and said, "All right. On the one hand Donny's going makes trouble in the group and it's not really necessary for him; on the other he gets something out of it."

This summation was fair, but it offended me; I began to stammer a protest. Everybody looked at me curiously and sympathetically, for they had often heard each others' characteristic opinions and now it was my turn to reveal myself. I suppressed my stammer by altering my voice and faltered in a high, strained tone, "The whole point of—of what she says is—the thick detail. You'd have to weigh it item by item. How? How? what do you do about incommensurate values? . . . Maybe if you *changed,* it would prove to be really necessary for him, as Mark Anders says."

Nobody said a word. The fire crackled and Harrison, the art teacher, petted his spaniel. I clenched my fists and now I was fighting mad, ready to demonstrate any absurdity.

Lawrence Dixon rubbed his palms wildly and sprang up and began to prowl. I looked at him in disgust. "In such a case," he giggled, "we cannot penalize happiness! Young Torgesson has a good relationship with his mother. That's his good luck. We must support the positive side. We cannot afford to quench radiance. It shines far. Shirley Thomas is made happy by it in turn. Do you want to reduce excellence to the level of misery? Hm. Hm.

"Furthermore, this happens after every Parents' Day." He unaccountably giggled. "It takes a week before they settle down. I say, Good! excellent! We do not want the troubles kept under. Let them out! It is an invaluable opportunity. What's more trouble for us in the short run is better for them in the long run. We have to live in the world we make, we

23

and our children's children."

This astonishing speech, full of the creator spirit, raised me to a glow of glory. "Yes! yes!" I wheezed. The others were more accustomed to Dixon's high style.

To me it was an infallible sign if a person said one true thing, for nothing comes from nothing, and the proposition, "we must not penalize happiness," was true. I gave my allegiance to Dixon. But what the devil was he giggling about?

"It's very well," said Caroline dissatisfied. "But I have only two hands, even if I weigh 130 pounds."

"You take out your aggressions on the children," said Dixon.

"Lawrence!" cried some one, shocked.

"That's the meanest remark you ever made to me, Lawrence Dixon," said Caroline. "You could have said it in private."

"I'm sorry," said Dixon, confused.

Bernardine brought cups and a pitcher of tea and at once everything became sociable. I was bewildered.

"What was the decision about Donny?" I asked Dolly Homers. "Is there no vote?"

"Vote? If there's a difference of opinion, it's permissive."

"Permissive to whom?"

"To Donny, of course."

"Ah. Does Dixon always carry?"

"No. But he's usually right. You'll see."

—I was not so sure. He spoke too close to my own sentiments, and my sentiments were suspect to me. Nevertheless, I was suffused with joy and pride at what seemed to me to be the big fact: that there was no vote! because all of us wanted, in a well-intentioned way, to reach unanimity. The aim of the discussion was to conjure up the good idea that all would spontaneously assent to. That there was this aim proved that there was a basis of mutual love.

"It is a beautiful meeting," I said, moved, to Mark Anders. "I never sat at a more beautiful meeting."

He was arranging music at the piano. "Do you sing? Lawrence says that you sing tenor."

"No, I can't sing. I told him I can't sing."

"But you *can* sing," said Dolly. "You sang the children asleep."

"I can't sing in parts. I listen to the others and follow their parts instead. I don't sing my own. I go off tune. I can only sing alone. I mean, I can't really sing alone either."

eight

I agreed to help Sophie Nordau's Group III with their play, *Race Problems.*

They had hit on a fine conception after seeing Griffith's *Birth of a Nation* and especially the scene where the negro soldier pursues the white girl, probably with no violent intention, and she leaps from the cliff because she is afraid of rape. The idea was to show how the anti-negro prejudice poisons and makes fearful and then brutalizes the souls of the whites. To treat the evils of race-prejudice, that is, not as usual in terms of the oppressed, but by looking inward.

They had created too many episodes and they asked me to be the critic. I came to Sophie's room to ask her how much technical help it was useful to give them.

She was distraught, her lovely thick hair was disheveled. After we had discussed the play for five minutes, I pushed the notes aside.

"What's the matter, Sophie Nordau? Did you get bad news from Sam—or none at all?"

"No. He writes—good news. I've been trying to write a letter to him."

She stood up and spoke firmly. "He says he misses me—my body. He masturbates with my picture. Things like that."

"Really? How long have you been married?"

"Nine years."

"Nine years! yes—Jerry's about eight."

"Why do you ask?"

"Why—I think it's strange. And a little funny."

"This is what I'm trying to write him. No—I'll read it myself."

I assumed that she wanted to omit or censor a passage,

25

but it was rather as if she needed to practice a firm tone of reading, as she read history to her class.

"Dearest Sam, We miss you very much. They miss you, and I miss you. I enclose new pictures that the doctor took.

"One sinks into this countryside, into it, like the rains; and after bloom the May flowers. It is out of the way here. Existence is remarkably well-rounded. I could tell you many humorous incidents. The group's creative play is going to be extraordinary—

"Look, Sam, you know that I think you, know you, to be every way a man. I should be *displeased, shocked, alarmed* if while you are there you did not have sexual relations with those women. You must come on many lovely women—I would fear something is wrong if you did not. I do not want anything, ever, to be wrong."

She stopped.

I said, "May I speak frankly? What you write there is fine, only—don't send it. What is the advantage of saying the obvious and spelling out a rotten situation? He knows how you feel; the fact that you can write it down shows that you know he knows it. He can take care of himself without advice."

"You don't *quite* understand," said Sophie. "I can't send that letter. This is the letter I must send him:

"Look, Sam I take it for granted that there are lovely women there and you will have those women—all the while being faithful to me, reviving my memory, waiting for letters, and so forth. This is bad. I do not want this at all. I do not want you to treat these girls as prostitutes. Because that is what it amounts to if you keep romantic ideas of me and don't give yourself as wholly as need be. See how learnedly I analyze it!

"Since you must have love—it is intolerable to me to think of my husband otherwise—please, for my sake really, do have it seriously. As we did. I am afraid of the consequences.

"It is so isolated here, so out of the way, so self-contained. This is when I see it close. But if I draw off a little, in imagination, to the vast perspective of the wide world, then we are crossed and infected by savage insanity. Destructiveness and self-destructiveness. It has deformed us to begin with. Can they blame us if we fall down?"

She burst into tears. I put my arm around her shoulders. "Sophie!—I shouldn't send that letter either if I were you."

"What letter should I send him?" she cried. "You're a man and I thought you could tell me what letter to send."

"I'm homosexual," I said. "Honestly, I can't face your feelings."

"Oh, this is something you tell yourself," she said impatiently. "Lord knows why you feel guilty—tho I could find out sooner than you ever will."

"All right," I said, nettled. "What letter do you *want* to send? I'm not the only one who's fooling."

"Yes! I want to say that I should like to have another baby. It's time. And what in *hell* does this war mean to us? And why did I have to come *here*?"

She shouted, in terrible anger.

CHAPTER II

The only real game, I think, in the world is baseball. As a rule people think if you give them a football or baseball, naturally they're athletes right away. But you can't do that in baseball. You've got to start from way down the bottom, when you're six or seven years old. You can't wait until you're fifteen or sixteen.

— BABE RUTH

one

Our young fellows came indolently to the ball-field, by twos and threes. Nothing with us was ever on schedule, and even when they were late they did not hurry.

Little Tony and Teddy chased each other around the bases, crying "Home safe! home safe!"

These little ones were a year younger than the age! a year younger than the age at which the principle of our game becomes important: to stand up there alone against the strange faces, and to venture on the dangerous bases, and to come full circle and get home safe.

Meantime the fielders, gatherers, reapers are crouching, the outfielders hovering like predatory birds.

One cannot do it alone. Brother! help!

— The sky was white and the grass was dry. A few came down the road. Davy and Michael emerged from the bushes along first base. A few girls played well enough to be in the game.

We played. They talked it up. Most of them did not play as well as I had expected. Nevertheless the game took fire. Davy Drood was easily the best—a beautiful outfielder who

29

ranged everywhere from the center and knew what was about to be hit and started with the crack of the bat; he was a place-hitter and it was impossible to keep him off the bases (but the others did not bat him around).

I was piqued at his excellence. I was, by choice, always on the other team. We could not lift a ball he failed to stifle. And it was impossible to keep him off the bases. My growing love for him was mingled with hatred and envy and I longed for him to drop the ball. Davy and I chose up the opposite teams, so we could hate each other. I longed to be the father of this perfection, repairing my damaged self — but it must be I who perfected it. The mixture of love and hatred fixed itself fatally and statically in my heart, like the twins who fought and could not be born.

Our tall boys stood up pathetically alone to bat, at the age of six or seven, facing the fielders. For one instant to blast the ball to hell.

To get home safe off the dangerous bases.

Droyt O'Neil was the biggest of the fellows and he was a strong hitter who could blast the ball almost to the brook. But he stood flat-footed off third base, and they picked him off by a throw.

Lefty stood up. "Yah Lefty!" shrieked Jeff Deegan from short. "Take off the wristband and see what you can hit! We know how you sprained it."

It was a mean remark. Being an innocent, I did not understand how they could love one another so, and be so cruel.

two

TWO EPISODES OF OUR BALLPLAYERS

Long after they were supposed to be asleep there were loud shouts and cheering from the large room. Lawrence Dixon rapped once and walked in. The flashlights winked out. He switched on the center light.

"What's up? Out with it!"

There was no answer. He looked them over and said to Lefty Duyvendak, "It's you. Stand up!"

The tall boy burst into tears. He was sixteen years old.

"*We* did it. It's not his fault," murmured some of the others.

"It was a rotten idea," muttered Jeff.

The boy's sobs did not abate, and their murmuring rose like the ancient chorus.

Jeffery Deegan got out of bed and, disregarding the director, touched his friend's head and said, "I'm sorry."

Droyt blurted from his corner, "He jerks off like everybody else, but he can't shoot. He tries and tries and can't. We laid bets to help him, to egg him on. So he was pounding away with the lights on him."

"Was it your idea?"

"I didn't bet, but I guess I egged him on more'n the rest." Droyt burst out laughing. "Why in hell don't you rap before you walk in?"

"It's not at all funny," said Dixon. "Don't get fresh, O'Neil."

"It *is* a little funny," said Droyt.

"It's not at *all* funny!" shouted Dixon. "You men know enough to know that it's serious."

"Oh Christ, we know that it's serious; you don't need to give us another lecture," said Jeff. "All the same why in hell don't you rap before you walk in?"

Dixon said, "I'm sorry."

"Well, what should we do for Lefty?"

"*You* don't do anything. Duyvendak and I will talk to the doctor. Go wash your face, Lefty. Do you want to sleep on the couch in the office tonight?"

"I cried out," said Lefty, "because of the loud click of the door. That's why I cried like a baby."

Another night, I went into their room to switch off the center light.

"Good night, lads," said I. In the dark, I kissed Lefty on the brow.

"Tell us a story," they called. "Tell us a story you made up."

"All right. I will tell you a story. But not one I made up. An old story—about the Greeks. The same Greeks that fought in the Trojan War.

"You remember the King, Agamemnon."

—I could hear them move forward with apprehensive

31

attention, because with a certain ring in my voice I said the words, *"You remember the King, Agamemnon."*

"Now after that war, he prepared to return home." And I started to tell them the *Oresteia* of Aeschylus: of the chain of signal fires on the mountain-tops, and of the messenger watching, and of Queen Clytemnestra lying in wait with Aegisthus. The image of the fires did not fail again to win belief and they settled back.

In his corner, Droyt O'Neil lit his flashlight. He began to work on the radio that he was assembling, but it was not to offend me, it was in fear.

I told only the bare acts of the story, but I did not spare any of the acts, the carpet, the bath, and the net.

And so finally I came to the disclosure of Orestes to his mother.

"Well," I told it, "the Queen was afraid. She threw herself on the ground in front of him, and she held him by the knees. He lifted up his sword. 'My son, my dear Orestes,' she cried, 'don't kill your mother. You'll feel sorry afterwards.' She thought that maybe he would relent, that means give in.

"But not Orestes! He lifted up the sword and he stuck it right in her heart!"

"Good! Good! Good for him!" screamed Droyt O'Neil with a joy that rings in my ears. "Oooh! I thought he'd give in just like everybody else. That's how it always turns out. *But not Orestes!"*

He leaped from bed and did a kind of dance.

The others were dumb with horror.

I did not dare to continue. "It goes on from there, the story goes on from there. But it's too long. I'll tell you the rest of it some other time. Get back to bed, Droyt."

I stood a moment, till they were quiet a single moment, and slipped away with my heart in my throat.

"Good, good," screamed Droyt O'Neil

PAUL GOODMAN

three

It was I who was yelling, *"Fair! Fair! Foul!* Whaddyemean, foul?" The ball had rolled to the edge of the brook. I don't remember who hit it. Our runners were streaming across the plate. There was no umpire. Droyt ran storming out to right field and jumped up and down on the spot: "Here's where it fell! here! here!" "Yes, even inside o' there, a little over!" "What foul? Who says Foul?" The other side roared with derision. It was inconceivable to me that I might be mistaken. My forehead was red hot. All were hoarsely bellowing.

"Joannie, did you see it?"

"Yes, I think I saw it," said the girl, the only spectator. "But I won't say."

"You won't *say?!* Whaddye*mean*, you won't say?!" Our boys began to jump up and down.

Davy's boys kept pounding their gloves derisively and saying, "Play ball! play ball!"

Tony and Teddy chased each other around the bases, laughing and crying, "Home safe! home safe!"

As if frightened by our vehemence, some of our boys began to waver. Lefty said he hadn't really seen it. Another said it might have been an inch one way or the other.

I picked up my glove and threw it down hard. "Jesus *Christ!* If *that's* the way you want to play ball! You'd think people had homers to give away."

"It was foul," said Davy Drood, over his shoulder, on his way back to the outfield. "If it was fair, I would have caught it. It was foul."

"O.K., O.K. Get the ball somebody. Let's play ball."

Our batter stood up there, whoever it was, whoever it was. The runners returned sadly to the bases.

Whoever it was, he had plenty of courage in his child-belly, for he hit it again, and we shouted.

The ball soared in what seemed to be the same arc, toward the same place, but this time I knew that Davy Drood would catch it. He started before the crack of the bat, and he raced behind the fielder in right, and he grabbed the ball out of the air.

The long arc of the ball was stilled. It was stilled.

But as for me—I was satisfied. With quiet curiosity I watched the runner vainly cross the plate, and the other one rounding third. The sun broke from behind the cloud.

There was the pause of the crack o' the bat, and the looming fielder losing his hat, the long arc stilled and life-in-death were there: there was no need but turn and stare.

I was satisfied. With quiet attention I watched the other runner rounding third base. I recognized—that—when the runner had rounded the bases and was fixed to start again—he had now rotated thru 360 degrees of angle: two whole straight lines. *But to do this he turned four times away from a straight line,* and therefore—

I walked behind the backstop and drew it in the dirt as follows:

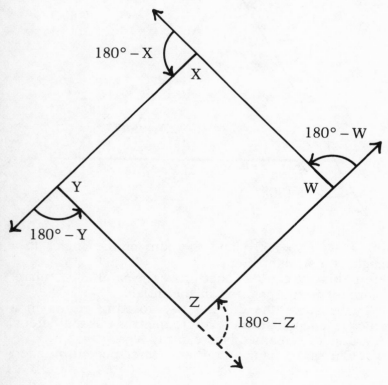

That is, turning away from the straight line each time, the runner had made the following turns,
$(180° - w) + (180° - x) + (180° - y) + (180° - z)$ and the sum of these turns equalled to 360 degrees.

Then, $720° - (w + x + y + z) = 360°$; and the sum of the interior angles of the quadrilateral equaled two straight angles.

They called out to me, "Hey, shortstop, play ball!" but with tears flooding my eyes I drew the theorem for the triangle:

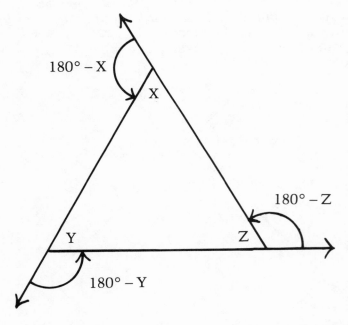

$540° - (x + y + z) = 360°$; and the sum of the angles in a triangle is a straight line.

From this one could at once prove the parallel postulate. I ran out to my position in the infield.

—To be sure, one did not use rotating points in a geometrical demonstration, but to me this was indifferent.

A grounder screamed between my legs.

"For Chrissake, hang onto them," screamed our pitcher.

four

I was walking back in joy with one arm around Davy's waist and the other around Droyt's, and Tony riding on Droyt's shoulders. *They* had won, but *I* had seen; and *I* was happy in my love for Davy Drood. Mark Anders caught up to us, and I slipped free and walked beside him.

"I can't make you out," he said in a friendly way.

"I can't make myself out," I said frankly, because I was well pleased. "Why?"

"Well—no offense—I should have thought—I should have thought you'd hate physical exertion. The way you burked the farm-work. But all right. But now you were screaming in that game like an Indian."

"Oh—but did you hear what they pulled!"—It was extremely pleasing to my image of myself to have been seen in that behavior of many years before, to which I had given in unselfconsciously enough. Now, not quite unselfconsciously, I described the incident in buoyant terms.

Mark Anders did not respond. We walked a few moments in awkward silence.

"If one gets into too intimate terms—with them—" he said at last, fishing for words in order not to be wrongheaded, "especially with *them*—I mean, it's hard to keep the proper distance."

"Ah. You mean one loses their respect and then can't teach them." I drove the matter at once to a logical formulation (an abstract one), as if I were going to gain great glory from winning a little victory in an argument. I was angry because he had dampened my joy.

"Take your own case," I said, with a simulation of earnestness. "You're fifteen years older than they; you have been to two colleges; you're a master of arts; you're a husband, a father, an experienced teacher. Isn't that enough natural distance without having to set up conventional barriers?"

He did not answer.

I was hot with anger and cold with anxiety. The anger was directed at myself; for the fact was that the argument that I was advancing with simulation, as if I were lying, was nevertheless my best truth, and I felt that it was true. Mark Anders' practice proved his mistake. With Sophie's group, just turning into adolescence, he did *not* preserve any distance; he gave himself wholly to them; and they loved, admired, and respected him. But with Lawrence Dixon's gang he was diffident, his words were often grating; he behaved as tho he were physically afraid of them (he was physically afraid of himself); and they hated and feared and did not respect him.

I thought that the reason for my own lack of integrity was that I was afraid that when he said, "You do not keep a proper distance" he meant to say, "You indulge yourself in physical contact with them." I was not wrong; consciously or unconsciously he did mean this. Even so! I did not think that this was wrong, tho I thought what I thought with guilt and dread.

My trouble was deeper, and more pervasive, and simpler, than I then feared. It was this: If I said a true thing, and I said many true things; even if I read it off from my plain experience or invented it by the spontaneous prompting of my heart and wit—nevertheless I did not feel that it was true! It was not true for *me*. It did not *justify* me.

As if a man should set up the syllogism: All persons are thus and so, and I am a person—yes! affirming both these premises—and still be unable to draw the conclusion, I am thus and so. How is this?

The cause of it is simple. I did not feel my body; and because our substance is the life of a body, I felt unsubstantial. And about the unsubstantial one does not draw true conclusions.

five

The recorders were infatuated with *The Little Shepherd* of Debussy. The climactic passage in the upper register was taken with various shrieks and howls, and the effect, in the earlier twilight—now that daylight-time was cancelled— was charming. As I started up the road Tony no longer stood in the road and cried "Daddy!" In order to feed my anxiety,

I went back to look into it.

"He's playing with Teddy in the block-room," said Dolly. "Don't go there."

"But I'm bothered because he's so quiet. Now he's adjusted to my going away. Maybe it would be better if he kept on wailing and chasing me. Now he has suppressed it."

"Not at all. It has nothing to do with you, don't be so vain. He chased you because he was afraid to go to sleep."

"Am I vain? Why is he afraid to go to sleep?"

"He was afraid to go to sleep because of the Dragnet. When he closed his eyes and began to drop off, suddenly Dragnet came in the window, with flying dogs and wolves on both sides. Then he woke up screaming. So he preferred to scream after you on the road, in the open, and put off the moment."

"There you are. What's happened to Dragnet?"

"We took care of Dragnet," said Dolly kindly. " 'Don't be afraid of Dragnet, little Tony. No, *be* afraid of him, and scream if you want. But I'd like to see him too. Take a good look, and draw me his picture. I'd like to know what he looks like—he must be scary. . . . He drew me about a dozen pictures."

She showed me a crayon drawing. It was terribly beautiful. Dragnet was scary. He had cavernous eyes, and at his four corners flew the dogs.

"Thank you, Dolly," I said.

. . . She drew back in alarm. "Hush! none of that!" she whispered. She put a bony finger across her lips. "People get crazy ideas. You know how Lawrence gossips. I can't, I *can't* let anything of that kind get to my sponsors. They'll make us *all* go back home. You can't begin to imagine what it's like—to watch your step—the way you Anglo-Saxons live."

I stared at her in stupefaction. She misinterpreted also the stare. I stiffened my shoulders against the duty to make everybody happy and satisfied.

"I don't bother about the older children," said Dolly. "But I detest watching Teddy grow up with American notions."

There was bloody howling below, from the block-room. I leaped downstairs.

The kids were battering each other with two-by-fours.

"Daddy! he's trying to break down the house you built. Make him stop." Tony had barricaded it with chairs.

"You bastard, you fuckin' bastard, you bloody fuckin' bastard!" screamed the Danish boy and threw a block in my face. I grabbed him. He kicked and pounded. His tough, squirming body was very strong.

"Go ahead, pound away," I said, "but not with blocks. I'm afraid of blocks. You have a claim to hate both of us." He battered me a couple of huge thumps with his head, then the body contact made him give in and he began to cry.

"Yes, little Teddy—it's all right, little Teddy," I crooned, rocking him. "Nobody can take mama away, you ought to know that, you're smart."

Tony wailed. For himself, for himself.

Dolly appeared and I got out, leaving them both wailing.

six

Because of the discovery I had made on the baseball field, I planned to start the course in geometry from the nature of the Plane, any existing visible plane—the blackboard or the floor would serve. What it means to move, or have direction, or have position and relation, on a plane surface. The salient fact (it was simply a matter of fact) was that on a plane four adjacent right angles, no more no less, complete the surface; or conversely, as I had discovered, that a traveling point can bound an area only by rotating thru four right angles.

(Besides this, I conceived an ambitious scheme—that was beyond my powers—of relating the nature of the plane to the definition of a straight line, "one that lies evenly," and to demonstrate that the straight line is the shortest distance.)

Because of my contact with Teddy's tough resilient body I knew that my soul was more resilient than tough rubber. I would rebound again and again under *all* the shocks of this miserable existence.

But being a frustrated and disappointed man, I was determined, before everything, to compel the young people—

whose measure of happiness annoyed me at the same time
that it enlivened me — I would compel them to respect this
abstract subject-matter. They must share with me my
respect for this beautiful subject-matter — that, also, I clung
too close to and stifled, so that I stifled my inventiveness.
(I attributed my failures to indolence, but I was not indolent.)

The phrases that I would use proliferated in my mind.
"Now for the first time in this school I want you to learn
something that is absolutely useless . . . In this class I'll
put up with anything except somebody saying, 'What's
the good of it?' He or she — do you hear that, Davy Drood? —
can get up and leave right now. . . . Some very great men,
some of the greatest men that ever lived, spent years of their
best effort on this useless study; we are going to try together,
we also — for I am just learning geometry myself, to — . . . Let
me write some names on the board —"

In my fancy, going up the road, I printed the names. But
I printed the name of Pascal —

"No — I'll rub these out. What I want you to pay attention
to now is just this flat blackboard. This flat itself — nothing
on it. Let's see if we can't find something about it that is
interesting. We mustn't be ashamed to say the simplest
thing. . . ."

seven

For two days following, Davy Drood cut the mathematics
class. I asked Michael why he did not come down.

They had the tiny room at the end of the hall on the
second floor. There was space for only a double-decker bed.
But the room was considered desirable and seemed to fall
to their lot without dispute, either because of their apparent
preeminence or because the other boys and girls felt a loving compassion toward them.

"He's mad at you in that period," said Michael. "He says
he won't come to that class."

"Why? Frankly."

"Well, you picked on him. 'Drood! did you hear that?
repeat it.' 'Drood, you're a grown boy, you know what a

reason is!' All that. He says you made him look a fool and made somebody laugh at him. He can't stand that, you know. He was so mad that he nearly cried—that's just my opinion, of course."

"Did I do that?"

"Yes, you did."

He looked at me, with his sophisticated leer—that was indeed sophisticated, but not in the way he imagined. "In my opinion, if it had been some other teacher, it wouldn't have been noticed. But you have the reputation of being gentle . . . Well, why? Frankly."

"Why am I gentle?"

"No, stupid. Why did you pick on him?"

"I did it because I love him. It's important to me that just he should get every detail. There, that's frank."

"I doubt it," said Michael. "If you loved him, it wouldn't turn out that he got mad. Besides, he says that the work is too simple, it's boring. He hates that."

"Well, is it?"

"Yes. It's not simple, but it's boring. Nobody sees what you're driving at. You keep on asking questions and never tell us anything."

"Hasn't anybody used that method here before? That's called the Socratic method."

"Listen, when you've been here as long as we have, you've seen everything. And we've seen that too. That only works when you're hopped up and have ideas. First you got to get us hopped up."

"Tell him that I didn't mean to pick on him. Or—that I did pick on him, because he has a good head and ought to learn something for a change. Or—"

"I won't tell him anything. Tell him yourself. It's not my business. If you ask me, frankly, he's lazy; he likes to sit on his ass and sulk and now he's got an excuse."

I went upstairs and rapped at the door of the small room. Davy did not bother to say come in, but I went in.

The room had the double-decker bed and a table and chair crammed in against the window. They kept their clothes in a dresser in the hall. The place had been built for a linen-closet, it was not a room at all. Two pairs of snowshoes were hanging from the ceiling. Davy Drood was slumped on the lower deck, practicing a studied disregard, and playing a dice-game. On the table was a little hectograph device he had gotten for his birthday.

"Oh," he said, "it's you."

The bed was neatly made, but it was littered with papers covered with lists of names and rows of figures. The youth rolled a pair of dice, and grunted, and marked down a figure.

"Do you play that game all alone?" I asked. "What is it? Kind of baseball?"

"Yes. How'd you guess? See, 10—he's out! Hartnett is up—10, after a 7 and with nobody on base, that's an infield out. Depending. See, 4. Ball one for Gowdy."

He stopped to mark down Hartnett's out.

"What! You played all these games today?" There were a dozen sheets covered with names and figures.

"Those! . . . Why, here's a boxful under the bed." He pulled them out. "That's only this season. I have six boxes full at our place up on the hill. See, 9. Strike one on Gowdy."

He was seventeen years old. He was the best athlete in the oldest group—which did not mean much, but he was a good athlete. He wrote the best prose in the school; he made the best paintings. Among many fine actors, he was a fine actor, tho he was handicapped by a peculiar thrill-less voice. He was medium small in size. He had thick lips and other irregular features all so purely modeled in a matte dark color as to win (not only from me) infinite interest.

"Strike two on Gowdy! Strike three! Struck him out!" He marked it down. "Chicago is leading, 4 to 2."

"Do you always play this game when you don't go to class?"

"Sometimes I just sit."

"What do you brood about?"

"Who says I brood?"

"I say so. How long have you been coming here?"

"Eleven years. I'm the longest one."

"Eleven years!" I cried. "Eleven years!"

"Yes. What's about it?"

"Eleven years! And you've been playing that game, and marking down the score, for six years? *Six* boxes full?"

"See, 4. Ball one on Collins. Sure. Why?"

"Why? It means something to me, but I'm not saying. It would be clear to you too if you'd just shut your eyes and think about it instead of rolling those fucking dice. Where'd you get the hectograph?"

"My mother brought it for my birthday. I don't know what to use it for."

I pressed a copy from the stencil. He had made a drawing of a steerman at the helm; the ship was keeling over.

"Listen, Davy Drood. One of us here is going to weep tears, and it might as well be me. I'm used to it."

I let the tear run down my face and wiped it away, embarrassed, but I did not turn.

"Lawrence Dixon's getting divorced," he said, "and Mae won't come here any more. Did you know that? Oh, you wouldn't know."

"Who told you?"

"Oh, we know it. She's to marry Frank Knightley."

"How do you study here? Double-deck too?"

"You should see it when they're all in here!" he cried with sudden animation, warmly laughing.

Almost every night after supper, the whole gang, girls and boys, crowded three deep into Davy and Michael's. It was the popular room.

I longed to be the second-father of this perfection, this misery. I was an artist; I wanted to touch myself there and make improvements, according to the material.

Also, by invidious comparison with my damaged self, I hated and envied him—because I was fatherless. But he also was no doubt fatherless (I knew nothing at all about it). He needed help, and sought for help, and I had an immense flood of pity and self-pity dammed up in me. Both compassion and self-pity. Also, I was indignant at what seemed to me to be obvious neglect: eleven years! Was this what our school was worth after all? If it could not make Davy Drood happy, whom could it make happy? Also, this crucial case was my justified vengeance for the hurt, past, present, and future, that that school dealt me; for *they* would say, "You did thus and so"; but *I* would say, "And what about Davy Drood? *You* had him for eleven years."

"Bungle! Bungle!" groaned Davy, as the dice fell 3. He took sides in the game, tho he played both sides. He marked it down.

I looked around. "It's interesting what you say about the hectograph—'I don't know what to use it for.' You know what that means, don't you?"

"You listen close, don't you? You catch everything and find a meaning."

"Of course. Everything has a meaning. Do you think there's not a meaning in the way the bed's made, *and* the papers strewn on it; do you think I don't know something about you from that? . . . When you say, 'I don't know what to use it for,' it means that there's some trouble with this thing that inhibits your ideas—inhibits means hold back. See, *I'm* holding back; look at my elbows. Maybe it's something about the thing, maybe it's something about the one who gave it to you."

"Oh?"

He said nothing, and I loved him for it. Any other man, woman, or child would have shown curiosity as to what something meant, what the way the bed was made meant, and the papers on it. But not Davy Drood. I smiled at the perfection of his defenses. I should have been disappointed if he had succumbed. Becoming a little happier, I hit on the right thing.

"Why don't you and Michael turn out a school newspaper—the *Blast*—no, the *Growl*. I'll show you what I mean. Here, look at this book: line after line neatly ruled. One little letter after another in each word, neatly spaced out, and one word after another filling up the line right to the edge. And each line under the one above it. Neat margins. Numbered. And then you turn over, and there's another page. All clipped to the same size. Do you know what *that* means? I'm a writer, and I know. It's a lot of shit all put in neat piles."

This caught fire. He enjoyed it. He repeated it. "One little letter right next to the one in front! No bungling! No typographical errors! What shit! rich, neat, smooth!"

One of the dice rolled on the floor under the table. I picked it up.

45

"We shouldn't make a paper because everybody knows the news anyway."

"Don't be childish," I said. "People want to see it said. In neat lines. This makes it have some sense."

He thought. "No. We'd get in trouble."

"A smart frenchman said that people would rather hear bad things about themselves than nothing at all."

He enjoyed this too and repeated it.

"I'll see you later," I said.

"Is that all?" he asked.

"Yes, that's all."

Any other man, woman, or child I should not have quit without kissing on the brow.

I learned again from Davy Drood what it seems I have to learn again and again, that one gains interest not by showing heartfelt concern, but by doing something objective and to the point.

CHAPTER III

What good can you expect from a day that
starts with getting out of bed.

— PETER ALTENBERG

one

Eliza was to come on the noon train, to visit Tony. I slept
badly, reviving the pain and agitation of the past year, that
I had finally fled from. I began already to hold my breath
for the moment that she would climb aboard and leave.

I dreaded that she would become pregnant by the man
she was living with, and this would mark the ending between us—a more definite ending than either she or I was
prepared to admit, altho unhesitatingly, as if inspired, we
took every step toward it. What I did not understand was
why it was precisely this happening, of her becoming pregnant by the other, that must mark that ending. But I was
swallowing the disgust of a very ancient treachery, before
I could remember (and that never came to pass); and I could
not breathe.

If it could have been achieved by a floating wish or a nod
of the head that would induce the floating wish, I should
not have returned to live with Liza. Certainly I did not want
her to be here at our school, agitating the calmness that I
did not yet feel. Yet hotly I painted to myself both these
unwanted pictures, in order to win a little triumph over the
interloper. Jealousy and hurt feelings made it impossible
for me to experience what I wanted, or what I was in fact
joyously bringing about.

47

two

Lawrence Dixon called an unusual meeting of the Staff for after breakfast, and there was speculation as to what was on his mind.

I for my part was not good for much at that time of the morning, even after a good sleep. It was not my custom to come down to breakfast at all. Awakened by Max's pounding the iron rail bent in a circle, I used idly to watch from my window the dogs gathering and barking, and the doctor inspecting his long line. They went in to eat, all was quiet again, and I dozed till the class bell. Today I was deprived of this last hour.

Dixon stood trembling before us, quite unable to conceal his feelings. His voice came from deep in his throat and was indeed his natural voice rather than the nasal tenor with which he used to nip one's ears. "I have important news," he said.

He read it off from a slip of paper, as if he could not remember the one sentence: "Today Mae, my ex-wife, is going to marry Frank Knightley. Our divorce was granted yesterday."

I do not suppose there was a single one of us, and not a single one of the kids, who had not already discussed this matter at length. There was an audible ripple of irritation that it was for this that he had interrupted the coffee.

"The problem," said Dixon, gasping, "is how to inform the children, because they are bound to find out sooner or later anyway. They will be upset. I am afraid they relied on us — too much, as it turns out. It's better if they hear the news by some formal announcement than by picking it up from hearsay and gossip." He could not go on.

"The man is quite demented," Dolly whispered to me. "He is living in a world of complete and total fantasy."

But what he said fitted into my bad dreams and I felt icy cold and nauseous.

Behind me, Sarah, the secretary, was describing the rigmarole by which all letters had been sent to California to be forwarded, in order not to reveal that they were going to Reno.

"All of us," cried Dixon, forcing his voice to a shriek, "all of us, I am one, wish the new couple every possibility of happiness. I have here a telegram from Mae wishing to be remembered to you all and saying that she can be relied on to do her best for the school in the future as she has in the past." He giggled.

By degrees the atmosphere changed from the grotesque to the embarrassing and to the pathetic. No one spoke.

Seraphia leaped up and threw her arms around Lawrence's body. She patted him and he patted her. I did not have the impression that this display was sympathetic to the rest.

She was again a small but opulent dark woman, like Mae, like the well known analyst, presumably like his mother. Tricked by the sameness of an external image, he would have surprises from them all.

She had been more or less present for two years, sometimes helping with the books in the office, sometimes doing the purchasing. It was not unknown for her in a drunken stupor to break a window at midnight.

—I am giving an uncharitable outward picture of these things, as one would give it to an applicant for a job, or get an outward impression of him for the job. But in fact we were not changing our places, not getting any new job, and we were not in a position to see uncharitable outward pictures.

Still trembling, Lawrence approached me and said, "Do me a favor. The one I am most concerned about in the whole school, about—this, is Davy Drood. You be the one to tell him. Influence him. He will listen to you. Make him understand that everything is—not changed. He is insecure."

"Do you think he would be very much upset?" I asked.

"Yes. He is the one that Seraphia and I are worried about, aren't we dear?"

"He *has been* upset," I said. "He already knows about it."

"Ah!" cried Dixon furiously, "his mother told him! *Damn* her!"

three

My first class of the day was Sophie's brighter 13-year-olds, whom I was beginning in Algebra. The chief determinant of our method together was the material fact that I had not yet had breakfast. We agreed to respect this inevitable fact and devoted ourselves to rapidly and thoroly running thru the exercises and problems in the textbook.

They were at the stage of adolescence when it still seems desirable to acquire the skills and attitudes of the grown-ups; they worked with a fury of sublimation; they came in with angrily precise questions and they found errors in the text. On especially sour mornings, I gave stiff tests, in which they invariably scored near perfection.

All of this enthusiasm, the thawing out of the Glacial Age (to which Ferenczi somewhere attributes the latency period of sexuality), redounded to my personal credit and reputation. It was among them, and thru their example, that I first became Oracular.

We met in the art-room, where the eastern sun poured thru the glass. They had the key and ordinarily were inside cleaning up the mess that Harrison had left.

But when I arrived now, the knot of them was gathered in front of the door, and Harvey Coldstream, the negro boy, was bitterly crying.

"*He'll* settle it! *he'll* settle it!" they cried when they saw me. "Don't *you* think that Harvey must be the slave on the slave-block?"

"Nothing else makes sense!"

"Don't get us wrong," said Adelman, "it's not to save grease-paint—"

"It's not for realism," said Jenny; they always knew exactly what they were talking about, I had ceased to be astonished at it—"it's the Symbol."

"Yes, it's the Symbol!"

"What symbol?" I asked.

"Don't you see? Here they are auctioning off the slave—'Step right up and touch him!' 'Good bones!' 'Big chest!' 'Lots of work in this baby!'—just as if it was an animal. And all the while everybody knows it's Harvey."

"That's not a play!" blubbered Harvey. "In a play it doesn't make any matter who's who!"

"What do you mean?" said Adelman. "There's such a thing as good casting."

"A play is an *illusion*," said Harvey.

"Oh! there's something in that." Smart Barney at once saw what he was driving at and changed his vote. They were infinitely judicious, they respected anything that was an idea. They were absolutely parliamentarian; on every issue they divided and counted heads. Their philosophy was a dogged attempt to follow the Eternal Reasons, like the stoics (and alas! the Eternal Reasons were nothing but my reasons).

"Sophie Nordau thinks you should play it."

"*If* I want, she said. But I *don't* want."

"What difference does it make who says what and who wants what?" cried Barney. "It's who's right that counts. It doesn't make any difference what *you* want."

They paused, and looked at me.

"I don't know the scene. How do you expect me to say? You know you mustn't ask me riddles before my coffee."

"O.K.," said Adelman the director. "Run thru the scene for him. Harvey strips to the waist."

"No, I *won't!*" The boy clenched his fists and shouted loud and true.

"Oh, *Harvey!* don't begin that again."

I intervened. "Please. He won't. He in fact won't. What's the use of talking theories?"

"But—" They hushed. The Oracle had spoken. ". . . All right, we'll get somebody else."

"Yes, do that."

The colored boy bent his head.

"All right," he said, "I will." The tears gleamed in his eyes.

We went into the art-room, that was littered with yesterday's drawings. Perhaps Liza would make a picture, I thought, while she was here.

four

When she got down from the train, looking beautiful in my eyes, and we spied each other, and she gave me her hand, I felt a lively pleasure.

It gave way at once to the beginnings of anxiety. I would watch everything from now on with mounting unease, and finally never draw a breath till she was gone—but what I was watching against, or watching *for* (it comes to the same thing), I did not know. She was too thin.

Her own good spirits lasted a while longer, and perhaps they would have lasted indefinitely, always, if my moroseness did not dash them. Perhaps what I was watching for was the moment that being with me made gaiety sad. She cried:

"I saw such a thing! Looking out the window at the drab old grass—then poof! bang! explosions of white, flame, purple—the box-cars on the other track going the other way; before you would take a breath, yellow, white, white, flame, *green!* Filling the frame, jumping out at you. Poof! Bang! You couldn't take a breath. Just this very minute. It's wonderful to be in the country and I'm happy as a fucking lark."

The train was pulling out. Her hands flew about the picture and made it clear. It was delightful to me to hear her describing something she had observed, as she used to. "Come in here, we'll have a cup of coffee," I said—I was annoyed that she did not at once ask for Tony.

It was a powerful bond between us, while it lasted, that she refused to bother her head and feel guilty about anything, whereas I, who felt guilty about everything, could not endure that anybody else should share the guilt and weigh me down. Eliza did not weigh me down in this way. Further, her forced unconsciousness gave me the opportunity to sit in critical judgment. But I would not express the criticism for fear of doing a hurt and being guiltier, so I soured my breast with plenty of unspoken judgments.

Nevertheless it was this same faculty of sitting in unspoken judgment, not without prudence and wisdom when my desires were not directly involved, that gave me great power at our school, among the children and adults both; for my judgments were strong, they burned with a quiet animosity.

Eliza saw at once that I had fallen in love with our school. I did not hide it, I made it clear that our people were the most well-disposed in the whole world, that no others were trying so hard to accomplish a good thing; that there were no other such demented people in the whole world; the children were beautiful and bright as could be; their plight was sad to break your heart.

And as we neared our school, the drab disheartenment of my inward struggles of the past year, that resulted eventually in my inability to want anything at all or to take any pleasure in myself, dragged down my steps, and I wanted only to flee from the presence of Eliza and from our school, for they were now inextricably bound. But I did not flee either. The next best thing was to begin devising little stratagems to hasten her departure before she had arrived. Before we turned into the back road, I pulled out a time-table and began to calculate the trains.

But Tony had been waiting where the road turned in, and now he flew to us shouting, "Mameee! *and* Daddy."

We had not thought of this simple thing. To Tony it was now an ideal picture: his mother and me together, with him looking on. An ideal picture, of what had never existed and would never exist on land or sea. I felt death in my heart, and Eliza did too. We took each other's hands, as Tony flew to her. There was nothing to prevent our enjoying our love except ourselves and our circumstances. Also the love that we did not enjoy was intervening elsewhere, and would continue to intervene elsewhere in the future.

"I waited a long time," said Tony, for he had come there at train-time, to lie in watch. Nevertheless, we had got there on time! before, as sometimes happens, one had swallowed his disappointment and gone back.

In both our hearts there formed the resolve, no matter how far we mismanaged our own affairs, not to disappoint *him* beyond a certain point. If only for his sake, we would remain amiably disposed to each other. We remained amiably disposed to each other because we had never given in, without reserve, to either love or hate. We still had some kindness and cruelty in store.

"Why shouldn't we live in the country all the time?" cried Liza. Tony walked between us, swinging on both our hands and making jumps. She said "we" as if it were obvious that we should live together again. Sore with jealousy and hurt feelings, I found solace in this little assurance. So our words and feelings and decisions remained always ambiguous; it was only our actions that seemed to be unambiguous — except that in the long run these too proved to be ambiguous (and this is the way one proceeds until he shortly dies).

At our school I firmly maintained the ambiguity. I told Lawrence Dixon, Dolly, and others that we were no longer man and wife, and I mentioned that she was living with another man. Also, I allowed no question but that we were man and wife and we were living apart for some trivial or unexplained reason. By this means I avoided recognizing my hurt feelings. Also, I did it because I felt guilty of the sexual coldness that had brought us to the breaking point. But everybody else seemed to understand the situation for simply what it was: that we were separated from each other and still tied to one another — nor was this unusual at our school.

To put this another way: it was important for me to be, and to make them admit that I was, the person who was happy with his wife and child (she being absent for some trivial reason); and also the person who had broken with his wife and was the sole guardian of the child; and also the person who had broken with his wife, but they two were careful not to separate too far, because of their child.

I was sympathetic with Lawrence Dixon's confusion; I was indignant at Dolly's mockery of it. I wondered how she could imagine that the decrees of a court eradicate the living actuality of the past.

five

Within a short time, as I hoped and feared, she made herself at home. She involved herself with Harrison and his art class and with Sophie's group rehearsing the general dance of their finale (by such means, when there are too many conflicts of plot one achieves harmony by going out of the medium!); she involved herself with Lefty, Droyt, and Jeff Deegan who were helping backstage. She called my attention to the beauty of the girls. There was nothing extraordinary about her success, because we artists always at once find ourselves a community, wherever the spontaneity of young people affords us a bridge (but this community is, like our art, an imitation of happiness). But also she became especially friendly just where I found it difficult, with Mark Anders, with the doctor, with Dolly Homers, on a level of witty courtesy that I could never attain—for, harassed, I drove too close, or, the same thing, defended myself too soon too deeply.

Meantime Tony, neglected, stood looking after her as she went about just as he had stood wailing after me in the road. With her he did not wail, because he knew that was how she was, as he wailed after me, because he knew that that was how I was.

Anxiously I consulted my time-table and proved that if we were going to have our talk at all, we had better go elsewhere.

six

She said that she was pregnant and she asked whether or not she ought to have the child. So my worse fears came to pass and still I was as anxious as before.

I did not say the sarcastic sentence I thought of, for she was already near to tears and I did not need to win this victory. But with impersonal judiciousness I said, "In such cases, obviously, the fundamental question is not about this child but whether you want to have a baby at all now."

I avoided taking her hand.

"Do you?"

A tear rolled down her cheeks. "A couple of months ago— yes! yes! But I don't think I love McWilliams. Not anymore."

I stiffened; I was not displeased that she should see that it was not altogether my fault that she had troubles. The

55

fact that she spoke of him by his last name repaid me for much hurt. I longed to ask for details. But I contained also this little triumph. "In the long run," I said, "the particular man doesn't matter either."

"That's what you say," she said bitterly. "That was your attitude when I was having Tony. I have no one to rely on."

I looked at her with hard hate, for I would not bear any criticism of any kind whatsoever. It was intolerable for me to have to justify myself.

She gave in and said, "No. I know that I can rely on you, in your way. You don't let anyone down. But I have no right to ask."

"What have rights to do with it?"

Presumably what I wanted her to say, in a burst of affection—and I taking her hand to hear her say it—was that she wouldn't have this child that would stand between us, but we would live together again and she and *I* would have the child, etc. At once my anxious ambition revived, to get her away from here as soon as possible. And counter to this was the soft dread that she would in fact go away and leave me bereft and alone.

"Sometimes you don't have any sense at all!" I said. "You could have spent at least a little time with Tony."

To my astonishment a look of remorse crossed her face. This I wanted least of all. I took her hand with simple affection, without sexual meaning. "I think it's pretty good for him here, don't you?" I said. I told her about the Dragnet and the pictures—that were scary but one needn't be scared, because they were only pictures and it was only a dream.

We were warm and content with each other. The pressure of the approaching train was very saddening. To be sure, with one word we could have arranged for her to stay over, but it was precisely within the limitation that she was about to go that we felt warm and free.

"We'll think about the other business, no? There's no rush."

"Are you mad? It's about seven weeks."

We kept regarding each other with the kind of strained benevolent smile—with only a few sentences—that was the closest that we two ever managed toward communication.

56

It meant: what horrors we get into; neither of us is to blame; we love each other on condition that all passions remain dissolved in sadness and do not explode; conversely, we can rely on each other indefinitely and need never fear rejection.

When the train came, it was with a sad and undesirous yearning, full of meaning, that we kissed good-bye.

And I at last took a free breath, because she was gone.

seven

Now, first, I felt the nagging woes. Something important was being moment by moment decided, and I did not control the course of it. Also, the embryo was forming, sporula, blastula, and gastrula. I was not at the scene of it: to intervene and prevent it, or to intervene and further it. What I loved was to postpone, but it could not be postponed.

Surely I had not done or said something.

I felt the impatience in the midriff, where I had hardly noticed it when I was holding myself back from speaking. If I had then not held back, I should have bitten and devoured something. Now there was nothing to bite and eat up but myself.

I wanted to have under control all the thoughts and decisions important to me, even the inchoate wishes in Liza's mind on the retreating train. My ambition was that of an animal-trainer in a cage, who has to keep them all under surveillance and control. But one excites another, unpredictably.

After a while the difficulties were too complex for me to control. I suffered sharp pains in the midriff, that I did not know enough to relieve by vomiting up everything that I had swallowed.

I clung dearly to little Tony, and this contact opened up a fearful but pleasing vacancy in impatience; but I was speechless.

eight

I got to my older ones, up the road, at about eight o'clock. By now I wanted to be there every night, at the time that they were doing nothing and preparing for bed. I invented pretexts in order to be there, but there was no need to, for I myself was the sharpest and only watchman to be circumvented. I invented a world of appearances in which every detail of my actions could be publicly scrutinized and explained away: if need arose; it was in this fictive world that I was unconcernedly moving; this was how I existed.

All were upset because of Lawrence Dixon's distress. The girls were sharply critical of Seraphia, whom they mimicked, even in front of her daughter, with bursts of hilarity that Lawrence Dixon and Lucy repeatedly had to tone down. Deborah Lowenstein, a very pretty and rounded girl, who was going to be an actress, isolated herself oddly behind the piano and wept. The boys, more moody, were irritated at the noise made by the girls.

I slipped into Davy's room. He was alone, and he was pleased that it was I.

It seemed to me that I could not do anything of importance to myself without devising some indirect method of approach, so that, if need arose, I could pretend to be engaged in the direct meaning of my behavior and speech. (Unselfconsciously I directly did many things of importance to myself.) I existed as if I were dreaming awake: and as if the form of this dream was the following: that my desires were the wishful dream-images, and my little devices were the secondary elaborations by which I made my desires acceptable to my own judicious scrutiny. But in fact these devices, by which one could interpret my behavior in what I thought to be an acceptable moral pattern, were really expressions of deeper wishes that I hid from myself: for I deeply desired to conform and succeed, and I only imagined that I desired to have my own way in conditions in which I must fail.

But Davy Drood turned to me a brightening face, and without method or indirection I frankly said what was the case: "Do you mind if I talk to you, boy? I'm so mixed up,

I can't see straight." I took my glasses off and laid them on the bed. "In this whole place there's no one I can talk to but you. Also, I don't give a damn if you repeat what I say; nobody's interested anyway."

I did not need to hold back from touching him; that is, I did not need to devise a maneuver whereby I should accidentally come to touch him—thereby falsifying also my voice and my thoughts. The clutch in my midriff was more imperious than the longing of my skin; I longed for him freely because at this moment it did not seem to me to be of any importance. I kissed the side of his head, indefinitely, as one might kiss a wall.

He courteously made a place for me to sit on the table.

Lawrence Dixon poked his head in at the door and blushed in confusion, and withdrew. To him it was obvious that I was talking to the boy as he had asked me to.

But I said to Davy, "My wife was here today to tell me that she was pregnant by another fellow she used to love. Name of McWilliams. We've broken up. I guess I love her, but I can't stand to live with her—and I won't. I got her away from here as fast as I could. I'm burned up with hurt feelings and jealousy about this other fellow. I hope they break up. She said she didn't love him. I knew that, of course; otherwise why should she ask me for *my* advice. But I was glad to hear her say it. I was pleased she called him by his last name.

"Round here I try to hide all this business and to give the impression that everything is just peachy. Why do I do things like that? One reason is this: it was mostly my fault that we didn't get on, because I didn't satisfy her sexually and I'm ashamed of it. Because now I'm homosexual. But it was her fault too. It's really never anybody's fault—I know that, no excuses. But I feel guilty and ashamed and I try to cover up."

"You're clinging to what you don't want," said Davy.

"Do you think I am? Maybe yes I am. But I've got to have something, not to be lonely."

"You're a dog in the manger," said Davy.

"Don't you make fun of me, Davy Drood," I said coldly. "I didn't come here for that, but simply to be loved."

59

"I'm not making fun of you," he said in a woeful voice. "It's sad."

"If she has this baby," I said intensely, "it's all over. I don't want this—I don't think she does . . . But why? I mean why am I so sure that it's this that make it all over between us— maybe it really doesn't. The idea of this baby disgusts me, I could vomit at it."

"Tell her not to have it."

"I *can't* tell her not to have it, because I know I'm doing it out of spite, and that would be too low, too low for my picture of myself." I was lying. I said, "If I told her not to have the baby, I'd be obligated to do something myself. To begin to love her again. You're right, I don't want to. I don't have the will to intervene, and even so I want to control everything according to my wishes. When I do intervene, it turns out badly. I was afraid of McWilliams so I worked myself into a rage and punched him in the nose. This fin- ished it between Eliza and me—and I suppose that's what I wanted too.

"When I talk this way, some new idea always pops into my mind that's more foolish than anything I thought of before. Then in the end I can't reject it and I do it—I do this one too—I do them *all!*"

—Davy was not listening to me at all. He was slouched in the lower berth and his face, leaning against the wall, was white. All his life they had kept hidden from him everything of importance to him. He did not know about his mother's lovers until he found them out by accident and spying. He was not sure whether his father had other children. His brooding was occupied not by these particular doubts, but by doubts. The dice-game was doubtful for only a throw, then it was made sure, throw by throw; and he doggedly masturbated those throws and marked down the score. Also he played both sides, tho he favored one side.

I gave him my trust entire (he never betrayed it). I did not experience one moment of frustration and rage, with Davy Drood, but that I would still speak frankly to him— so far as I knew. For I began by saying, "I'm so mixed up I can't see straight"—taking off my glasses and setting them down; and after this anything would be easy, for this was

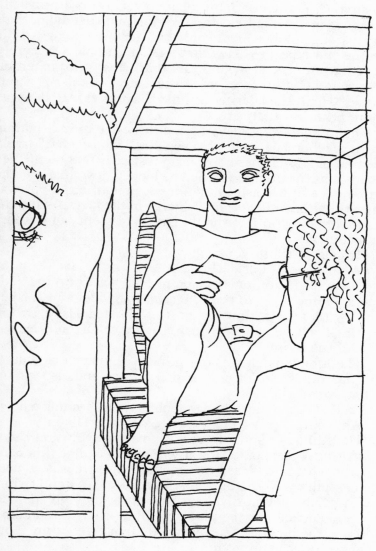

Lawrence Dixon poked his head in at the door

the hardest thing in the world for a person like me to say to anyone; it was too hard for me ever to say to myself.

By a sure instinct—my hunter's instinct that did not fail me if I let go of myself and did not force my feelings—I hit on the one appeal to Davy that was irresistible: I sincerely gave him my trust. When I saw that he was not listening to me, and that his face was white, I stopped talking about myself. He flushed darkly, against the plaster wall. He was more beautiful than fire.

The moment that Davy Drood turned to me a brightening face when I came in, this was the limit of what I freely desired of any of these boys (the rest of it was compelled by my ancient troubles). When he looked now, like fire, the experience of it was beyond any desires of mine but was an intimation of the original energy of the heavens and the earth: drawing on it, I should have had plenty of wisdom and courage.

He said, "I think you're good."

"What—good!" I cried.

Lawrence Dixon rapped, and put his head into the little room. "Time to go to bed," he said. I slipped onto the bed and, without a feeling of guilt, embraced Davy Drood, patting his head and bare neck. Lawrence Dixon filled the rest of the room.

(The judicious part of my mind was glad to be able to arrange this scene of perfect conformity and also having what I wanted.)

I said, "I can't tell you how much I love this young fellow."

"Ah, I knew you would," said Lawrence Dixon.

"He thinks we should put out a newspaper," said Davy, inventing a pretext for me. I was astounded at this complicity, where, so far as I was concerned, there was no need for complicity. My astonishment produced a painful twinge in my penis and I hastily drew back my arms. Only momentarily. I carried out the play and clung to my well-being. I kissed the boy on the eyes, good-night. We wormed our way out of the tiny room.

If his round eyes (no fools) judged that I was good, I *was* better than the unmagnanimous thoughts that had been consuming me alive.

Lawrence Dixon said, "Seraphia and I would like you to have a drink with us. It's been a hard day for everybody."

I came to a hard decision about Eliza. Whatever my unknown motives were, I had the satisfaction of coming to the worst decision, of leaping into the rejected possibility that vaguely presents itself, and that, once it has suggested itself, I always end by executing.

CHAPTER IV

one

The Staff Meeting was now a familiar circle of the twenty of us, with Harrison petting his spaniel and the German doctor's puzzled face as he took down from the shelves one of the American classics.

The children were supposed to be asleep: they well represented our anxieties (as we represented theirs).

At the blackboard, Mark was giving a talk on teaching the elementary operations in arithmetic. His proposition was that it was better to teach by "flash-cards"

$$\begin{array}{r} 4 \\ \times\ 3 \\ \hline 12 \end{array} \qquad\qquad \begin{array}{r} 15 \\ -\ 8 \\ \hline 7 \end{array}$$

than by tables, $4 \times 1 = 4$, $4 \times 2 = 8$, etc. With "flash-cards" the pupil learned certain numerical "facts," which were then subject to instant automatic recall, without losing time by inaudibly vocalizing the table up to the point called for. Certain stopwatch experiments tended to show that the recall was in fact more immediate and also more accurate.

Sophie was knitting and counting. Having finished a row she said, "He can't check up by going thru the series. That's what I always have to do."

"Yes, that's a bad habit," said Mark. "Really he either knows or he doesn't know. Going thru the tables is a compulsive habit. Even if he knows the answer, it produces

65

doubts; and if he doesn't know, he rarely comes out right."

"Well, I've learned a lot about numbers by going thru the tables," said Sophie simply. "Yesterday I discovered that multiplying was a kind of adding."

Mark was a little taken aback to find the Group III teacher without instant automatic recall, but he said, "You're right; the relations of numbers must be explained too. Now what I would do," he improvised, "is this: first bring out the relation between multiplying and adding, using numbers up to 4. Then use flash-cards to teach all the facts up to say 15 × 15. Then prove one of the higher numbers, 8 × 9, by running thru the series. This has the added advantage of an experiment in confirmation; proof is exciting."

I heard this with admiration, for proof of a brute fact is indeed exciting and throws everything into connection better than a routine series. Mark was a good teacher. I did not see how there could now be any disagreement.

"If I use these flash-cards," said Caroline, the Group II teacher, "will they give up counting on their fingers? That's what I tend to do."

"Yes, I think so," said Mark. "Counting on the fingers is just the extreme form of compulsively going back to the beginning and doing everything over."

"What," I said ominously, "is wrong with counting on the fingers?"

He looked at me in blank surprise. "What do you mean?"

"Why, fingers are things. There has to be *some* connection between the numbers and the things, especially if we take the numbers out of their own series."

"I'm not sure I understand," he said.

"Neither do I, really. Just an impulsive thought. Perhaps I'll come back to it. I'm sorry."—The fact was that I was ashamed to present the subject in too philosophical a way, a way that in the end might be irrelevant. I retreated, as I often did, by contributing something of my own to the point of view to which I was perhaps opposed. I said, "Don't you think these cards could be made by the kids themselves, as part of their art-work? This would give them a more material meaning."

To my dismay this was picked up by Harrison. "First rate!"

he cried, pushing away the spaniel. He at once began to improvise (we were all good teachers): "First of all, there's no reason—we have to make up our minds to it right off the bat—there's no reason why those cards shouldn't be bright and beautiful, instead of the things you're showing us. Four times Three!—this *fact*, as you call it, this fact has a certain *feeling.* The usual way in the work-books is to draw animals, isn't it—four groups of three bears—I think I've noticed such things around. We must try to get some beauty out of the abstract numbers themselves."

This roused interest.

Mark closed his eyes in pain. His own point was being lost forever. For now to the distractions of instant automatic recall they were adding art-work and animals. One could envisage Stevie's "numerical fact," and Gene Istomin's, that would have feathers.

There was no help for it, because each teacher had to contribute according to his lights. All of us truly wanted the best solution, and therefore in the long run we should surely hit on it—but it was a hard row to hoe.

"Will you please explain, Mark," said Dolly Homers, "*why* it is necessary to have instant automatic recall? I myself can't see the use of adding up so fast unless you're a greengrocer. I myself can calculate quick as light, but I learned it when I worked in a creamery."

"It's a language," explained Mark patiently. "Please don't be sarcastic, I'm doing the best I can. You don't want to have to think of the grammar every time you speak a sentence. That's why recall should be instant and automatic."

"I suppose I shouldn't speak because I can't do long division," said Sophie placidly; "but honestly, I find every single problem interesting, and it doesn't make any difference to me if I spend ten minutes on it and even have to go back to the beginning. Is that bad?"

My own bother with the discussion was that, instead of pressing to a decision, I could not drive from my mind what each speaker had said and seeing the development of the dialectic towards the most ultimate issues; yet these seemed always a little irrelevant to the immediate issue. Also, I knew a little too much; for instance, whether arithmetic is a language or a scientific subject-matter in its own right, I knew that this was an ancient question, and very much had been said about it for many centuries. But I was ashamed to burden the discussion with such considerations.

Suddenly Lawrence Dixon leaped to his feet and began to prowl, and I realized that this would be the end of the end. "It's the old question," he cried, "the difference between the classical progressive education and the new progressive education, and *how* are we to compromise between them and get the good points of both. The older progressive education tried to draw out the child, to go at *his* speed, to follow *his* interests, and encourage *his* feeling; the new progressive education tries to adjust the child to the realities of the environment, while protecting his personality. Both are great, both are necessary, but are they compatible?" — This distinction was uppermost in Dixon's mind; last night he had elaborated it for hours to Seraphia and me; whatever Mark would have said, he would have come to it. Yet in a sense it was not irrelevant. "No doubt of it, no doubt of it at all, we must expect every graduate to be able to add, subtract, multiply, and divide with accuracy and rapidity. But *where* do you draw the line? Next, shall we teach spelling again?"

"I *fail* to see the point of bringing in spelling," said Mark Anders, raising his voice a little.

"You yourself said that arithmetic is a language."

"We are *completely* off the point," said Mark. "The question was not *whether* they ought to know arithmetic, but *how* to get them to learn it, whether by flash-cards or by compulsively running thru tables."

"You say 'compulsively,' " cried Lawrence Dixon; "are you sure you're not projecting? The tables are compulsive; I think you have a splendid idea there; but to me the automatic response you're after is even more compulsive! the quick adjustment of the newer progressive education is even more compulsive! But *this* compulsiveness you can't see, because you're projecting."

Mark clenched his fists till his knuckles were white and he began to tremble.

"Please," I said heroically, "*can* we get back a little closer to the topic?" I began to improvise rapidly. "Sitting here, I've been thinking of the whole mathematics curriculum, and I wonder whether some of these disagreements couldn't be resolved if we reviewed the whole matter with a more progressive attitude, I mean of course *both* the older and the newer progressive education—"

A good idea came to me in a flash. (The bother was that I was indolent and not fundamentally concerned; I would suggest an idea but I would not do anything toward preparing a syllabus or training a teacher.) Nevertheless I said with enthusiasm:

"Fundamentally, it seems to me perfectly pointless to begin arithmetic, algebra, geometry, and trigonometry separately, the way we've been doing; rather than develop them as an integrated and continuous calculation of more and more complicated *real*, I mean material, subject matters." —This was of course quite the contrary of my attitude in the geometry class; but then I too had been different, I had not been so close to Davy Drood and I had not come to a decision about Eliza's embryo. Certain important events had intervened; and it was not irrelevant, I came to see, it was not irrelevant to how we taught arithmetic what passions were uppermost in the soul. —"Mark Anders is 100% right about calling arithmetic a language. It is the language of science. From the very beginning they should get the habit of using numbers and geometry for counting and measuring real scientific materials. For instance, age 6 and 7, they count blocks and by arranging them learn to figure simple areas. Age 8 and 9, we begin to swing pendulums and to slide a key down a string and time it with a stopwatch; or to figure out the ratios of a bicycle.

"The object," I cried, "is for our graduates not to feel like foreigners when they see an equation in the middle of a page of type. That's what I meant, before, when I said it wasn't a bad idea to count on the fingers."

Suddenly I realized that I had decided against Mark Anders, even tho this had not been my intention. I said frankly, "Sophie is right. A real problem, for instance the rate of a rolling ball, is worth taking an hour or a week to figure. You could even start every time from the beginning, and count on your fingers."

"Bravo! a hundred percent right!" cried Lawrence Dixon, rubbing his hands enthusiastically.

We *were* right, in the long run, in the big way, given the energy that in fact we did not have free to dispose of, and knowledge to carry out the plans that in fact we did not possess. But we were improvising with words. I felt guilty at having conceived precisely what seemed to me to be a true idea. I had started to speak in order to alleviate the tension between Dixon and Anders; the outcome was otherwise. But the fact that *this* consideration occupied me, rather than the correctness and practicality of my proposal—it seemed to me that this in itself proved that my proposal was impractical and irrelevant. If it had come to a vote, I should in shame have voted for Mark Anders.

"Yes, he's perfectly right," said Caroline. "It's the same problem I have had with Harriet Silver"—this was the turtle-girl. "One reason she's afraid to talk is that she soils her drawers. Of course we have to get at the psychological cause of this, but meantime the doctor and I are working on the material facts: One of her troubles is the crowd and hurry in the toilet, so now we arrange for her to use the infirmary toilet in the morning during the first class. It's quiet and she can take her own good time. I'm pleased to say that it works like a charm, and soon she'll be in better shape."

This unexpected communication lifted the weight off my shoulders. Not only mine; for everywhere there spread a glad smile. I was only mildly sympathetic when Mark Anders folded his notes angrily and said, "I take it it's agreed we are *not* to use flash-cards, but—" He was going to say, "But to wait for some chimeric pendulums to be swung and to calculate the ratios of bicycles." But he cut the sentence short.

"Why, I always use flash-cards," said Caroline indignantly. "It's accepted practice."

"Do you?" said Harrison gladly. "Can I assign it to your kids to make up a set?"

"My point," said Mark acidly, "was not to use them because it's accepted practice, but because tests prove that they are more efficient."

70

"Oh, if *that's* the point," said Dolly, who disliked Mark, "it's not much of a point. The intuition of a good teacher is better than a test with a stop-watch."

Suddenly the lights were turned off.

Thru the door, in the darkness, advanced the blazing glory of a large birthday-cake, lit with a forest of candles. We sang, "Happy birthday to you, happy birthday to you, happy birthday, dear doctor, happy birthday to you!"

In the rosy light, brought up close to his face, the doctor flushed and paled with surprise. He faltered back, and sat down.

Once again the miracle was accomplished, of a sociable community amongst us—instant, automatic—that made me think it would be *easy* to achieve the many good plans we had, that we conspired in with all good intentions. Yes, not despite, but because of our differences. As if we knew this sociality (from the beginning!) by an instant automatic recall; we had not learned it from flash-cards, and we did not need to run thru the series of accidents by which we lost it.

The lights were turned on. The doctor, sitting on the sofa, was gasping for breath, till one felt a certain alarm for him. It began to be explained to him that according to our custom he was supposed to blow out the candles on the cake, but first he must make a wish.

"I haven't the breath to breathe with," he said, "how do you expect me also to blow out candles?"

On the wall of his room the doctor had an absurd needle-point sampler:

Humor ist wenn man trotzdem lacht.

"And a wish? what wish shall I now make? So. I wish—"

"No no," we cried; "you mustn't tell us the wish. The wish is supposed to be a secret."

two

Now this great cake had been made that morning by the older girls in Bernardine's kitchen. She invited them to come and learn to cook—just as she discouraged them from asking for lessons on the piano.

Having many collaborators, she concocted wonderful and elaborate things. In general, if the dietician allotted to each child four eggs a week, Bernardine preferred to include them all in custard cream-puffs, that were gobbled up, rather than to serve them boiled or fried, to be picked at. Surely something was wrong with this, but it was not certain what it was.

I rapped out the secret signal, and the door was opened to me. The first class was over and Bernardine poured out the coffee I longed for and produced a cinnamon bun from our private store. We understood each other; I did not need to thank her.

The four girls were flecked with flour; and now they were whipping the yellow batter and grating oranges. Seraphia's daughter had golden hair and her blue jeans were dusty with flour. She had been weeping because her mother had been drunk; she beat the batter all the more vigorously with a wooden spoon that sounded C and G. She was fair as day. When she noticed that I was looking at her, she blushed and took some utensils to the sink at the other end of the kitchen.

Claire, a frizzly-haired small mulatto girl, imitated every move of Seraphia's daughter. She could not endure to have any space between them and she followed her to the sink. Afterwards, when Seraphia's daughter left to go riding, she watched out the window for her to reappear outside, and she tapped on the pane to attract her attention.

I poured Bernardine a cup of coffee and made her sit down to keep me company. Our staple morning conversation was her irritation with Dixon: today he had mislaid the key to the car; when she found it for him, he couldn't make the car go anyway and had to 'phone for the mechanic. She was irritated that a grown man did not know enough to check the sparkplugs himself.

72

I screwed up my courage to ask what I wanted to ask for many days: would she give *me* lessons on the piano? I could not play a note. To cover my confusion in asking, I invented the pretext that there were such long pauses in the day, because the kids never came on schedule—this was how Lawrence Dixon ran things—I ought to put the time to use, and I could practice.

(It is now some years since then, and now falteringly, inaccurately, I play sonatas of Mozart; and when "nervousness," as it is called—it is the buried feelings that revive, stirred by the images I remember—makes it impossible for me to sit and write another line, then playing the beautiful song makes me more quiet. For he does not create a strong tension before he resolves it, but he relaxes the tension soon: and at once surprisingly, more relaxed than the relaxation there is a deeper relaxation: and he looses feeling by no apparent violence, but as if with gentle words.)

"You don't know anything?"

"Not one note."

"Do you know harmony at least?"

"Nothing. Nothing."

"Good! then we can start from the beginning." And she named an hour.

She colored darkly, because a lad in the other room had begun to play *Chopsticks*. But Deborah's eyes lit up, because it was Lefty, playing with great violence and speed—as he masturbated, with a fury that came to nothing.

"*They must stop playing this Coteletten Waltz*," said Bernardine angrily.

"This what?"

"This song he bangs—it is called the Coteletten Waltz."

"Bernardine! it's *Chopsticks*."

"Please. The *Coteletten Waltz*—there are variations by Borodin."

Seraphia's daughter left and Claire rapped on the window to attract her attention. Afterwards, she worked happily in the corner by herself, wearing a little smile.

Deborah and Queenie, the two other girls, were speaking of the three boys, Lefty, Droyt, and Jeff Deegan. Deborah wanted the embraces of Jeff; this colored all her thoughts.

73

In his brusque way Jeff was courteous and affectionate to her—but all the same the three boys always vanished together. Perhaps indeed she wanted all three, perhaps all the boys in the group. I liked her; the longing she breathed was like what I myself felt. But she made me uneasy. The boys were afraid of her.

I sat at one end of the table; Bernardine stood at the other, pouring milk from a can.

My pipe was clenched between my teeth. I should have said, if I had observed myself—which was not unlikely, for I spied on myself as well as on the others—that my jaw was thrust forward watchfully. But it was thrust even further forward than that; it was clenched, I was looking on, with hatred. The pipe-stem had the scars of many teeth. A present hatred for objects not present (for what was there to hate in these lovely girls in the sunlit room where Bernardine treated me with esteem); *also* for these girls present, happy with their boys—except that they were not happy. I looked at Bernardine and my jaw fell back a little, to the place where I was simply watching:

She was pouring the milk from one can into another. That is, she was standing like a column, and her arms were performing the act of pouring. For she held the act away from her. She did not cringe from the act; she did not cringe from anything; but she did not *give* herself to it, bending forward with neither the head nor bosom (as one gives oneself to a child) nor with the belly (as to a man).

But she was *frankly* performing the act of pouring out the milk, without giving herself to it. As if a Trojan woman, whose husband, father, infant, have been lost in the carnage, by the insane cruelty of Pyrrhus, and she herself has been taken captive—what! shall she cringe? She is a princess. Shall she forever weep? A person must live on again, such as it is. No! frankly, graciously, amiably—noblesse oblige— she pours out the milk for the stranger knights. Only she does not give herself to it. The knights too courteously hold back.

So I watched it, my pipe less firmly clamped in my jaws. The lovely girls were putting in the oven the batter of the birthday cake that would eventually wear a forest of fires.

The daughter of Seraphia had left, and the frizzly-haired girl left off tapping on the window. Lefty was rhythmically playing *Chopsticks*, not otherwise than he masturbated (nothing came of it). Bernardine poured out the coffee I longed for after the first hour, and I did not need to thank her. I did not know that I was staring with a present hatred for objects no longer present.

three

The doctor blew out a few of the candles and made a dark swathe in the flaming forest. (It was not easy to win a wish against so many burning years.)

He sat heavily panting, letting go in sighs the breath with which he could not wish. We feared for his heart and regretted our murderous surprise-party; but he had the knack of not containing his feelings, and he groaned and wheezed and sighed himself to composure. The party sprang alive. Hoshi and Bernardine brought in a great bowl of punch and Lucy followed with a great white pot of coffee. Mark Anders beat the sparks up the chimney. Sophie cut the cake and I carried round the plates. The doctor heaved a last deep sigh and said, "*Ach*, I ought to know better than talk politics at a party."

The punch was very strong and good. Harrison was soon loudly explaining why the girls fall in love with the art-teacher: "The dears express their unconscious thoughts in their paintings," he said, "and then they attach their deep feelings to the teachers, as if I were responsible. It's not our fault, it's a special occupational hazard."

"Why don't some of them react negatively and hate you?" asked Mark's wife.

"Oh they do, they all do!" he cried. "It takes the form of making fun of me." He was easy to make fun of. He used to reproach his spaniel for not being a hunter and the dog mortified him by running away from mice. "Look what one of the dears sent me this morning!"—he produced a card hand-printed with the following legend:

J.J. Sturgeon
Plastic Surgeon
by an amazing new process
he can add
2 Inches anywhere!

"*I* sent it!" cried Dolly gaily, and began to giggle as if demented. I tried my best not to be near her.

I sat down next to the doctor, trying by proximity to convey the deep affection that I felt for him.

He was overcome with confusion and emotion. Ordinarily he spoke adequate academic English, but now he was unable to find words to express himself, except the one word, "A servant! A servant!" that he muttered again and again. — *This* was the role that he had assigned himself, and that he moved in; and now he was the honored guest of the party.

His frightening escape from Germany had fallen just at the age of a turn of life — he "lost everything" just when some men retire and break down. From that time on he was "realistic," without pretensions. The result was that at our school he had assigned himself a role that was foreign to the conceptions of simply every one of us. Finally he recovered speech sufficient to say, "Except I did not choose of my own free will!"

But not one of us was here of his own free will! Not the director, not the staff, not the children. Perhaps, partly, it was the interdependence of bondage that made so close-knit our friendship. The armor of the ego was pierced and we mixed the blood of our wounds.

Harrison was laying down the dictum that a teacher would not have sexual relations with a student because his position gave him an unfair advantage. This did not square with the common opinion that he had had relations with one of the girls (Claire); in fact his remark was accepted as a confession of remorse and better judgment. I thought that his dictum was correct, but I said, "Yes, it is an unequal advantage; but what if the teacher falls in love — and he can't help himself — or herself?"

I said it as a confession before the fact, to call attention; as a threat; an alibi, whereby I could later say, "But I *told* you so all along."

"Don't drink to that!" cried Seraphia

Lawrence Dixon would not let drop his thesis of the Staff-meeting. "You see, it's a good school," he was declaiming, he was drunk. "Every one here is devoted to it and well-intentioned to do the best job. Again and again the toughest problems are solved by a creative community!

"The individualities are strongly marked. You might even call them eccentric. All the stronger is the inventiveness of the community.

"Hm. But there is a fatal conflict between our characters with our persistent pasts and our growth in the living present. This flaw is pervasive, in the staff, in the children. I have it, you have it, they have it.

"Hm. There is another conflict, between our good educational practice and the crazy mores of the world. I shouldn't be surprised, I shouldn't be surprised at all, if there were a close relation between our damaged characters and the crazy mores of the world.

"Do you want the truth? I am not afraid of the truth—I will drink to the truth—" He filled another cup. "The truth is that we are engaged in a job really beyond our wisdom and available energy. The results are dubious."

"Do not drink to that!" cried Seraphia, to my astonishment, and she knocked the cup out of his hands. "Apart from people like us, nobody is doing anything about it at all."

The cup splashed full in the lap of Mark Anders, whose face was a study. Dixon wailed with remorse and produced a handkerchief to repair the damage. —He and Seraphia were on the way to becoming really drunk. Everyone else (perhaps not Dolly) seemed able to contain his liquor quietly.

There were noises outside. Some of the boys were abroad. The watchman was chasing them.

We went out in the cold fall night, and lights were flashing up the road.

I knew that it was Lefty, Droyt, and Jeff Deegan, out to steal the properties from Morton's Theater.

four

The three youths had trapped me, in Davy's and Michael's, stretched out in the upper berth. For during an interim, and when the roommates were away, I used secretly to come here to write a line. The upper berth, away from the world, was Michael's; it was untidily made, whereas Davy's neat corners would show signs of derangement and betray I had been there. Up there, if I held still, I would not be seen by anyone who came in for a moment. It was convenient for me to write in this room, for here the hunting spirit was a little calmed. I stretched out in this vantage point of a little calm to write the symbols of disturbance.

But they found me. "We want advice," said Droyt.

"If we tell you something we want to do, will you keep shut about it even if you're against it?" said Jeff Deegan.

"No. I won't promise such a thing."

"We'd better not tell him," said Droyt. "Let's go."

"O.K. Close the door behind you."

"Please?" said Lefty, whom I could not well resist.

"Listen," I said, "if you tell me something, I'll make up my own mind. Personally I doubt if it's important enough to have to make up my mind about at all. You know me, generally I let things take their course."

"He won't blab," said Lefty.

"We'll do it no matter what you say," said Droyt.

There was a summer theater in the neighborhood, now closed. They had been exploring it, jimmying the greenroom window. They planned to borrow the spotlights for the Group II play—the lights were needed especially for the dance. They would sit up in the loft and work the lights. (It was indeed not a matter that I had to make up my mind about.)

"We'll put them back soon's the play's over," said Jeff.

"What! you won't even keep them for your own play?"

"No; we'll borrow them again."

"You boys are out of your minds," I said. "Don't you think Lawrence Dixon and Mark Anders will ask where the lights came from?"

"No!" said Jeff positively. "They won't even notice them."

"What? How do you not notice spotlights? I suppose they have gelatines?"

"How much do you want to bet they don't notice 'em? The only one will be Sophie."

"You are completely demented. Mark Anders will ask where the spots came from and then there'll be a stink. Not that he cares about property any more than I do, but you can't run a school and steal other people's property. It's all the same to me—but if you ask my advice, no."

"O.K. Put up or shut up. How much do you bet he doesn't notice them? Bet you five dollars."

"You don't have five dollars."

"I can get five dollars, don't you worry."

"Great!"

"You said yourself," said Lefty—and my heart sank, for I wondered which of my random sentences would now return—"you said yourself that property belonged to the one who can use it. What the hell good is it sitting there all winter?"

five

They had done it and they were fleeing thru the night. It was more important to me to know what they were up to than to go back to that stupid party. But by the time I slipped away and went roundabout, all was quiet.

There was a light on in the little room—I longed to see my boy. But I could only stand below and stare with frustration.

It was cold and I had drunk a good deal. I went back toward the party.

From the old building poured the music of the piano. They had prevailed on Bernardine to play. With fulness and sweetness she was playing dances of Lully and de Chambonnières. The ornaments fell with a weighty sweetness that seemed to my ignorant experience incredibly lovely and difficult. It seemed to me that she was one of the great musicians of the world. It was preferable—it was preferable to listen to these tones out here, alone, under the window, where one could unashamedly respond to them.

One did not get the impression that she was holding the keyboard away from herself—nor that she held it too close. But she gave herself to it. She played it.

Later, later I got back to my room. The door next was open, the light on, Dolly and Harrison were in bed together. It was as if, drunken and asleep, they were concerned to be seen. I shut my own door.

Tony was sleeping with the moonlight full on his face. If I could stay—

It seemed to me, if I could stay at this distance and this nearness, as I had all day, with no blundering step or fright, I would become progressively happier. It fitted me well, this distance and this nearness. What happened to me, and what I made to happen, would regularize itself, if I could stay here. The ornaments of the music sounded weightily in my head. I had a better clarity than I was used to have. Yet I shifted from side to side in bed and could not sleep. I got up to smoke my pipe another time, agreed to burst into tears, but I could not, because of the way I clamped the stem in my teeth.

FOR M.C.

Fumbling, a late learner, on the keys,
yet plausibly enough the pomp and grace
of the antique dances sound in my ears; and yes
sound afterwards the secret melodies
of the soul: of his that all at once at ease
came to be, or his that sound like distress
but he knew they were cries of happiness,
or his whose noisy madness made him cease.
Bernardine! thank you for these elements
which you, their mistress, with even passion
make into music (oh, too rarely heard).
The octave and the fifth and the third
that awkwardly my hands have learnt to fashion
suddenly speak out, and the heart attends.

CHAPTER V

one

I took the early train to the city, to act out a resolution that had lasted fifty or sixty hours. It was simply this: to tell Eliza to have the baby, since this was what she intended in any case, and that I, if, or when, the other man failed her, I would be the child's safety and his father.

In the city I stopped at a tavern for a drink, and the glass shook in my hand. I wrote.

> Why shouldn't I, throttling myself
> in middle-agitation, make my brief
>   meditation (may it be
>   acceptable)—like the
> raging alarum-clock so struck
> silent by its late wild shake
>   that now has even stopped ticking
>   the seconds rushing thick and fast.

It was well that I came to Eliza so early in the morning with a friendly proposal, for she was in a frantic way, a little beyond self-control. She either talked away from her concern or glanced it with witty remarks. She was living at a friend's house where she did not feel welcome, and she sat on the edge of the bed as if she also slept in the bed without touching it. I spoke frankly and warmly, as I could when I had the upper hand, even if the upper hand over only my own feelings. I had marked out a picture of myself in which I believed; it was easy for me to convey such a picture. So,

83

making my friendly offer, I clung to the past with a deathly grip and comfortably mortgaged also an indefinite stretch of the future, treating our facts of life as tho I were a dramatic artist arranging a dramatic scene.

Yet she and I both knew—and it was this complicity that made it impossible for us to break with each other—that these incidents were indeed dramatic scenes and not our facts of life. We were play-acting. The effective causes in our lives were the miserable pasts that we kept repeating in this scene or that. In the present we were ceasing to live altogether.

I felt constrained and uneasy in this house where I sat on the edge of a chair and fished around for a pretext to get away—as at our school, I had fished for a pretext to get her away. But I did not dare to go because she was too disturbed.

She made conversation about Dolly Homers, of whom she had become immoderately fond, compensating for her resentment of Tony's foster-mother. "Don't you think," she said, "that she's a little—" she touched her brow with a finger: dippy? My heart sank, for I took this to be a projection of her own state (I wonder whether it was not a projection of my own state). But to humor her, I told her of my first meeting with Dolly, when I too had taken her for a slightly deficient and prematurely aged fifteen-year-old.

I had a crick between the shoulders from living on the edge of the chair.

"Look Liza," I said, "if you want to have the abortion, here is the money for it." I laid my month's check on the table. "But I don't think you intend to."

The money loomed on the table; it was in our way. I was not very stingy, but the long habit of poverty made me close and measuring. To have done the simple thing, to give the check into her hand, this was impossible for me: simply to give something or to take something; but I made use of intermediary stations, like table-tops, just as fearsome primitives deposit their barter on the shore while the others hide in the bushes.

I folded the check and put it in the pocket of her blouse.

"No. We'll get along." She gave the check back to me, in my hand. This action, unmaking the embarrassment and relieving my economic anxiety (for this check was all the money I had), served as the forepleasure that made me relent. I put my arm about her—the pain stabbed me in the back—and she wept.

two

Mark Anders spent his free day suffering his asthma and using a machine to alleviate it. The attack seemed to come sometimes if he had taken even a single drink the night before. Many of us were annoyed when, at a party, or whenever conversation was animated, Mark would cut us short by beginning community singing; for tho the singing was often warm, lulling, and unifying, it could also be childish and boring. But the fact was that he did it partly selfishly, as a measure of prudence, to forestall the drink or the argument that would excite him. Like the rest of us, he was intensely sociable and erotic, but he was unable to get his need outside his skin, in perversions, art-works, or fantastic programs.

Their baby chose that morning to wail forever.

The doctor came, and Mark said about me: "It's his perpetual smile that gets me down. Whatever comes up, he's happy about it. If it's a bad fix, he understands and sympathizes and smiles with relish at the interesting problem. If I contradict him, he takes my side and smiles with appreciation of my point of view, and also with anticipation of the way he's going to refute it. He behaves as tho he had heard all that a hundred times before.

"Perhaps he has! I don't think he makes any pretensions. He knows what he's talking about—I've tested him; he doesn't say he's read what he hasn't read. There's always a meaning to what he says; but he knows that too—that makes it worse.

"Well! if he really knows more than any of us, what the hell is he doing here? Why doesn't he go somewhere and make a name for himself—because he won't make a name in education. What's here for him? He can write—he can write anything; but he doesn't write as well as he thinks he does.

"Personally I like him. His smile isn't superior. It's not his fault if it makes me feel inferior. But why is he here? why does he hang around here? He has homosexual tendencies. All right! if he does anything open we'll get rid of him—because we won't have any more Typhoid Marys. I swear, I'll take it right to the trustees. But I won't get any satisfaction out of doing it.

"Everybody else laughs, he smiles. I hate his smile. He thinks everything is a learned joke that he relishes. No, not privately—he wants me to relish it too and to love him.

"The question is—does he turn Dixon around his finger? or does Dixon turn him around *his* finger?"

This was all he could say before he lost his breath and had to be still.

The doctor knew somewhat more about smiles. He sat quietly in the big chair for a while, puckering his lips experimentally and baring his fangs. Then he said, "You can't get that smile so easily as you think, it probably took him more than twenty years to work it out. When he does like this—that's sucking. You see he clings with the lips here—it's what you mean, sucking for affection. But then he swells these upper parts here—that's growling and getting ready to bite. Then he's sucking in the lower lip—masochist, no? But also hissing out, spitting. No no! disgust! *Why* is he so disgusted? He is disgusted with women. Banal! banal sucking and spitting out and vomiting. Even so, this smile of his is not so banal; it is not so easy to make this smile. So.

"It is in the eyes. There—there. He is perplexed. Everything is doubtful, but everything. This he would never admit to anybody; he does not know it himself. There are no lateral wrinkles of astonishment, and even the worry between the eyes is not very deep. The whole strain of it is carried by the smile, the eternal smile. You note how the corners of it are softly rounded; he does not know whether to laugh or cry at what he sees—what he doesn't see—thru his glasses. Ah, Mark! a strong mind! It takes a strong intellect to be as doubtful about anything as he is about everything. As he is about everything. When really everything is so simple, so simply terrible. He smiles and is self-confident. You think he feels guilty and is not self-

confident? Obviously, obviously, but superficial. He is really
confident—a continuous masturbator, it goes without
saying. He believes in magic, and that *he* has the magic—
but he has forgotten the formula. Age two. An artist, no?
Maybe after all, *he* is right and *I* am wrong? See, he has
power, he drags me into doubt too. You don't like what he
writes? I have read what he writes and I say this: He would
write something great if he did not think every moment
that what he is writing is so great.

"I cannot altogether catch it. Some of that smiling is
genuine pleasure, and this one cannot catch without feeling the pleasure."

He smiled broadly at this beautiful simple thought: that
the smile was really a smile. "Ah, there! you see? it is a smile
of pleasure! because he is *interested*. A pity! a pity!

"How long can we be driven away again and again, before
the heart breaks, and the sweet flower on the lips is frost-
bitten? Let me tell you, it happened to me. I was on my way.
I slept in a barn. 'Lord! Lord!' I groaned, 'how long can this
go on?' Some kibitzer was lying in the loft overhead, and
he shouted in a deep voice, 'Two years!' I was thunderstruck.
Two years! Two years? Well, two years was not so bad.
'Then,' he said, 'then you'll be used to it.' "

three

Our Doctor had a large discourse. In treating his patients,
he was alive with every sensory and motor power: he mimed
their symptoms, grimaces, and convulsions, like a great
child; he knew what the children could not say and the
adults would not admit. Also, he was suspicious of his
intuition and he pursued every alternative diagnosis to the
end, making many tests. He prepared beautiful slides and
verified the tests on the spot, by himself—explaining that
he did not trust American laboratories, but in fact because
the answer he wanted, or rather the question he wanted
answered, suggested itself only in this activity. He was
certainly over-anxious about prevention, checkups, daily
examinations, so that he constrained the free spirit that

belonged to our school; yet perhaps he was not excessively over-anxious, considering the careless sanitary arrangements of our poor school, and of the wide world.

But when one saw him at home, in his little room with his wife, one was astounded. He stared helplessly about and could not find anything. He could not brew a cup of coffee for his guests, but lounged back mortified. She had to do everything. He would say, "Ah, tobacco? wait, I'll get it—" and make an abortive motion forward, meantime holding himself back so violently that his arms trembled on the arms of the chair; and she would say with a melodious little cry, "no, *I'll* get it!" and she would bring it. This comedy was carried on with a baldness probably impossible with Americans.

What he could not face was the pity that he felt for himself, that was not unjustified in his case—nor in any case, I think—but it was unadmitted; it stood between him and any burst of open laughter, or any impulse of gratitude. He laughed only at his own little jokes, which he called anecdotes, and which had the following form: "Shall I tell you an anecdote, it happened to me—" that is, "what happened to me is a joke."

four

Returning to our school, or to any place important to me, I was full of fears. Fears that in my absence an accident had befallen Tony or, more strongly, that I was unmasked. I would come to be confronted with my misdeeds made known, even if (especially if) there were no misdeeds but only abortive desires and subterfuges. I was the tamer of the beasts in the cage, unable to attend to them all—I ought not then to go away. Transparently I wished for the child's hurt, and for myself to be punished for it when I came back to my neglected duty. Yet it was not so much a physical injury that I vaguely imagined, but that he had stood wailing in the road after me and would not be consoled hour after hour—thereby publicizing his need and my neglect. Most strongly, I wished that I were at last unmasked, my

homosexual aims and intellectual pretensions and acts of
envy, and the clever pretexts that I employed to spend an
hour in Davy's room; that I was confronted with my ac-
cusers: yes! in order that now, open and above-board, I could
win them to me by true and loving persuasions. Unmasked
and punished, in order that we might live at last in social
peace (my boy the living sacrifice built into the wall)—no
more strangeness, and I to have all my desires with general
applause (for I did not lapse so far into the persecutory mania
as to forget the aim of pleasure).

I watched the faces of the first persons I would come on,
whether or not they showed the signs of my disgrace.

But Davy Drood was running toward me on the road. I
started with fright. But his face was glorious with wel-
coming, and he shouted "Hi!" as a boy can who has marked
your absence and is glad to see you again, with such a ulula-
tion in the syllable as to shiver the bases of the hills.

I did not allow myself to give way to delight, but I put
on my cordial face and smiled, and I tried my best to get
away. "How is Tony?" I said at once. "I must go there right
away."

"Where are you going? He's in our kitchen with Bernardine. Or maybe he's with the girls upstairs. We can't get
rid of him."

"At *your* place? how did he get there?"

"Just came, walking up the road."

"Hell! that means he was crying and looking for me."

"He wasn't crying. I saw him—he was just walking and
looking."

"Does Dolly Homers know where he is?" I asked in alarm.

"Oh yes, Bernardine 'phoned her and said she'd keep him.
I was the one who 'phoned."

It was impossible for me to retreat into dismay. The way
was blocked. My breast was rent and my eyes flooded
because of the goodness and love of my friends.

"I'm glad to see you, Davy Drood," I said in a low voice.
"If I were any gladder, I'd kiss you."

Relentlessly, he threw his arms about me to kiss me
indeed, but I pushed him away. For I *meant* it, in my way,
and I could not allow a pretense. But perhaps he too meant

it, simply. Supposing, that is, what I wanted happened *also* to be the case—nevertheless it was necessary for me to push him away, holding my breath, with clenched fists.

I was flustered and unable to retreat into sorrow, as a child is when one violently tousles his hair. I resolved, with an iron determination (withdrawing to my last ring of defense, benevolence, that had served me well in the morning with Liza), I resolved to do as much as I could to make the youth well and happy, to procure for him the girl and the courage, to have at least the beginnings of the sexual experience whose lack reduced him, with all his gifts, to misery.

I resolved to battle according to common reason for the sexual opportunity of these dear young people, disregarding my own twinges of guilt and despite the fact that my own desires and behavior (too blinding for me to distinguish what in them was love and what was fright and what was envy and what was hatred), despite the fact that my own desires must compromise my efforts. In that mood of grateful love, on the road returning—surprised by ordinary well-being when I was set for disaster—I could perhaps even have foresworn my own future small satisfactions—small to me even in prospect—in the interests of the young people. But it was impossible for me to do them any good, if I did not, as a comrade, strive also for my own pleasure, tho their good was still probable and great and mine at best improbable and small, and tho my efforts on my own behalf must jeopardize my efforts on theirs.

five

Soon enough I had the opportunity of thwarting my dear boys and girls in what they took to be their chief group pleasure. Returning from my free day, I was counsellor for the night, and they had chosen the evening to go to the weekly movie in the village. The bus was to stop for us at seven-thirty. The movie had been approved at the Staff-meeting, while I sat dumbly listening.

Now I said: "We're not going. Not while I'm the counsellor—you won't go to a Hollywood movie."

For a moment this was disregarded, or regarded as a jest. Then there was consternation in the dining-room.

"We thought the movie was approved at the Staff-meeting," said Ralph Ross, the poet's son. "Wasn't it approved?"

"Yes, it was approved, over my minority body. But now I'm alive and in charge."

"You're not *serious*? He's not serious?"

"What's wrong with the picture?"

"I don't know anything about it. I never even heard of it. I won't take you to *any* Hollywood movie."

"What? are you serious? You don't know anything about the movie and you won't? He doesn't know anything about the movie, and he won't! I ask you—" appealed Seraphia's daughter, "*what* kind of intelligence is that?"

They stared at me; I had taken them so by surprise that I had every advantage. I said "No," and sat tight. After a while I only shook my head from side to side. They became angry, and I became angry.

"Well, for God's sake, let's at least discuss it. Don't sit there shaking your head like a dummy."

"Certainly. I'm willing to discuss it. Let's quietly discuss it all night if you want."

"Meantime the 'bus will come and go and we lose anyway."

"Yes, it will and you will," I conceded.

"*You* don't even have to go to the movie, if you don't like movies. You can wait outside and drink ice-cream sodas. Don't we have *any* rights?"

"Do you think the movie will hurt our morals? Don't be naïve."

"You don't get the point," I said. "*I* can take movies or leave them. And I don't give a fuck about your morals. I refuse to lead fifteen dollars to a Hollywood movie to encourage them to continue. It's as simple as that."

I had been bitten by a bug and was prepared to be absurd. They were so dumbfounded by my stubbornness—for I was the easy mark who went along with anything and everything—that they became incoherent. If one of them had said something shrewd, I should have given in, but no one did. Soon I began to enjoy myself. I patiently explained that I was an artist, I belonged to the artist-class, and Hollywood was the class-enemy to which I could not contribute fifteen dollars and the presence of thirty heads, without committing treason against my dearest friends.

"*What* friends?" they screamed. "*What* are you talking about?"

I was willing to name them one by one. It was seven-thirty and the 'bus came and went. Lefty, Droyt, and Jeff Deegan took the 'bus anyway, without my permission.

"Fuck you, we revolt!" shouted the others, and they scattered and began to make thunderous noises upstairs. I was deserted in the dining-room, among the overturned chairs.

Only Michael remained, or rather came back with more tea for both of us.

"What will you do to Lefty, Droyt, and Jeff Deegan?" he asked. He had a sadistic interest in tortures and punishments and he always asked this question.

"Why, nothing. You know I never do anything about what's past."

"Then we all could have walked out and gone when the 'bus was here."

"Certainly."

"Don't you like *any* movies? Don't you think it's an art-form like any other?"

"Ah!" I began to tell him of the movies in the pantheon, of *Potemkin*, and *Man of Aran*, and *Joan of Arc*, and *Le Sang d'un Poète*. I was willing to make a list of a dozen or even two dozen. What I liked to impress on him, on them all, was that one's positive judgments must be accurate and concrete (tho one is entitled to generalized negations). So we profitably talked, while the noise quietened and my good ones began to laugh again.

six

A delegation of the girls, Deborah and Seraphia's daughter, came with a flag of truce.

"Since we couldn't go to the movie," they proposed, "can we stay up late with a dance instead?"

"You can dance as long as a double-feature movie-show," I said. "But why do you ask my leave, since you bring down the records and dance every night anyway?"

"If we have the counsellor's permission," said Seraphia's daughter, "then it's a formal dance, not just dancing. We can decorate. It's a dancing *party*, for the whole group. Especially tonight, when we don't have to dress again, because everybody was dressed for the movie. That's what made it so bad, what you did—not that we missed the movie, but you made up your mind after everybody was dressed."

"You're right. I'm sorry. I don't understand these things."

"We know you don't, and we make allowances. You ought to follow Lawrence Dixon. These are just the things he understands perfectly."

In a few minutes they had organized a beautiful formal dancing party, with streamers from the chandelier and a buffet of soda and crackers. The phonograph was enthroned under the great mirror, and they chose an arbiter who would also, at the proper occasions, switch off the center-lights and play a flashlight. Formal dress meant clean tight-fitting sweaters without rips, or bright blazers, and pressed skirts and slacks. The arbiter flickered the lights and they came into the ballroom in a troop, and the machine at once began to play a fast neat foxtrot. Before my astonished eyes, their rainbow youth dissolved and coalesced into this dreamy pattern.

I sat down heavily and pressed my hand in front of my eyes for the waltz when it came, proved to be *The Invitation to the Dance*, in the orchestration of Berlioz, and the boy asked the girl, and she rose, breast forward, for the opening beat of the first waltz—rising in anticipation on her toes, and off they went. But they knew also nervous Latin-American steps and wild rug-cutters, and they could organize a Virginia Reel. At our school.

Lawrence Dixon wanted them to learn to be "gracious hosts and hostesses," not so much polite or expert as loving amateurs, loving sociality and unafraid to indulge in it. And they had learned it, to unblock a kind of orderly spontaneity that one did not see in other places, than at our school. I was a little piqued that one did not see it also, for instance,

93

in their Latin and History; but that was not their fault; we chose the curriculum and the burden of proof was on us — to unblock by these disciplines their lovely desires. (It could be done, but how to do it?) I had been a fool about the movies. For indeed it *was* their morals that I had been concerned about. That is, their style. One did not have to fear for their Style! They had plenty of Style. What they abstracted from those movies—things that I did not understand and likely would never be able to understand (because my own adolescence had been based on contempt for what was popular)—what they abstracted they turned to a stylish use.

I danced with Gracie, a pimply gangling girl who danced poorly but was not abashed by it—it was part of much else that she had to put up with, and she had learned to take it lightly. Lightly, already she danced better, tho she would never achieve that combination of deadly seriousness and pulsing vitality that most of the others put into the routine steps, with little invention. (Indeed, these routine steps are danced well only by fifteen-year-olds.) She horsed a little, as an adult does who has any life left, trapped in the too simple exercise. Regarded as a grown woman, and not by comparison with the others, she was not so unattractive after all. And this was the peculiar glory of the friendliness, the endogamy, of our school: that Gracie, without shame and without having to invent new defenses, could skip the steps of development, could agree cheerfully to have missed the beauties and dissatisfactions of twelve to fifteen. Nobody hurt her; and she too proved to have a style.

But the others moved and breathed with the earnestness and the abandon that came from a perfect mating of the form and the meaning: quite unconsciously to them, their sexual play became more and more overt.

Smirking, and also shyly blushing, Deborah Lowenstein asked me simply, "Will you dance with me?" and offered her arms. Her feelings were hurt because once more Jeff Deegan had gone off with the other two; maybe he would have done so even if he knew there was to be a dance. Jeff danced stiffly and correctly, he did not like to dance; perhaps he did not like girls, or perhaps it was only Deborah who embarrassed him.

"– he won't embrace with <u>any</u> one"

With this heavily serious young lady, it was inappropriate to make light conversation. Her facile tears moistened her eyelashes. So I said in a low voice, "What do you think of the shore-people you've been studying with Lawrence Dixon, the way they make love and carry on *their* affairs?"

"I wonder," she said, with thought heavy on her brow. "I don't know what to think of them." We glided across the floor. "I don't like it," she said positively.

"What don't you like? I think it's pretty sensible, not to regard a sex-partner so exclusively and so tragically, but take him just for what he is, somebody it's pleasant to be with and full of pleasure to embrace."

"Yes, it is sensible—when you put it that way." Her manner was affected, but so habitually so that it was a warm and rich style, if one did not mind the histrionic style. She was unfairly overpowering for these boys, but they had their own naïve defenses. "*Some* girls," she said, "think there ought to be more romance."

Her eyes sparkled. "Oho," I said, "that's why I wouldn't take you to the movies, they put impractical ideas in your heads."

"It's sensible," she said, her voice choking just a little, "but I never *can* be with the boy it's pleasant to be with and full of pleasure to embrace. What if he won't?"

"Why won't he? I shouldn't think *you'd* have any trouble, unless the boy is a zombie."

She lowered her eyes at the compliment and said, "You don't know Davy Drood—"

"Davy Drood?"

—"he won't embrace with *any* one."

All of this, the whole dialogue, she had been maneuvering up to the revelation of this name, thinking that I might be of use. I was surprised to hear the name, but I said, "Well, that's so much the worse for him."

The number ended. Lucy, the housekeeper, appeared in the archway with a young woman, with spectacles, dressed in a russet suit. I went over to them at once and was introduced to her daughter Veronica who had that very moment arrived from the West Coast; this was Veronica she had told me of, and we two would have a lot to talk about because we were both so musical. Another number started and I asked Veronica to dance, but she stepped back in confusion, she had just gotten out of the taxi. I went out and carried two bags in from the porch. "I'll see you," I said, and pressed her hand.

I was claimed by Claire. By this time I was warm and was enjoying myself very much. It was a fast jumpy number that I was afraid I was going to miss because of the newcomer, but she smiled and went upstairs.

With such music, the angular out-ankles farmer's style that I danced — that I had learned in Milton, Vermont, and never learned any better — was not odd or out of place; I gave myself to it confidently; and Claire and I bounced and jumped as fast as they played, and banged into other couples, and had fun. I was a poor partner because I failed to lead; on the other hand, I danced the dance as a whole, with a beginning, middle, and climactic end, so that I danced well if I knew the record and could predict its progress. The music I could control — this was my artist style — but my partner I could not control; so I protected my joy by letting her go completely free. And this suited Claire.

My kids liked me because I was having a good time.

I did not think at all of Eliza. I thought a little of Veronica.

seven

Davy Drood did not dance. He stayed to himself along the wall or in the back, not sullenly, but left out. Once or twice he quit the party and went upstairs, but soon returned. Then he left and did not return. It was as if, after a last look at the company, he intended to devote himself to dice-baseball, marking down the score.

It did not occur to me that he did not know how to dance. Yet so it was, and, being Davy Drood, he was too proud to ask to be taught or to risk the awkwardness of trying the rudimentary steps on his own. But how had this been allowed to continue during so many years at our school?

What was impossible for me was — to do nothing. I bounded upstairs and unceremoniously entered without knocking.

He was not playing the dice-game, but was lying stretched on the lower berth staring at the bottom of the upper berth, his hands behind his head. In the same impulse as I had gone early in the morning to help Eliza, and had sworn to help Davy and the others on the road, and had warmly danced the fast number with Claire, and had bounded up the stairs, I said, "Why aren't you dancing? Are you afraid even to touch the girls?"

"Do I have to dance?" he said hotly. "Why don't you mind your own business? Can't I have a good time my own way?"

"You're not having a good time. No shit with me. I have the right to all the shit. What are you afraid of?"

He said nothing and I was afraid that he was offended and was going to be sullen. But altho he was dark and secret in every way, there was no sullenness in Davy Drood. He was simply trying to answer my question and he could not define the vague feeling. I always misread him, in fact I knew nothing at all about him but acted according to my desire.

"I can't dance," he said.

"You *can't* dance?" I cried. "Everybody can dance!" I was taken aback by this remark from the mere surface of his circumstances. Always I expected at once to hit on something more fundamental; but he, when he tried to be honest, could see only the big obvious truth, that I was often too stupid to explore, for of course the surface expressed everything. (Apart from my emotional confusion, I was intellectually unfitted to play the role that I had elected.)

"Well, answer me this, Davy: don't you have a feeling for any of all these pretty girls?"

"I don't like any of them."

"Not even just to kiss? or to feel with your hands?"

He fell silent. With an effort he said, "Deborah Lowenstein. I'm hot to touch her breasts. And to suck them." He bit his lips.

"*Why don't you do it*"—I spoke with an edge of triumph. I believed in magic, the doctor was right; the fact that it was her name that he mentioned and his name that she mentioned (out of pique because Jeff Deegan had gone away with his friends), this was the sign of success; by this sign, if one had the courage, all barriers would fall and resources spring ready to hand—just as when I first set eyes on Davy Drood he was searching for the ball in the deep grass, but I walked to the ball and handed it to him. "Why don't you try it? And do you think that she wouldn't like it?"

"How do you manage?" said Davy. "You were dancing with her and pressing against her. I watched, her breasts were *flattened*. That's when I went away. I'm not blaming you, don't get me wrong. I don't think there's anything wrong in it. But even if I could dance, I'd stay far back, like this—"

"Look Davy. I'm more than ten years older than you. When I was your age I was much worse than you. And now I'm in a bad way, you know. I want to make sure that when you're ten years older, you won't be like me. I want you to be happy and goodlooking and smart and lucky, like Davy Drood."

I wanted results; I wanted to get him to begin, so I was willing to work on his pride and self-esteem; later I could return to the biting criticism which alone, I knew, could be effective with him. I knew this, I was not completely a fool, I somewhat knew what I was doing; it was only the place, the time, the opportunity, and the characters involved that were inappropriate. (I am not apologizing for this past, tho I should not today act in the same way.)

Besides, to flatter him with words was like caressing him, as I was not going to do.

He said, "Now I know what I'm afraid of. I've been thinking just what it is. If I propose to one of the girls, or try any funny work, she'll push me away, and I'll be made a fool of. Then she'll talk and they'll make fun of me."

"I'll make fun of you now. Don't you see, you fool, that the girls are furious because you freeze on *them*? You know as well as I that you're the leader of the class. You're so damned conceited that you've become afraid of your own shadow."

He got up. He was fiercely excited. He grabbed me by the lapels of my jacket and shook me. "How do you know she won't make fun of me? Can you be sure of that? That's just your opinion and I'm left holding the bag." He sat down cursing.

"If you have to know, she told me so. That's what we were

talking about when we were dancing."

"*She* said so? *What* did she say? What were the exact words?"

I was flustered. "I don't remember the exact words. Don't get so excited." I was frightened at his vehemence; I had imagined that it could be accomplished suavely, with every defense of my ego intact, and his defenses falling serenely away by magic.

"You *tell* me!" he commanded. "Don't squirm out of it. If you don't tell me, I won't ever talk to you again."

"Is that a threat? Hell to you, Davy Drood! You're not doing me any favors."

"Can the shit. I know your type. I know what you're after. You'd better tell me."

So. I dumbly opened the door to leave. I had not meant to be taken for a certain type, but to be regarded for myself (according to a fancied image of myself). I was hurt and I wanted to go away.

But Davy Drood bent over the table and began to sob, to sob out the loneliness of the evening when all the others were at the party dancing and he was lying in his lower berth staring at the bottom of the upper berth, with his hands behind his head. His sobbing was loud, but it was not perhaps loud enough to be heard above the fast loud music—except that Michael was standing at the foot of the stairs, intensely curious but hesitating to come up, and he heard the voice of his friend.

"There's nothing to tell, Davy Drood," I said. I was not angry, nor desirous, nor well-intentioned; I had no feeling but death in my heart and a little kindness that made it hard for me to go away now. "She said only that she was sad because you kept away from the girls because she would like to embrace you."

It was hard for both of us to face each other again tonight. But his need was so great that he began to plead with me, with almost a whine in his voice, and I could not leave, altho again I felt a crick between the shoulders. "What do you do when the girl's there?" he said. "Please don't go away for a minute. What am I supposed to say first? How do I get to put my arm around her shoulders?"

"I can't tell you *that.* You *do* that."

"No. Tell me. What do I say?"

"You just talk, the way you talk, about something interesting—interesting to her—don't talk too much about baseball."

"No. Tell me what to say?" He was pleading, not demanding. I wanted only to get away. "Should I try right off to grab her?"

"Oh Lord!" —This beautiful subject! this beautiful subject that should be a delight to discuss cheerfully, not without jokes, and to pass on from one to another our lore and style, in the interest of more pleasure and happiness on earth—this subject was now hateful to me, disgusting. I hated myself, and I hated our school. I should have wished the buildings of it to burn to the ground and sink into the ground. What I wished was to be far from here, with my child, in a desert place, and no more longing and no more possibility. I gripped hold of myself; I gripped the table till my knuckles shone, and I said coldly, trying to be friendly: "Don't *force* yourself. Don't try to make any motions that you don't have an urge to. Otherwise it turns out badly— we'll talk about that another time. Just be friendly, and feel friendly, and do what you feel. Don't be afraid because there's nothing to be afraid of. A girl likes to have her breasts touched lightly. You'll know what to do when you do it."

I could not. The pain stabbed between the shoulders till I gasped.

—As I think of this scene, trying to describe it, I feel mournful. But what I should be feeling is anger. Anger that this lad, so beautiful and gifted, should at the age of seventeen ask these pleading questions; and that I, one of the good wits in America and a teacher by my artist-instinct, should be trapped into fear and guilt, by a love mixed with repulsion: that there should be dismay and withdrawal instead of joy and eagerness. What has been done to us? Any other than I should have been the friend of Davy Drood; and apparently, if not I, there was not going to be anyone.

Michael rapped and came in. Davy straightened his face and said, "He's been trying to persuade me to dance, and now I'm going to give in and try." He slipped past

101

us and went downstairs.

"I'm not intruding?" asked Michael pointedly.

"No, I have to work," I said. I went to pace the hall, for I could not go downstairs and I could not stay in this room and I could not leave the building because I was their counsellor.

eight

The 'bus returned with the three young fellows. At first they planned to sneak in, but the lights were ablaze and they decided to brazen it out and make a noise. I came downstairs.

"Was it a good picture?" I asked.

"No," said Droyt frankly, "it was silly."

"Did you have a good time?"

"Of course we had a good time."

"Last dance," I announced. There was a groan, but the arbiter obediently chose *It's Three O'Clock in the Morning*.

They were tired and went to bed without a fuss. Lucy marshalled the girls and I the boys. As usual, I went into the big room to say Good-night and switch off the light.

I choked with anger that swept over me at last after all this sorry day. In their raid on the Morton Theater the three had taken not only the lights, but swords, a chinese costume, a pair of gourds. These were in plain sight on the wall.

"Jeff Deegan. You lied to me! —I didn't think that *you* would be a liar."

He blushed darkly.

"Skip it!" I said. "Skip it! . . . Good-night, boys." I switched out the light.

Shaking with rage I went below into Lucy's room and threw myself into the big chair. Her daughter brightly made conversation and seemed to be a pleasant girl, but I boorishly answered "Yes" or "No," staring at my hands.

CHAPTER VI

one

I was content, on the quiet Sunday evening, not to go over
to the other school and make peace with Davy Drood. Soon
they would all be here for the Assembly in any case. It
seemed to me that I had now lost them both, my wife and
Davy, or had given them up (it came to the same thing).
But, or therefore (it came to the same thing), I could not
help smiling. Smiling at my own character as I noticed its
operation, it wreaked itself so inevitably; it was a beautiful
machine, like a bicycle. The doctor was right; at bottom
there was no deception in my smile. Simply I was *interested* . . . We should see, when he came, how we stood, I
and Davy who "knew my type," the devil he did.

Meantime, it was a good interim to practice the five-finger
exercises that Bernardine had assigned me—a new art, about
which I knew nothing at all.

Our Assembly met in the lounge, the ground floor rear
of the big red building. One went in the little entrance, down
and up the ridiculous steps, with the puzzlement and unease
of the dream of Difficult Access—and merged suddenly into
this spacious and handsome room, opening out thru French
windows onto the pond. The red sunset was pouring in. And
the walls were decorated with the art-works of children.
Tony's *Dragnet* was there, his cavernous eyes borne toward
you by the four flying wolves.

I was practicing the slow arpeggios that wind from the
lowest to the highest and return heavy with tonality; or

103

supposing one goes the other way, they end screaming with tonality.

My piece was the little minuet in G-minor from Bach's *Anna Magdalena.* "No matter how slow you play it, still it sounds," said Bernardine. Soon Joanne, one of the algebrists, came early to the Assembly, carrying her recorder; and she stood at my right shoulder and played with me. The sun had set and one could hardly see the page.

At the return to the G, but now it was G-Major—

played softly, one could shout for joy, or jump from the chair with excitement, or be quite still—depending on one's temperament. Was it by such easy means that one achieved such effects?

two

The Assembly started to collect in numbers and they switched on the lights. The tempera and crayon drawings spoke from the walls—deeper than their makers knew, as Harrison had said; in fact, near to free violence.

At the Assembly the lower groups sat in front on the floor, and the greater ones and the Staff on benches behind and on the sides. But I sat on the floor with Tony and Dolly Homers' boy on my knees. The chorus and the recorders massed behind the piano.

Davy came in—the big ones were always late. He was radiating victory and hope; he wanted to speak to me at once. At once! But I waved him away and he stood far in the rear, studying a picture of his own, the largest steersman he had ever painted, on a tilted yellow deck washed by black seas. Everybody was present, even Veronica who had just returned. We sang *Greensleeves*. I watched Davy critically: he did not sing, because he had a poor voice, and wherever he felt incapable he withdrew.

The youth seemed alien to me, neither one of the most interesting nor one of the most beautiful.

While Mark read Bryant's *First Snowfall*, we passed around the new picture. It was an aeroplane by Knud, Dolly's oldest boy, an aeroplane in the sky such as Group II drew by hundreds. But to Knud had happened the following: he slammed the classroom door and came back to the dormitory speechless with rage, and he took out his best thing, the model-plane sent from Copenhagen, and he smashed it with his fists and crumpled it with his hands and bit it with his teeth and ground it underfoot, and then he burned the fragments in the middle of the floor. The soaring plane that he drew, that we were passing from hand to hand, was such as one would then draw.

The chorus and the instruments sang *Absalon*.

I was becoming very gloomy. The two small bodies heavy on my knees were not alien but very close. It seemed to me that always I felt this division, between my personal longing and this pattern of social creation that was also my personal longing; and I would not be happy at our school any more than elsewhere. I was not interested enough even to look critically at Davy Drood. I sank my forehead on the kids' shoulders. In an infantile voice Annie was reading the Group I creative-writing; but these pieces were always disappointing—"I am a Jack-rabbit"; "We took a walk across the bridge and saw the leaves falling off the trees"—because in everything the voice of Annie, who took down the dictation, sounded very loud. We had heard the seven-year-olds babble more post-Hebridean fancies, more flesh-tingling threats, thrillingly filing the teeth of death, than ever were conveyed on Sunday nights.

But the tales of the Second Group were excellent! one looked up and bared one's teeth.

Caroline had the knack of inspiring them, she had a "method." It was to discuss some simple and shocking fact of life, as that boys and girls often try to kill their baby sisters and brothers, and then to get them to write something. (It began to be clear to me that, with her blundering literalism, Caroline was a great teacher.) This week of "sibling rivalry," as Caroline entitled it, Katerina Jamison, aged ten, fair-haired and blue-eyed, had written as follows: Beverly became angry with her brother and she chopped him up into a hundred pieces with an axe. She buried the pieces under a tree. Then she was frightened and sorry and tried to put the pieces together again, but she couldn't. They wouldn't fit, some were lost. But a frog jumped out of the brook and hopping from one piece to another, showed her how to put the pieces together. And when she put them all together at last, it was not her little brother but Prince Charming.

We did not like to applaud the efforts of the children, but

this pleasant tale was like a little copse,

and we flushed and clapped our hands.

Davy Drood clapped and cried out with pleasure. Who was it cried out? It was Davy Drood. There was no use in fooling myself. The fact was that here, whatever else he was to me, was a youth who needed help, and he could be helped, he accepted help; and I could help him, and did offer the help, and was going to offer it; and *therefore* (whatever else) it was impossible for me not to love Davy Drood; because this is what love is. I understood it and stopped holding my breath and at once the tears flowed down my cheeks.

The Third Group, Sophie's, were very literary and mannered, and she could not make them unbend. Mostly the girls wrote day-dreaming romances and the boys sports stories in the style of cheap magazines. But this week Schuman, the boy who was the most dialectical of them all, surprised us by describing the stems of pond-lilies that entangle you in swimming; they go slimily down thru "slabs of darkness" into the "breathing mud," and "things are germinating there that will crawl out later on the land."

—As an author has pointed out (Jekels): there are two kinds of pity, the weak pity and the strong pity, and in me they were at that time inextricably mixed. The weak pity is masochistic; it is the desire to suffer the disaster oneself and then cry for oneself. But the strong pity, the compassion, is out-going; it is the realization that the other has suffered the same disaster as oneself (perhaps, even, I myself inflicted it), and one gives him aid, to make whole at least him.

Among Lawrence Dixon's big ones, Michael had written a delicious account of a cow-auction held recently in the neighborhood. He hit off the sadistic patter of the auctioneer, and he dwelt on the personal rivalries that raised the bidding to everybody's disadvantage. But what was best in his piece was his portrait of the cow, dumbly shifting amidst the eulogies and the bidding. His piece was already in the way of true composition, and I conscientiously jotted down notes for correction.

There was a recess for the youngest ones to leave.

Lawrence Dixon also read a piece of his own. It was one of a series combining the physiological psychology of the Yale Institute for Human Relations with the incidents of our school and the seasons of the countryside. In these extraordinary productions one met such terms as "goal gradient," "mental set,"

association of
the apple-pie on the window-sill above,

hard by accurate observations of birds and leaves and the discomforts of large boys cooped up in a study-hall. But while he was in the midst of reading it with great earnestness, a door slammed, there was an immense clatter, and Harriet—the small girl who used to hide in her pants like a turtle—arrived an hour late and cried out cheerfully, "Hiya, everybody!" In a month at our school she had found her voice.

The recorders played *The Little Shepherd*. The chorus sang a number of the *Peasant Cantata*. We sang half a dozen songs. And the Assembly was over.

three

Davy whispered gleefully, "It worked. Just like you said."
He had cornered me, but I extricated myself. "Not now,
kid," I said softly. "I'll be over later. I have to help Dolly with
the kids."

"No. Now. Just one minute."

"What worked? what did I say?"

"I touched her breasts and she liked it."

"Who? whose? what do you mean, you touched her
breasts?"

"Debbie's! Debbie's! Don't you remember?"

"Yes, I remember. Where?"

"What do you mean, where? Here—the nipples—" he
touched his own, not mine. "Oh—in our little room. We
jammed the door and Michael looked that nobody barged
in for half an hour."

I relented and did not try to get away for a moment. "Poor
kids. That must have made you nervous."

"No!" He cried it out with pleasure, the same cry that he
had spoken after the little tale. "*She* didn't care, even when
O'Neil tried to force his way in. I'll get even with him. And
I don't care a fuck." He said it with better than bravado.

"Good for you, Davy Drood. Did you have an erection?"

His face went blank. He stopped. "Was I supposed to? Or
not to?"

"It doesn't matter one way or the other," I said. "I'll be over
later. Now I have to get out of here."

"No!" he pleaded, grasping my arm. "That isn't what I
wanted to talk to you about. Debbie and I, we want—"

I broke loose and extricated myself. "We have lots of
time—" I said.

I kissed him on the brow, ostentatiously, in view of many.
For whatever my feelings and whatever my unease, I was
going to ally myself (tho not quite identify myself) with my
answerable love; but certainly I held it away from myself,
at my fingertips.

I was jealous. How quickly he had come to say, "Debbie
and I, we want—" relegating me, no doubt, to the role of

their instrument. What the devil did they want? I was not happy enough myself to bear the savage insolence of the young ones.

four

Our Assembly was always like this. Fairly monotonous but not dull; and very affecting, not only to me. Thru painting, song, and words our obscure feelings became obvious. And we were almost unanimous in singing the old songs.

Our Assembly was a festival of very true communication, considering that it was a formal occasion. Or perhaps, at our school, the fact that we could hit on the formality made our communication most true; for the communication was the function of a community that existed (so far as it existed), and the formality was a likely arrangement, a natural convention.

But what was missing from our Assembly was gaiety and urgency. There was every art, but not the art that decorates the present moment or that prophetically suggests the moment after the next.

May the creator spirit not turn away from us, and may the happier generation not regard us as beneath contempt and pity, but we needed these arts, we needed these universals (as I need them still and write this, and therefore write it), because we did not dare to be concrete.

five

As I came up the narrow stairway and my head rose above the landing, it flashed into my mind that Dolly was demented. The two kids were wild with delight and could not get over staring at each other and staring in the mirror and shouting. She had bisected their pyjamas down the middle seam and sewn the diverse halves together, making one suit yellow and blue and the other blue and yellow.

"Look at *me!* Look at *him!*" they shouted, leaping from one bed to the other. Dolly laughed, and fell silent, and laughed.

"She says we're Hallowe'en," said Tony.

"Not Hallowe'en, harlequin! stupid!" cried the little Dane. "Isn't he silly?"

"No, you're silly!"

I did not belong in this company. I had to go downtown with Dixon and Seraphia. It was not the night for singing; we had already had enough of community songs.

six

The boy was lying in wait for me. He appeared from the sere-leaved bushes that had once been thick with forsythia.

I was pleased to see him. It was exciting to touch him in the night; but the air was cold.

"It's you again. You'd better be getting back before they start looking for you. I'll walk you down the road."

We walked hand in hand. On the left the black brook meandered away from the white road.

He withdrew his hand and came to it directly: I was to get him a contraceptive at the village drug-store, if he needed it.

"Why, yes—" I said spontaneously enough. "That's the kind of thing that a friend does for a friend."

"When? tomorrow?"

"Oh? . . . Why tomorrow? I'll have to discuss it with Lawrence Dixon, but I'll do that as soon as I can."

He cried in alarm, "Don't do that."

"Why don't do that? He might not say No. But even if he does say No I'll do it anyway, since I've given my word. He'd be wrong."

"No no!" cried Davy. "Don't mention it at all. Don't do it at all, then."

"Why, I must mention it. It's important, don't you see?"

"I'm sorry I asked you," said Davy bitterly. "What the hell's it his business—after all these years?"

"Davy! it's for your own good. You ought to have a decent

place; it's not pleasant outside in this cold weather. It's not so simple."

"It is simple," said Davy. "You yourself said so, and you were right. Now you keep saying, 'Why, why?' You know damned well why. No, don't!" he cried. "Don't mention it to anybody, and don't do it. Anyway, she won't, so what's the use?"

I took his hand, dumbly, to show that he had support. He had trapped me saying "Why, why?"—which I said because I did not know. I was puzzled—but I could not find the answer without initiating new complications—whether his request expressed a physical urgency or was an idea in his mind. If he failed (which was probable, the first time, in such circumstances) it would be unfortunate if his desire was not immediate and strong. The thing was to slow down. But now he had no time. And my guilty involvement made me too weak to talk plainly and take the upper hand.

"You hardly know this girl. Can't you wait a couple of days?"

"I've had nothing but an erection ever since!" he cried, "ever since you mentioned it before. You were right about that too. No! Don't mention it to anybody, because she won't anyway, she's afraid. Forget it. Forget I ever asked you for anything. I should have known I couldn't rely on you. Don't you mention it again or I'll never be your friend again."

I seized him by the shoulders and squared to him in the darkness. "See here. This is enough of this hocus-pocus. Listen carefully to what I say. I'll discuss it with Lawrence Dixon no matter what you think, because it's more important than you think; it's a matter of policy. I'll discuss it with him tonight, at eleven o'clock sharp. Whether he says Yes or No, I'll do what I can for you. What you want is perfectly sensible and, you're right, it's simple. Furthermore, she's not afraid. You're the one who's afraid. Don't be. I'm your friend and you *can* rely on me. I'm not such a good friend as I should be or as you deserve, because you're remarkable; but just now I'm saying the best I know how. Good-night, boy."

He called after me, but I would not look back. I was

animated by my forthright speech—you could see the breath in the night—and I was ashamed of the falsehood distorting it in the past and in the future.

seven

I was stopped outside the door of Dixon's office by loud angry talk between Dixon and a young woman. I turned away, not to overhear it, but almost immediately Dixon strode out, heated, his face contorted, and he said, "Wait outside; I'll get the car."

The young woman began to cry and came out; it was Lucy's daughter Veronica. Seeing me, she tried to stop crying but could not; but instead of hurrying past as I expected, she stood leaning against the door weeping, looking like a bedraggled schoolgirl. I could not walk away, so I said, "Can I get you something?"

She sobbed that Dixon wanted her dog to be operated on. Then calmly, drying her eyes and wiping her glasses—in a gesture exactly like her mother's—she explained that Dixon would not let her keep the dog unless she were spayed, because there were too many dogs.

"Oh, forget it. Disregard it," I said. "Don't take him so seriously. He can't remember one day to the next."

"But it's done already!" she wailed.

"That's too bad." I could not think of any special consolation. "—That's strange. If it's done already, what were you shouting about?—surely you were quarreling. I couldn't help hear the voices."

"But I didn't get angry till afterwards! I never do. That's the trouble with me; in everything." She began to cry again, one last burst, but already brightening considerably, as an April day brightens during the rain.

I put an arm round her shoulders. "Come, come. Why don't you come to the village with us and have a drink? Or maybe you don't want to see any more of Dixon tonight?"

"No, I'd like to. Let's go. As long as he didn't see me crying I don't care. If I have to stand him tomorrow, I can stand him tonight. If I sit in front of him and smile, he'll eat his heart out," she said savagely.

She fixed her face and we went outside. Dixon drove up with Seraphia. I was pleased to have someone else to dance with than Seraphia, who tended to melt and to have to be pushed around.

eight

At once, before shifting into second, Lawrence Dixon began to praise me for the job I was doing with Davy Drood. Davy had been seen — imagine it Seraphia! — trying to dance, and that was all because of me.

"How *did* he dance?" I asked curiously.

Beautifully! — (Lawrence had not seen it either). Before I had come, the boy had been retreating into himself and regressing sexually; but I, Dixon praised me, proved to be exactly what he needed: a kind of big brother with such a brilliant intellect that Davy did not have to be too proud to take my advice and imitate me. The latest thing was Davy and Michael's film society: they had got up a collection to rent famous old films from a museum in the city; they sold blocks of tickets printed on a hectograph.

"Did they do that?" I cried out. "He never told — I didn't know anything about it. I had nothing to do with it." But I changed color and sank back in my seat, and, full of ease, took Veronica's hand.

Full of ease — for my attachment to Davy was such that the greatest possible satisfaction for me (I do not mean the satisfaction of the keenest desire, for that could not be satisfied) was for him to caress me by imitation, to regard the fact that I existed, to become what I fancied I wished I were. I took Veronica's hand — for from the beginning the pattern established itself that, given comfort by Davy, I could give myself to Veronica.

I took her hand, without further desire, *pro forma*, since we were together in the back of a car.

nine

"I am glad you got to know Vonny," said Lawrence at the first opportunity. "She needs someone like you. She is shy."

"Shy?"—it did not seem to me that she was shy.

"Yes. You'll find out. I remember when she was so high—isn't that right, Seraph?"—it was striking that he asked for her support, confirmation, or approval on what must have been a question of fact—"she used to hide in the corner and stare at us."

Seraphia was Lucy's oldest friend. Veronica used indeed to sit in the corner glaring with sullen hostility at the men who came, brooding over the lurid unknown that went on in her absence. Year after year she was sent to a convent boarding-school, returning only for the holidays.

When she danced, she was resistant in one's hands, over-controlling the rhythm, anticipating the beat. Yet if, as I was too disposed to do, I ceased leading and let her go free to dance her solo while I danced my solo, she at once showed signs of panic anxiety. Then she would softly, and even languorously, yield, but in such a way that she no longer moved at all; only an explosive would make her budge. But on the other hand, if the music was fast and bouncing and free-limbed, a polka, she would dance it with breathless gaiety, her face highly flushed.

According to my puritanical standards, she drank too freely; I felt a revulsion when she became flushed and talkative. But in fact she did not drink too freely, for she did not give way to any deeper feelings.

One did not know, one did not know—in this engine of delayed reaction—what smashing blow would fall.

I became uneasy and irritable, my confusion again began to engulf me. I was poor company at a little party; it was impossible for me to have a good time. There were too many ties—it was I who gripped to the ends of them: Liza and my sister and Davy Drood and Veronica, and all those other possibilities, necessities, of involvement. The soldier leaning at the bar.

My lungs were bursting, what I wanted was air, free air. I got up abruptly—but went, not outside, but next to the soldier at the bar, and stood there frozen and apprehensive, longing for a sign of love from a stranger, where no such sign would be forthcoming, and in circumstances where, even if it were forthcoming, there would be no opportunity for gratification. It was eleven o'clock.

ten

"Lawrence, I am glad to have this opportunity," I said. "I want to talk to you about Davy Drood."

I was glad to be able to broach the subject not with Dixon alone, but with the others there, with just these others there; they put us both on the spot. Publicity was the end of hocus-pocus.

"We just now," I said, "have a chance to do something worthwhile for Davy. The main thing he needs, of course, is to accept and affirm his sexuality—with our approval, because he is afraid. Well! He has found a girl he wants to have sexual relations with, and she too wants to. We ought to encourage them by furnishing contraceptives and also by giving them a convenient occasion together. What do you think?"

Dixon's face was frozen.

"It needn't even be a general policy," I said, "but only the special case of Davy Drood. Remember he's seventeen years old. The girl is fifteen."

"No," said Dixon.

"I'm sorry you say that. Remember, you can't stop them from doing what they want anyway. Don't you think we have a duty to provide decent circumstances?"

No one said anything.

"I never heard anything so fantastic in my life!" cried Seraphia. "What kind of school does he think we are running?"

"Hush, Seraph," said Dixon, "it's not fantastic at all. If— if it were only Davy, I might say Yes. How can I say Yes for the girl? I ask you that. Who is the girl?"

"I'm damned if I'll tell you who the girl is!" I cried. "Aren't you ashamed to sit there? Afraid of the parents. You know

115

that everywhere they carry on anyway. What's the good of your school if it doesn't provide better circumstances than the average? Where else is a boy supposed to learn to use his powers?"

Dixon began to rub his hands and wring his fingers, with a grin of delight.

"You had him for twelve years!" I shouted angrily. "And now look. Nobody cared for him, till I came." This I ought not have said.

"What about the girl? what about the girl?" insisted Seraphia.

"I don't give a fuck about the girl!" I exclaimed, quite beside myself. "She's not such an innocent, I know. None of the rest is either."

"*You* know!" cried Seraphia. "How do *you* know?"

"The reason you're so excited," said Lawrence Dixon, with the peculiar vibrancy in his voice that sounded during his flyers in interpretation, "is your homosexual attachment to Davy. This is just why you have homosexual tendencies, in order to have sexual relations with women by proxy, thru other men. Exactly. Now you want to use Davy Drood."

I was pleased; I was only too eager to air my guilty secrets, and I exclaimed, "Right! this time you hit the nail on the head. Why do you think I have been forced into this stupid way? Not thru *my* doing—but just because when I was at the age of the boys in Lawrence Dixon's group, instead of their encouraging me to love my girls honestly and honorably and gladly, they frightened me, and shamed me, and thwarted me, and made me guilty. It happens that I can remember the exact incidents that did the work! Very banal! But that was not at a so-called progressive school."

"You think you're a friend to Davy Drood," said Dixon, rubbing his hands with what looked like almost delicious joy, "but in fact—you're saying it out of your own mouth—your motives are envy and hatred!"

"Who's projecting now?" I started to cry out, because these were his feelings towards me. But I cut it short; I was afraid to fight it out, I was dependent, I could not risk losing anyone's benevolence, even when I knew that this benevolence would vanish in the crisis. This was not yet

"What we have devised is a trap".

the crisis. I became moody and icily hostile.

I had not planned that my reasonable plea on behalf of Davy Drood should lead to hot words (tho I had hoped it would lead to revealing my own motives). I had not really expected Dixon to say Yes; yet sometimes, just in the teeth of the worst complications, he could be expected to do what was outrageous and courageous, quixotic and correct.

Coldly hostile, I was able to see the evening laid out in its anatomy. "If it were *only* Davy," said Dixon, "I might say Yes"—this was obviously a lie that he told himself, and therefore it must be interpreted as the opposite. Surely it was because it was *precisely* Davy that his face froze. And perhaps because it was precisely I who asked. And also, therefore, he made the precise flyer in interpretation. He had loaded me with praises: that is, he was jealous of my friendship with Davy. Why *was* he?—for it did not seem to me that his interest in the boy was erotic like mine. He spoke rather like an offended father who finds that a stranger has told his child the facts of life, when he himself has failed in the duty. I ought not to have let myself say, "You had him for twelve years!" Not yet. After all, it was Lawrence Dixon's school, that is, his father's school.

Because I could see the situation a little clearly, I was able to hit on a cruel sentence to begin again, and break the silence. I said in a low voice, "The kids are right, I thought they were wrong. Do you know what they say? They say that it's really worse for them here than at a strict place. We encourage them to unblock their feelings; we let them know that sexual pleasure is beautiful and fundamental to everything else. We raise the tension. Then we say No. At another place they would not have expectations, they would not be tormented."

"Who says it?" cried Dixon. "You're putting it in their mouths."

"Oh no I'm not. Let me finish. What we have devised is a trap. If they were at some other place, they'd manage all right. They'd make the adjustment to concealment and subterfuge; they wouldn't give their feelings away—then the smart adults could imagine there were no such things. Meantime they'd perfect tricks for sneaking out; they'd have places to go to; and they'd protect each other with sadistic punishments for stool-pigeons. Am I making it up? Am I making any of it up? But at our school—nothing. Freedom!"

"If that's how you feel, why don't you get out?" said Seraphia. But Lawrence Dixon said, "No, Seraph, it's his school too."

He looked groggy, as if I had fished up beatings of his childhood. He said, "Is that how it is? Is that what they say?"

I became frightened that he was going to break down and give in, and leave me with Victory on my hands. I did not want Victory. I was unable to wield it.

He said, "I don't deny it! If a fire broke out and burnt our school to the ground, they might be better off.

"Probably we are trying to prevent their pleasures simply out of resentment. Maybe all of it is a rationalization."

I did not press my plea further. "I am sorry we got so heated," I said. I got up and walked to the door for a breath of air.

The soldier preceded me outside and got into a car. I loitered near and he held the door open for me; but since it was now impossible for me to go with him, I smiled sadly and smoked my cigarette, adding such and such more drops of poison, unacted out desire, to the misery of the world.

eleven

Veronica clung to my arm with a heavy pressure, as if I had distinguished myself by some heroic deed and therefore had the strength to support her.

However it was—with what could be called cunning, if she were not ingenuous—she encouraged me to speak of the boy for whom I would have chosen to suffer and die, but not to relax a muscle of my pride.

CHAPTER VII

one

The morning lay still on the fields and hills. None of us watched the sun rise. (Into the gorge) the light hardly filtered, altho there were no leaves on the trees. Under thin ice and in the open the black brook glided at its ease. The branches of the big sycamore scratched the upper windows of the big red building.

Abed, my body was rigid, my head thrown back and legs akimbo, and fingers taut above my genitals: I lay in the form of a lute.

But in my dreaming head shone our old pot-belly stove with its flaming crack. I opened the door of it and the door broke off in my hand. It was disintegrating and the fiery coals poured out over the floor.

A voice was screaming "Fire!"—a voice unrecognizable, because one did not use to hear voices in such extremity. By the time I looked out the window to identify her, she was vanishing round the corner of the house, but her fleeing streak was still fading across the road. Max had begun to pound the iron tire for the alarm. More clangs than the hour of the morning. It was a fire, no dream.

I could see, across the road, a little smoke curling from one of the basement windows of the red Assembly building. I pulled on trousers and a sweater and shoes I did not lace. Max continued to bowl his iron bowls.

Outside was no one but Seraphia. I was the second. "Are the babies out?" she screamed, and she plunged into the

121

entrance where that narrow winding-stair began. At once, before I could follow, she reappeared, choking, followed by Sophie and the small children, choking and coughing: Sophie was carrying one and there were the five others, all in gray pyjamas. One could see at a glance that the six were there, not yet crying, but I slowly counted them over. Now Mark and his wife and their baby had emerged from their entrance. Mark in his bathrobe was pitifully directing a hand fire-extinguisher into the dark more thickly smoking window. As if in answer, the first tongue of flame flew in his face. Max left off his clanging and the six children began to cry. In an instant there were many people. I did not see clearly what to do so I jumped on a bicycle leaning against the sycamore and pedalled down the road toward the high-school to 'phone for the firemen, for the other 'phone was in the burning building in the black smoke.

Riding away from the scene: I felt that it was incumbent on me to do what was brave or highly reasonable. (Feeling so, I would never be the hero, if occasion arose, who reacts before such feelings.) I thought: "if I could do them a great, irreplaceable service, then this would count for me when I am exposed and about to be expelled."

By the time I hurried back, they had organized an un-skilful bucket-line from the stream, were dashing spilling pots of water into the hot golden basement windows. I joined this line, gasping for breath. A good deal of water was spilled and all knew that this activity was useless. As we carried on the regular activity, it was possible for each one to recover from the psychology of the social emergency to his private concern.

"There goes two years' work!" half laughed half cried Mark Anders as, next to the window where he had taken his stand from the beginning, he aimed pots of water with no inspired accuracy. Was it his apartment and furniture, or his file of cards and his career, that he thus lamented? Whichever, it was evident that he thought of his life and action according to a rational schedule unique amongst us.

They had brought Lawrence Dixon by car. He walked back and forth in front of his father's building, rubbing his hands maniacally. Then he said (as we take refuge from the present to the cause), "Where did it start? In the boiler-room, I knew it!"

"No, not in the boiler-room. This window. That's where the coal is."

The whole school was out, kept back along the wire cowfence, down the road, across the road, in lines. The rule was: each child has to touch the fence. The big girls and boys began to come up the road on their bicycles, some on the cross-bars.

"Here come the firemen!"

As if in answer, the first sheet of flame flew upward over the face of the gaseous building. We fell back in fright. We were content, now that there was an excuse, the presence of the experts, to give up our meaningless bucket-line. I ran across the road to find my boy, to make sure. He was with Teddy and the other small children. Dolly and Seraphia had gotten them oversize warm coats. It was impossible, unwise, to keep them from the spectacular scene, tho they had not had breakfast.

We helped with the apparatus, quickly ran the pipe into the brook and unreeled the hose. A fireman braved the darting flames to point the nozzle of the hose into the window. But no stream of water came because the pump was connected in reverse; instead, there was a hiss—of air, and bubbles gurgled in the brook.

At this moment Mark Anders gave the order to Caroline, to count all the children, one by one.

Gusts of flame, first sporadically, but then with a certain regularity as if it were a breathing beast, flew from the first and second floor windows. By some interplay of the drafts, the gusts blinked alternately on the left and right sides. Frequent sheets of fire washed over the whole facade. The stream from the hose caused a kind of hissing on the surface of the fires.

One of my unlaced shoes stuck in the mud, in the brook. I paddled for it in the frigid water, in vain. I hobbled back, my left foot bare, and stood close enough to the bonfire to warm myself by it. I held my palms out to it.

"The coal! that's what it was!" importantly said the captain of the firemen to Lawrence Dixon. "We had three, four fires like this. You overloaded the bins!"

"Yes!" cried Dixon, with the edge of joy that comes from seeing the middle-term, "I told them to bring the usual load. He said four months or nothing; they can't deliver in wartime."

"Same story! Spontaneous combustion!" cried the chief with deep satisfaction, as if there were no fire after all.

"This isn't getting anywhere," said Dolly to the fireman. "Douse a bit on the sycamore, so we save at least that!" He obediently played a stream on the tree.

The sparks were leaping high into the air.

"What's about it spreading?" we asked the chief.

He raised a professional finger in the breeze. "No chance of it!" The sparks were falling into the brook, with little hisses.

Caroline returned to Mark with her report: "All present or accounted for," she said cheerfully.

"Count them again!" said Mark Anders in a strange voice. "Bring me a written list."

The sparks were leaping high into the air and across the brook toward the house in the gorge, where Caroline, Veronica, and a few others lived. The dried grass finally ignited. I began to hobble toward it. Max was charging there with a spilling bucket in each hand. I painfully hobbled across the bridge and we doused the grass with bucketsful. Madly Max pounded with a broom, he pounded out the little tinkling fires, but still he pounded as tho he were pounding the earth, or still pounding the iron tire, more than was necessary. He was dumb with despair. Because I had no other recourse of feeling—and he could hardly speak English in any case—I touched his oil-stained sleeve. He was crying.

Caroline, who lived in the house in the Gorge, came over hot with fury. She stamped her foot. "I won't! I won't count them over a third time, a fourth time, a fifth time. Twice is enough. Each time you'll get a different number, sometimes less than there are sometimes more than there are. Does he think it's a lesson in arithmetic. Look! now look what he's doing. He's lining them up in groups."

So it was; across the bridge, in the pasture, they were being lined up in groups, in size place, so that Mark Anders himself could count them. The big ones, Lawrence Dixon's boys and girls, were not lining up but were hopping around hooting at something. I was glad that I was not near enough to hear and know. No one had as yet had breakfast, tho it was an hour since the alarm.

The fire was no longer an exciting spectacle, for it had made every conquest and was blazing in triumph. The building was burning evenly from wing to wing and from the foundations to the roof. The fire was in the stage of monotonous fascination: a spectacle for the subliminal attention, endless pleasure. Free rioting. Consuming, without hope or fear, all accumulations. The inner drafts were now even and there were no more alternating gusts at the windows, nor any gusts, but steady puffing of the thousands of little mouths of fire, quicker than a dog's panting, quick as fire. Nor no more windows, but a skeletal frame for the fire. Certain gases did not ignite at once, but came alight, so there were brighter puffs and streaks of fire interposed between us and the darker licking fires. Also paler sheets of fire, transparent to the streaks and tongues both. This was the wished-for, the dreamed-of fire—there were black places—the magic fire; the thought of it, when there is not yet a fire, rouses suffocating anxiety in the breast and throat, but afterwards, when there is a fire and the fire had made all its conquests, it is lulling. The firemen have put down their hose, they stand and watch. Here across the brook, I can see, across the burning building, that the over-topping branches of the sycamore have caught fire, like a little tinkling diadem, but no one is concerned to save the sycamore or to save anything. Max and I and the children (oh, and I hope Mark Anders!) stand and watch the relax-ing fire. The whole of the fire, the burning building from end to end and from bottom to top, is reflected upside down in the pool where the brook widens as it glides at its ease. If Max and I were over there, with the others, we could not see this reflection of the fire in the brook, as well as the naked fire itself.

After a while, a large central part of the framework fell down with a sound and an uprush of fire—everybody cried out—and there was left, surprisingly, standing in the midst, the tall brick fireplace and chimney in which there was no fire. Also, we on the other side, could now see the sycamore revealed, its brown and cream badly scorched with fire.

two

It was not easy, it was impossible, to take up the routine after the fire (the fire was of course still burning). But it was necessary to keep them in classrooms, not playing in the live embers. There was a danger that the gaunt chimney would topple and murder someone; but one could not set a reasonable boundary line, for the chimney might fall clear across the road.

I set my algebrists to calculating the arc of the maximum crash. We took the height with a transit. For safety's sake, we saw, we should have to dynamite it. But really the only problem they were interested to solve at their inquisitorial, sadistically curious age, was "What started the fire?" that is to say, "*Who* started the fire?" I told them the chief's theory of spontaneous combustion, but they would not be satisfied with an impersonal agent.

But it was a terrible question to ask, "Who started the fire?" For such a question comes soon to be, "Did *you* start the fire?" And what can the answer be, that rises stifling in the breast and throat, except, "Yes, I—I started the fire." Or I could have projected the guilt at once, onto Lawrence Dixon. Only last night he had said, "It would be better if our *whole* school burnt to the ground." But it was Mark Anders who started the fire, *playing* with fire, pounding with his poker at every staff-meeting and making the sparks fly up; and I knew why.

"Spontaneous combustion!" cried Adelman scornfully. "Because they loaded too much coal in the bin and the pressure was too heavy. *Who* loaded it in? What about *him?*"

"He couldn't make more than one delivery this winter," said Harvey.

"*Why couldn't* he?"

"Because of the war and gas-rationing, stupid."

"All right! Then it was the *war!* Why didn't you say so

in the first place?"

The new theory, that it was the war that started the fire, was intensely satisfactory. The class (ages 13 and 14) seized on it with enthusiasm. The images of the war were great, terrible, fiery enough to carry the emotional charge of the experience of the fire. And the war was a properly guilty object. Brought up in the bedrock rationalism of our progressive education—where we taught them to be simpleminded about what was most gross, leaving subtleties for subtleties—they were, at 13 and 14, all pacifists, violently aggressive pacifists. The war, whatever else it was, was gross foolishness—inefficient, solving no problems. Those who caused the war should be torn limb from limb. It was intensely satisfactory to abreact the suppressed excitement of our fire by prosecution of the agents of the universal fire.

"Then who started the war?"

But they knew all about this, in all its complexity, the chains of events, the western sellout of the Weimar Republic, the depression, the defection of the German communists in 1932; or that the big war could have been stopped at the Rhine or in Spain, except that the British and the Americans preferred to let it rage; and then this Hitler and the psychotic personality of the German people. They knew it all, in a large way, taught by the radical parents of some of them and by our good teachers. Yet it was a terrible question, "Who started the war?", because soon it came to be the question, "Did *you* start the war?"

"Spontaneous combustion! Spontaneous combustion!" I insisted, with the sportive attitude that meant, they knew, that I would defend this paradox against all comers; that I would defend it behind prison-bars and also (this I did not myself know) on pain of death. They loved to bait me into this attitude.

I made them get back to the point, the spontaneous combustion of coal in a bin too heavily laden. Yes, the pressure, the ignorant heaping up, these were factors (and if we were thinking of the spontaneous combustion of the war, we should have to look for the pressure and the ignorant heaping up). But also, one had to look into the nature of coal: what gases were there, and what fine particles of dust? And

127

how was it that pressure generated heat?

The thirteen- and fourteen-year-olds in our class, such keen algebrists and so astonishingly largely informed about the universal world, were seething under pressure. It was a pleasure to be their teacher. But one did not have the feeling with them—as one might with the children of six or seven—that they were like wildflowers of the field, blooming with the powers of all the heavens and the earth. Like Max, one could pound the earth in dumb despair.

three

Lawrence Dixon, who had only in a certain sense started the fire, was flushed and seething with ideas and problems. "Shall we cancel the Parents' Day? No, just the opposite; we must especially have the Parents' Day. It is the great opportunity—amid the smoking ruins, etc.—to get funds for the New Building."

"New Building? What new building?"

"Is there to be a New Building?"

"What about the insurance on the old building?"

—The shell and fixtures of the old building were covered by insurance, about $20,000, tho one could not replace them now, if at all, during the war, for 50 or 60 thousand. Mark said, ominously, "It must be a fireproof building."

"All right!" cried Dixon—we had the habit, that the kids acquired from us, of crying "All right!" just when it was all wrong—"All right! $100,000. What's $100,000?" Meantime the insurance did not cover four grand pianos and Mark's laboriously furnished apartment and his carefully selected library of a thousand books. It was generally agreed that there must first be indemnity for private losses, and of these, first for Max and the dishwashers who had lived in the top storey.

Impulsively, in the beloved social euphoria, I was going to blurt out that I knew an architect. I restrained the impulse and bit my lips.

A moment later, rationally controlling my feelings, I suggested that I knew an architect, a great and famous one, who, if I asked him, would come up here without fee and estimate the costs and say what could be done, and even draw some sketch-plans for discussion. He would surely do this because I had described to him our school, what we aimed at, the kind of people these were, and he had felt left out—he would be only too eager to collaborate, without a fee. But then, I had to warn them, we would have to take his suggestions seriously, and not have impractical notions.

Dixon grew enthusiastic, my words often had the faculty of arousing him; and my heart sank, as often. But as usual he said good things: We had a tremendous opportunity! he said. We would create a building, an example, that just because it was functional thru and thru, inside and out, would have the highest style, would express our best ideals. We would have scheduled meetings with the architect, and every member of the Staff would think out and put forward his notion of the functions that such a building must house, serve, express. More important, every young person in the school must be made to see that his behavior, the steps he took, his feelings, were influenced by the plan of the building; therefore he had a concern in deciding the plan. Not in a general way, but in detail, this building must express the habits, and the freedom, of the ultimate users. It was our duty to look into the manner of similar buildings everywhere, in foreign countries—the architect would recommend magazines, bibliography. The disaster was salutary because it made us turn sharply on ourselves and ask how, under what conditions, we were moving our bodies about. (One would have thought, to hear him, that there had never been any complaints about the heating and plumbing.) All morning he said, he had been reminiscing about that old building, many images had flashed into his mind, outlooks, corners, things that he never thought he had noticed but there they were in recall. There were many unpleasant associations—many beautiful ones, of course! But a new beginning! And we had the chance finally to introduce, relevantly, the class project that we had sometimes entertained—perhaps especially for the third group—the layout of rooms and buildings, technically, socially, biologically. Perhaps my friend the architect—no doubt he was a very busy man—tho what building was going on during the war?—("War buildings," I said drily)—perhaps he would come up once a week and lead the discussion? Find out what he liked to eat, once he had tasted of Bernardine's artistry, he would come back for more. Later—of course this was anticipating—when it came to the actual construction, there would be the opportunity, the need—need was the real educational opportunity—for every one of us, child and Staff, to lend a hand. How soon could my friend arrive? Could he have any sketches by Parents' Day, not serious studies of course, but just an idea—for fundraising purposes?

Caroline said, "If you're thinking of having dormitories, let me tell you right off this way is the best way. You can close your minds and not waste time. Here, I'll draw you a picture: You have the bedrooms round an open space, this is the meeting space for parties and so. Besides, it is easy to supervise from there. That black spot is my desk. There are either doors or just openings depending. The arrow's the way out. I figured it out long ago, so I might as well horn in first."

It was as much as six hours since the first alarm—the Staff-meeting had been called after lunch—yet now suddenly Sophie flushed and trembled and faltered on her feet, with shock. Yet it was long ago that she had awakened smelling smoke and thrown the door open and cried out for her youngest, and led them all out of the building. The recall of it overcame her, after a delay. The Doctor made her lie down. She took a drink. Her eyelids fluttered.

"I'm better now," she said in a good voice after a few minutes. "It spread so fast—you wouldn't imagine it. You think you'd have time to pick up a few things. But the smoke. That's from the open doors, isn't it?" The Doctor bundled her in a fur coat and took her upstairs.

Seraphia sat mopping her brow and saying, "Thank God, there were no kids hurt. Thank God for that. Every time I think of it I get weak."

"Where is Torgesson?" said Mark in a strangled tone. "I didn't see him just now—I looked for them all. He's the one I never counted in."

"Jesus! Mark Anders!" said Caroline. "He's in my group. *I* ought to know—he read the map in geography two hours ago."

"He didn't come to lunch!" cried Mark. "Don't tell me he was there and I'm crazy."

"No, he didn't come to lunch. I said he didn't have to. I sent him back to sleep because he couldn't stop yawning."

"*I'll* go to look if you won't!" snapped Mark, and he struggled into a coat.

four

It was my coat, my second-best coat, a ripped sheepskin that surprisingly fitted him across the shoulders; I should have thought he was larger. He was wearing old pants of mine, several inches too short. I recalled that (it seemed years ago) Dolly, who was outfitting the small ones, had asked if she could take things of mine, for Mark.

Mark looked at me and said, "Thanks for these clothes. I'll give them back tomorrow, soon as possible." He went out.

"If he begins to count again," said Caroline, "I'll scream. Thirty-*eight!* thirty-*nine!* Skiddoo."

He came back. He was framed, as one is, in the doorway; attended to; seen. His shoulders were narrow in the coat.

"Oh yes, Torgesson, the one was Torgesson," he said and closed the door again.

Watching him out the window, I could see that he was going to count again.

I said to Dixon: "I think you'd better walk after him to cheer him up. I would myself, only we—" But Lawrence, I realized, was not a likely friend either. I came suddenly to feel that, in our beautiful sociality, if once there was a need, rifts appeared, and impassable gulfs. The atmosphere was unfriendly and chilly.

Assuming (so I speculated) that the obsessive counting was masturbating—for security—in the emergency— What emergency? Mark, of course, Mark and his wife were the only ones who had lost anything vital in the fire. "There goes two years' work!" he half laughed half cried it, directing

131

the ludicrous little chemical-gun into the cellar. I tried to intuit my own reaction in a similar misfortune: suppose *my* dear manuscripts burnt up (so I hatefully conjured them out of existence). I would feel defeated, an oppressive weight on my shoulders, unable to give lively attention to anything, no crispy smile. As for the furniture, the idea of a home, if that was it—I had lost my home, such as it was. But Mark, tho his shoulders were pinched in, held his head high, was more than attentive, was jumpy. When the fire was at last blazing unconstrained, having made every conquest, he did not stand and watch it with endless pleasure. That was when he made them line up in the pasture. But by then he was already counting; he first got the idea when the pump failed to produce—aha! (I could not feel myself into this character.) Security against what? Obviously he was experiencing a fearful responsibility: the need to prove to somebody that he was guiltless; he had not failed, nothing had happened. Did he hate the children so, that he wanted to lose them? Again, why especially Donny Torgesson, who had been the subject of a Staff-meeting, whether or not he was to go home to his mother on the weekends? Ah! aha! but no! on the contrary! Turning it this way and that, I knew nothing about it at all. And even if I could shrewdly guess where it was all tending (and what my inability to empathize with it meant), what could I do? Meantime someone, I, ought to do Mark a friendly service. Surely! the spontaneous prompting of the heart, without reflection, that was the right way, the human way! I felt no spontaneous prompting.

I put on my own, first-best, coat. "Is there anything I can do?" I asked simply.

"Is there anything *he* can do? No, there's nothing special for you to do."

Indeed, when it came to the primary arrangements, to clothe the unclothed or to reorganize the rooms so those without shelter would have shelter, or that the functions of the office could proceed, there was nothing special that I could do. But I had daydreamed of doing some irreplaceable service, so that when I came to be exposed it would count for me, when I was about to be expelled.

"You'll need my typewriter temporarily; it's under the bed."

"Oh, yes, the typewriter," said Dixon. "That's indispensable."

I planned to walk over to my big ones; but then we should start to talk, all over again, about this fire, and it was coming out of my ears.

five

The coal was burning briskly, healthy red flames in the early-winter day. From time to time pieces of what had collapsed collapsed further. The iron pipes were twisted in Z's and an A. The brown and cream patches of the sycamore were blackened up, but one could not predict whether the tree would ever again give forth green leaves. The chimney had no cracks; to my eye it did not look like a present danger.

"There you are! I was looking for you." It was Michael. I was not displeased to see him.

"Now look, Michael—don't ask me my impressions of the fire." I spoke with a buoyancy that surprised me, for I hadn't imagined that this was how I felt, but it is only the social situation that reveals us to ourselves. "I know that you're covering it. 'Where were you when you first heard the alarm?' In bed, stupid, alone. I know the whole questionnaire by heart. Please, some other time—never."

"The chief told me that the coal would go on burning five, six months—rain or shine."

"I don't believe it," I said.

"I wasn't looking for you to talk about the fire," said Michael.

"No?"

"Something else."

"About your movies?"

"Oh, did you hear about that?" he said with a flash of pleasure. But then he resumed looking at the flaming coal.

I shrugged my shoulders and also looked at the flaming coal.

"You're making a mistake," said Michael, "the way you fuss around Davy. You're going to get in trouble.

"Don't be angry. I know it's none of my busi— No, that's what I always say; it *is* my business."

. . .

"Well, say something. You're mad."

"I'm not. It's your business."

He brightened and became more voluble. "You know, everybody talks, especially the way you carry on, without even making any pretenses, way Shep used to. Then one day, even so, bing! bang! Take my word. Uncle Michael has been here nine, ten years."

"Do you really think I don't make any pretenses?"

"Yes. Do you?" he asked, surprised.

Because of my guilt I made such pretenses as spoilt my satisfaction. Because of my idea of myself, I refused to make such pretensions as would be useful. It was grim; I had to smile at the neatness of it.

"For God's sake, Michael, look at it my way once. If I can't—make advances—fuss around, as you say—if I can't make advances when my heart is in it and I feel like it, and I can't make advances when my heart isn't in it and I don't feel like it, when am I supposed to make advances?"

"I don't dig. Is it supposed to be a joke?"

"Yes."

"You embarrass Davy."

"Who said so? did he ever say so? did he?"

"No. But it must."

"How do you know so damn much, what's what?"

"Well, somebody said somebody said anybody's afraid to be alone in a room with you."

He had come to the point. Now I was angry.

"Who said that? Come on. Talk or don't talk."

"I won't tell you."

"Hell you won't. Are you sure that *you're* not the one who first said it?"

"Me? I never said it. It was Jeff Deegan."

"So. It was Jeff Deegan."

I was discouraged and I counter-attacked. "Michael, shall I tell you what the trouble with you is? You're jealous of

Debbie, what's her name, Debbie Lowenstein. You're burned up at Davy. This puts it up to you, doesn't it? To look at yourself. *He* has a girl and what have *you* got? So I'm a likely devil—it's *my* fault."

. . . He was badly hurt. He was only fifteen years old. I had to mollify him at once, and I said, "Why don't you get yourself a girl of your own? You're a handsome boy—and you certainly have the smoothest gab in the group; as you know."

But I saw that this tack made it worse and worse; for his jealousy and inferiority were of course pervasive. I said, "Why don't *you* get *yourself* etc." and meantime it was I who was doing everything for Davy Drood. And touching Davy Drood, but not touching Michael deVries. It was coldly unfair. It couldn't be helped!

I touched Michael's hand, but I had no pleasure or desire in this touch, and this too was obvious.

"Don't feel that way, Michael," I pleaded. "You know I'm fond of you. Really I'm probably fonder of you than of anybody in the whole school. Davy's a pain in the ass, sometimes I could shove him under a desk and leave him there. But— Excuse the language."

It couldn't be helped!

"But—" said Michael.

"We'd better get going. We were supposed to have French at 2:30."

"The others'll be even later."

Suddenly he burst out laughing. We went down the road. I waited curiously to hear what breastworks, what general defense, he had now repaired to. Always I was struck with astonishment and admiration at the ingenuity, the valor, the culture with which these young ones made it all right again. It was only I whose defenses roused in me only disgust (and that was the measure of *my* ingenuity).

"It's a comedy!" shouted Michael; he was convulsed, laughed heartily, almost without a block. "This love-shit with a capital L, you can just sit back and roar." He found his full gab again. "Claire can't sleep and she prowls in the hall, Debbie gnashes her teeth behind the piano. You've got brains and you act like an ass. But for *nothing*, for *nothing*.

135

"This love shit with a capital L,"

An idea in the mind. Davy is fit to be tied. But the richest! the richest is Larry Dixon and that black cow Seraphia — oh, rich! rich! you could write it in a book and nobody'd believe it. How the Gods must be laughing!"

He was laughing with a good voice, no edge of sour grapes or revenge. I for my part envied him where he stood, at about the age of ten, at the height of contemplative power, where indeed most of us, as the case is, would do well to have stayed, for from there down we get only more idiotic.

"You're wrong," I said. "That's all they put in books and everybody believes it."

One had to restrain Mark almost by force from sounding a fire-drill the same evening. The Doctor had to say No, categorically. We settled for a continuous regular nightly tour of inspection, till such an hour as every counsellor and teacher was back in his rooms. We drew a duty-list.

By night the leaping flames of the coal did not look so healthy and cheering. The sparks flew high and far in the wind. "I shall watch it, tonight, every night," said Max.

CHAPTER VIII

one

To those with wider experience, the fight between Jeff and Davy was a typical incident of Parents' Day.

At meals at the upper school, a line formed at a window from the kitchen where Bernardine and her assistants served the table-monitors who held out their trays. There was always horsing and pushing for position.

Davy Drood was on the line and Jeff Deegan pushed his way in front of him; that is, he either did or he didn't. "Quit it," said Davy, or "Sore loser!" Next moment he had struck him behind the ear. The Irish boy was surprised and dropped his tray. Yet he must not have been altogether unready or unset, for he drove a blow to Davy's heart that knocked him flat on his back, and one does not throw such a punch unprepared: it is pent up. Perhaps as he cut into the line Jeff also made some remark.

They helped Drood to his feet. "Murder him!" said Ross, the poet's son, in his ear, and pushed him forward. Shoving aside the tables, the boys formed an enclosure; others, and some of the girls, stood on the tables to see. The mugs of milk tumbled to the floor.

Davy Drood was gasping and flushed, but would not stay still. Jeff's olive face was pallid, he stood waiting on guard, a little taller. It was a bad set-up (tho a good match) because everybody knew that both youths were indefinitely wilful and courageous; nothing was to be discovered by confronting them, no test of superiority or unsuspected temper;

139

nothing but the technical matter of which, by skill or force, would seriously hurt the other, who would not give up. But we were not connoisseurs.

The sun fell into the room thru the leafless magnolias. Davy fought tigerishly, spitting and cursing—his disadvantage was that we did not bite in fights. Jeff was always pale and silent, he strode toward him and drove a hard blow to his mouth. Davy bled. Jeff hit him again, a blow on the cheekbone that made the head snap back. But Davy lowered his head and charged flailing into the belly of the other who stood too upright, and he hurt him.

Our kids had no pleasure from this punishment of their brothers (if it had been two of us they might have worked up plenty of lust for it). The girls looked with disapproval at Debbie who was, perhaps, the cause of the fight. If she felt, as no doubt she did, the stifling excitement natural to a girl in such a case, it was not heightened by the admiration of the rest.

The two broke free from each other and stood back a moment with flaming eyes and hoarse breath. There had been momentary cries, no hubbub. No one cheered them on now.

It was as if the perceptible falling away of the sun behind a distant cloud disturbed them. Jeff stepped back another step into those against the wall. Davy turned away and pushed his way thru the crowd and could be heard pounding his way upstairs. He slammed the door of his room. Jeff moved his tongue in his cheeks; he remained solemn and would not say anything.

Bernardine said they might have bread and butter, but she would not serve them Sunday Breakfast in such circumstances.

two

It happened that the first of the parents to arrive that morning was Davy's mother, who drove from the city with Michael's mother and Mr. and Mrs. Thumim.

I had been passionately expecting her.

Davy was badly marked up and had to tell her about the fight. Later, Michael described the scene to me. Ann Drood took it sensibly. She suggested camphor for the bruised lip, and at once she drove over to the infirmary and got the stick of camphor. She laughed at him a little because he was such a sight. Michael's mother was more alarmed; for a while she looked at Davy's face with dumb horror (and Michael was glad that it wasn't he). Ann Drood insisted on keeping the matter within its proper bounds; she wanted to save the young man embarrassment. As soon as she could, she reverted to the regular order: she had brought the wax for the snow-shoes. She went down to the car and got the wax. Davy brought down the shoes from the wall.

It was not that Ann Drood was unfeeling or uninterested. On the contrary, she took Corny and Ross aside and asked them how Davy had acquitted himself (Michael was mortally offended that she did not ask *him* this). Had he acquitted himself, in their opinion, like a man? She did not ask who won the fight, and she was not interested in what the fight was about.

Next on the agenda was to look at the still smoking ruins. Soon Ann Drood was walking across the bridge with Dixon—and this was the first that I saw of her. I came by casually, but they were, of course, animatedly discussing the drive for the New Building.

"Here he is! the new man," cried Lawrence. "Surely Davy has told you about *him*."

"Yes, he has," said Ann Drood, and gave me her hand. The hand was a worker's hand, but well cared for.

Davy had refused to accompany them on the tour of inspection. He had to put himself in order. He was now able to grin at his marks. He wanted to get to work on the snow-shoes that needed six, ten, twenty coats of wax.

So he sat there in the carefully-made lower-berth, that now had a few bloodstains; and he began to polish the two pairs of snowshoes—one for him, one to lend (me)—with a chamois cloth, thoroly rubbing their long lengths. My poor one who—yes!—had manfully acquitted himself in the fistfight, and would yet again acquit himself manfully on many occasions, no fear of *that*. He fixed his attention on the details of the job; he also oiled the thongs. It flashed across his mind that he was meeting Jeff on the porch — this was horribly awkward — the Ionic whorls of the porch-posts were like small high breasts. Obviously at a school like ours one could not bear grudges.

But for Jeff Deegan, no parents came at all. There were no living parents, and the relatives he lived with were very poor, in chaotic surroundings, etc. — that was why we had him. Now he usually stayed during the summers too. It no longer struck him as especially unfair, or as a subject of hatred or envy, that the parents of others came. He took Parents' Day lightly — except for throwing a savage punch to the heart; he had made a good adjustment to the situation. The fact was that he was the particular favorite of *all* the parents, inevitably, because he was wonderfully handsome in the dark Irish manner, he had a winning personality, solemnly frank. Also, without ill-intention, he continually spun a web of cunning private interpretations.

These then, Davy and Jeff, were the two who had had the fight before breakfast on Parents' Day, the ones who, if I could achieve my smart schemes, were supposed satisfactorily to embrace Debbie and the other lovely girls.

three

But it was Sophie's day. In the afternoon her group would give its play, prepared for months. In the morning her parents, the grandparents of the two children, were going to be married.

It was a brilliant day, hardly chill for December; ice melting in the brook, white clouds: more like the forecast of spring than like a renewed Indian summer (for sometimes it is necessary for the meteorologists of the spirit to put the beginning of spring before the winter solstice; how else to live thru January and February?).

When Sophie's parents — she was nearly thirty and they looked to be in their early sixties — first came to America, they were socialists of that period, with anarchistic wisdom, no friend of the State, Religion, Private Property. They had

142

great hopes in the innate dignity of individuals and in their
natural social groups. Such persons did not submit to legal
marrying—any more than the man submitted to military
conscription, so long as there was a corner of the world to
escape to; he came to America. But alas! in the land of
freedom Jake Landsberger helped organize the electricians,
he rose to a position of respect and respectability in trade-
union politics, which is not dissociated from governmental
politics; and now there was a little private property and the
problem of inheritance.

The couple were delightful; they had courtly manners that
seemed to be showing off for company but were usually an
habitual overestimation of the company. Jake had assidu-
ously perfected his English in 1908, and he still spoke the
slang of that period. Minnie still did not speak English well
and was fearful that by not catching the nuances she was
likely to cause offense. It was impossible not to show them
that they were with friends by making fun of them.

"You see, Jake," I said, "now you are in the trap, like all
the other fools. First you begin to compromise by sitting
down with Federal mediators—"

"On our terms!" protested Jake. "They came to us; we
didn't go to them. In 1912—1923—the Norris-LaGuardia act!
Why shouldn't there be orderly process, due process?"

"Naturally. Look what happens. Next—wait, let me talk,
I'll soon be finished, then you can say your say—next, as
if by magic, you own a little property. An accident—it's not!"

"A fortune it's not!"

"And now you have to protect the inheritance and you
get married! Really, no fake, did you foresee it?"

Minna cried out in alarm. "I told you, Jake. They think
it's wicked. We should think it thru again." She lapsed into
Yiddish. The matter was too important to be treated as a
mere convenience. It set a bad example.

"I'm joking, Minna, I'm joking," I protested.

"He's joking, Mama," said Sophie.

"With her you mustn't joke," warned Jake. "Everything is
earnest."

"I'm very sorry."

"With me you can joke!" cried Jake. "Please, go on, I'm

interested. You say one thing leads to another. Minnie, you go with Sophie and meet people."

Corny's father, the judge who was to marry them, came to be introduced.

"You see, Jake?" I nudged him, "a Judge."

"What kind of judge is he?" said Jake thoughtfully.

"He's in the Appellate Division."

He puffed out his cheeks and blew. "The Appellate Division is not so bad! We went to the Appellate Division in *Jaspers vs. Tin and Tube*. We won, didn't we?" He spread out his hands.

"*Adelman!*" I called. My algebrist was flying by, shirt-tails out. "Come here, Adelman. This is worthwhile. I want you to meet Sophie's father, Jake Landsberger. He's vice-president of the Electricians. He says that the Appellate Division is not so bad as the rest of the system. It's a nice distinction, let *him* explain it."

"Adelman? Ephraim Adelman's boy? I am pleased to meet you. I used to know your father. Sophie mentions you."

It was passionately moving. Again I saw—what had to be brought home to me again and again, and *was* brought home to me again and again—that we were the salt of the earth, the "lunatic fringe," as we would say (but let no one else dare to say it!); and that the target-center of us was just in our school, in such schools, so that here all gathered together and proved to be acquainted. Acquainted? Lovers.

But Adelman, judicially, more judicially than the judges of the Appellate Division, was interested only in the line of argument. He asked a few probing questions that showed he knew all about it, more than anyone else could possibly know. Not to show off, just to establish himself.

The old man was on his mettle. With marvellous grace he did the impossible: he simplified the technicalities to the understanding of a smart boy and at the same time sharpened the distinctions to the shadings and subtleties of an intra-party faction fight. I had expected the boy to run rings around the old man; instead I was rocked by the fact that both of them began to fish up arguments that cast light on matters of fact. It seemed grim that Jake Landsberger should be wasting his time with the Electricians (of course

Parents' Day

I do not mean the electricians) instead of teaching at our school. And the *whole* truth was that we were all teaching at our school.

Adelman got heated and began to shout: "That's what you *say!* that's what *you* say, Landsberger! 'Win here—hold 'em there!' And Bang! tomorrow! tomorrow they drop a bomb on my *head—my* head—" he pounded his head as if the chief concern of his hot idealism was his head. "*Your* fault!"

"*My* fault? *I* drop the bomb?" said Jake, sadly.

"I'm sorry," said Ephraim Adelman's son. "It's a manner of speaking."

"Now I have to go and get married!" said Jake merrily.

People had begun to gather in the gymnasium. Many had known about the wedding and had brought gifts. For my part, I was furious with Sophie, who had not told me. It was just for this event that I could have written a poem, an "occasional poem, the highest kind—" said Goethe; truly, if it is indeed an occasion *for* one, with people one comprehends, in institutions whose principle one can at least partly affirm. Jake and Minna would have liked my poem.

It was Parents' Day, they went in family groups. One could see the strange resemblances and variations. I bethought myself that I too was a parent and could parade my boy, who was as beautiful and gifted as any. I galloped upstairs, but he was out playing.

Dolly was in a black mood. Seated at her desk she was writing one letter after another, the script tinier than ever. Outside it was so bright, and almost warm.

"It's almost time, Dolly, if you don't want to miss the wedding. They're collecting in the gym."

She turned like a spring, that loosens with a sound. "I am *not* going to that wedding."

"Why not?" I was a little frightened.

"It is simply disgusting. The idea of it! What can have possessed Sophie Nordau? What do they take themselves for? In school, in front of all these children. Has she taken leave of her senses? Or even publicly at all. But these are my standards, of course. Maybe I'm old-fashioned."

"Are you serious, Dolly?" What she said was without precedent or connection with anything she had ever said.

145

"Yes, I'm perfectly serious. Are you?"

"Where is Tony?"

"He's at the barn. I'm ashamed to go out there and appear with my children."

I went slowly downstairs. Too sad and oppressed; I did not intend myself to go to that wedding. I thought of my own mother —

She was dead a very few years. She had died in Florida, just at the winter solstice, and I went down there. I thought of Mignon's song,

Kennst du das Land?

and I sang it over. The oppression of it was relieved, but the sadness only deepened. There it was always summer season, and I saw palm-trees for the first time.

I remembered that, once, I came home as far as the door; and inside my mother and the little boy were noisily playing at a parade, with the blare of a horn, the bang of a drum, and a marching song; and I could not turn the knob, for fear that suddenly I should hear the silence fall.

four

Michael made a comedy of the fact (it was a fact) that I would end up where there was the best food; and Mrs. deVries had indeed brought a bottomless hamper of turkey-legs, bananas, sandwiches, and vast thermos bottles.

"What's wrong with that?" I cried. "Fritz Perls says that if the food tastes good life tastes good, and he means it literally."

Ann Drood said, "Now I have time for you. I have been looking forward to it."

We found a place around the back, out of the wind, in the sun, quite comfortable, if one had hot coffee, which we had. The two women and their sons and I and Tony and, I think, Corny and Seraphia's daughter. But they were all so beautiful (not only our group), for on the face of one was sensibility, of another reason, of another humane suffering, of another animality, of another childhood, etc. It was desperate of us that we were not simply pleased, but had to bawl for pleasure.

I was compelled by Ann Drood. She had the same wide-apart eyes and matte skin as Davy, but more regularly good-looking features. Her eyes were gray. Her deadly traits of matter-of-factness and social intelligence were evident, but they made her erotic attractions only the worse, for I longed to be hurt and ruled and kept in order, "breathing," as Harold says, "the wine-currents of being guided." I had no defenses against this cruel mother. Unfortunately—or fortunately (it comes to the same thing in this sorry story)—she was too old to be physically desirable, at least at a first meeting.

Always it was not these boys that I was bent for, but in the end the mothers of these boys. *This* was the respectability, the regularity, the due process leading to acknowledged power, that I, who was unkempt, rebellious, and begrudged, was fantasying when I fathered myself onto Davy Drood and the others—to be the cause of their perfection, to unmake the damage in myself. And now the mother was here, the source of well-being, no fancy but the thing itself.

In the company of Ann Drood, it was possible for me to sit near Davy, to play with his hair, and not be always conscious of him. Soon I was not conscious of him at all, except as a means to make myself important to his mother. I was surprised, but not with a pang of surprise, suddenly to notice that he was no longer there. (Where had he gone?) Ann took it as a matter of course, that he had his own little business to attend to. Her sentence was, "Now Davy, don't let me interfere with any plans you have." I judicially marked down this sentence to her discredit.

Yet all the better if he was not there. (But where had he gone?) Ann and I could talk about him the more intimately. Ordinarily, as with Veronica, if I talked about Davy Drood, it was for the erotic pleasure of keeping him in the imagination and in the throat. But with his mother, I talked about him, clear-headed and voluntary, in order to touch her.

—Yet these feelings I was aware of, were not my true feelings at all, but just the opposite. With Veronica, to talk about Davy was a preliminary pleasure, that I could feel, in order later to fuck the pretty girl, as I deeply wanted, and could act out but not feel. But with Davy's mother, my desire to reach her, using Davy only as a means, was really a concern with my child-self, and soon it brought me back to touching Davy Drood.

I said, "About Davy—I hope you won't be offended. You will be, but it's my business and you'll find I'm not afraid to speak my mind."

"Please. I'm all ears."

"Somewhere along the line—it's hard to put one's finger on it—you hurt him by requiring too much. You demanded too much. You wanted him to be a man too soon. Not your fault, of course; a child is a nuisance and a person has his own work to do."

She showed a sign of annoyance. I was on the right track.

"Perhaps you don't realize, Ann—I'm sure you don't—what a figure you cut. So sensible, understand—I'm not being sarcastic. To a child it might seem—hard. Not *you* hard, but it hard. Cold. No? You *are* cold.

"Anyway the fact is sure: your Davy, who is a remarkable young man—I couldn't deny it if I wished to—has a persistent feeling that he is quite inadequate. He can luckily excel in almost anything, but if there's something he can't excel in, or even can't do right off, do you know what he does? He runs away and hides. He can't sing, so he won't sing. He can't dance, so he won't dance. And—what goes with that. I have no bright thoughts what to do about it; he's not exactly in a formative period. But we ought to call a spade a spade."

"How do you know so much?" said Ann Drood. "Really, I'm not annoyed. But you seem to forget that it's a very complicated world. What about his father?"

She ought not to have said this and baited me. "Now I'm really going to annoy you," I cried. "And you'll never speak to me again. And I'll be sorry. I'll make a conjecture; if I'm wrong I won't say another word and you'll be getting off easy.

"I don't know the first thing about Davy's father, he never mentions him. *Why* doesn't he? Only what everybody knows—that he was nothing but an artist. I am too. *We're* on the other side of the fence. But you, understanding nothing, expected of him so, and so; and you didn't go out to him here, and here. And after a while he wasn't even a man—instead of buoying him up and supporting him, as you can!"

"I beg your pardon!"

She turned her face away and made a clean, terrifying smooth curve from the deep throat to the tip of the chin.

Partly I had not reckoned with the pleasure of the scientific chase that always makes us go too far too fast. But of course I knew I was right, and why not say so. I wondered whether she would hit me with the lunch-box or just get up and leave.

Fortunately there was an interruption and she lowered her eyes. Ray Lowenstein, Debbie's father, came walking toward us across the dry grass.

(But of course! I nearly cried it aloud. Davy and Debbie had chosen the opportunity to decamp together. It was a pleasant idea, caused me only a faint pang; for it meant that Davy had departed not just to avoid his mother; on the contrary, her presence had been an incentive. And then, my guess at their relationship was not accurate either; and that was good.)

Ray asked if it was I. We introduced ourselves. He wanted to know whether I knew that Deborah had ambitions to be an actress. I assured him that when her group came to give its play, Debbie would have not the least role. Despite our assurance, he felt that he was intruding, and he left.

"You mean," said Ann Drood, "I belittled Davy's father and this has made him insecure about his own masculine role."

"They are commonplaces, aren't they? That doesn't make them false."

"I tried to guard against that."

"But you still do it. Asking Corny whether Davy acquitted himself like a man in the fight. Hoping for just the *opposite!*" I cried. "To unman him."

"Just now, you said I required *too* much! They get you coming and going, don't they? That's another commonplace, isn't it?"

"Ann! I'm not trying to blame anyone. What do you think I am?"

"You don't know the first thing about Davor's father, you

yourself admitted as much," she said angrily and got up. "You don't know what I'm afraid of. And I'm certainly not going to discuss it here, now. His father and his friends. I'm not sure I like you, either."

I too got up and said roughly, "Look, Ann Drood, you're a Marxist, aren't you? Then you know how it is: in the end it's the most mechanical interpretation, the *most mechanical interpretation*, the most unbelievably banal and mechanical interpretation! that hits off what happens."

By this time she had recovered her aplomb and said, "Look, as you put it, I have to drive down to Ollendorf's to get the fuel-line blown out so I don't get stuck in Croton. Won't you come along with me and we can talk on the way? But don't let me interfere with your plans."

"Please, may I?" I persisted. "I have no plans. I'm useless here."

We got into the car; Tony climbed into the back.

"You know, that was not very newsy, what you were telling me," she said as she drove along. "I can't imagine why I lost my temper."

"I didn't hope it would be newsy. I don't even care if it was true."

"Don't you? then why bother talking?"

"Just to get into closer contact with you quickly, Ann. We have so little time on Parents' Day. Even at the cost of making you dislike me."

She considered this a moment, for I said it quite ingenuously. "You're very attached to Davor, aren't you?" she said.

I toyed with the question. Should I tell her right off that I was sexually attracted to her son? that indeed (but this I would not say) his interest was to me a matter of life and death? With everyone else at our school, I felt guilty—I had to conceal myself or by reaction violently reveal myself. With Davy's mother my interest was a matter of simple fact, that I would mention or as yet omit to mention, as prudence dictated. It was not that I relied on her to take a tolerant view; but that in this relationship, with her, it did not make so much difference whether or not the roof fell down. The big devil had driven out the little devil.

Nevertheless I did not mention it.

"Modern society", said Lawrence Dixon, "is
sick in three basic functions: Community,
Economics and sex."

five

In the genre of the quixotic, of the valorous and fundamentally relevant in circumstances imprudent and ludicrously irrelevant, of simple logic tossed on the seas of uncontrolled associations of ideas, Lawrence Dixon's appeal for funds for the New Building before the Group III play was his supreme effort during the period that I had the pleasure and pain of hearing him.

This time we were all there, the whole school, both the school and the parents, in the old gymnasium our theatre.

He began with reminiscences of the burned building dear to them all, but pointed out a number of its deficiencies, especially what proved to be the grand one: children lived in it and it was not fireproof. Luckily we had now a warning. (He did not point out, what scarcely needed pointing out, that the building we were now gathered in, with its dormitories upstairs, was a still worse firetrap.) He went on to describe the idea of a New Building, a model of function and beauty, repeating the things he had said prematurely at the Staff-meeting. He drove home the educational value for everyone, of planning and constructing, and paying for, such a New Building.

So far he was excellent. There required only to give some rough figures of the cost, and to sit down.

But once on his feet, it was impossible for him to sit down. Not that he was long-winded; on the contrary, Dixon was usually rather elliptical and rarely boring. But therefore the only way for him to continue, if he could not expatiate, was to tackle ever new subject-matter.

"When I think of what we stand for," he said, "I realize proudly that we are pioneers." There was a changed ring in his voice and I turned pale; it meant that he had left his notes behind and from here out was sailing on his own. "I have become obsessed, obsessed with the thought that we do not go far enough; we do not dare. All right! we are to have a New Building!"

—He had said the fatal words, "All right!"

"Modern society," said Lawrence Dixon, "is sick in three basic functions: Community, Economics, and Sex. At our school we have community." He giggled. "We teach community because we have a community. Our people communicate; we are sensate. Our assemblies are beautiful; the unknown conflicts rise to the surface, and we reproach them against one another. But what's the good of it if, because we fail in the other two functions, we ourselves *create* the conflicts with which we reproach one another? As I am reproaching us here, now!" He rubbed his hands and giggled.

"So what are the *two* most important issues in modern life, in modern evaluation and reform? the goals of modern education! Remember, I am looking forward to the future, but the future is upon us. *Sex and Economics.* In these aspects is our school a preparation for life? are we doing the job?

"Remember, in progressive education we hold that only life is a preparation for life. Childhood is not a previous, preparatory, inferior condition. It is a life in itself, with its own demands, its own laws."

And he proceeded, with perfect directness and continually mounting hysteria, before the curiously assorted audience, to argue that the children could not live because their parents did not make them economically independent and our school did not grant them sexual autonomy. As always the most terrible blunder was a stylistic one. "We shall want fireproof dormitories!" he cried. "For what? for what?" This naturally became a byword.

Yet—it was astonishing. Some of the audience—the new parents—stirred uneasily; but on the whole there was little disturbance. They all knew Lawrence Dixon well, they had heard him many times.

As for me, if I had been one of those parents (as to be sure I was), I should confidently have given over my child to Lawrence Dixon! quite apart from the truth or falsity of anything he said. For the man whose mind could so freely, so uncontrolledly, proceed from somewhere to somewhere, obviously getting wilder but never getting lost, such a man might prove unbalanced and erratic, but he could not have a settled vice of character that could do any harm in the long run.

Fortunately the ending was better than the middle.

Lawrence bethought himself that Sophie had a play to give and it was her day. He pointed to the coming presentation (which he had not seen) as a demonstration of what we stood for and could accomplish.

He was warmly applauded. Pledge blanks would be mailed in a few weeks.

The lights were dimmed. There was the magical hush.

That afternoon I was not backstage, but I knew this moment well. The scene is set; something has been omitted, but it is too late to remedy it now. The arrested feelings vibrate in the breast—one contracts the breast—it is stage-fright. But they will flow in wild joy if the first words ring true. And with these kids they will ring true. One does not wish his actors and actresses good luck; this is nefarious. But it is not nefarious to touch a shoulder and when the curtain rises to burst into (silent) tears.

The play, *Race Problems*, did not deceive one's expectations, nor Dixon's confident pointing to it as a proof. What! it was a composition and collaboration and execution by a sampling of the best intellects and the freest expression in the United States. I am writing soberly. Of Adelman, and Leila, and Harvey with his grotesque I.Q., and Netty Fieldston, and Schuman; and teachers who could not, in the end, suppress the secret longing for paradise; and others who fled from the tyrant. In our school, the heart-center of the "lunatic fringe," as we would call it, but let not the others dare to!—we at-sea and demented ones, we poisoned ones who at least suspected how it was with us, not like the others; refusing to resign our creative natures that would, in the end, draw on the energy of the heavens and the earth, first the earth then the heavens; lonely, yet surprisingly we found ourselves acquainted thru a hundred connections. Here was the proof of it! that we were the salt of the earth.

The play was not what they give us on Broadway, nor what comes out of California. It was not even the play that I, or my friends, write in isolation and execute in conditions that do not allow of fraternal conflict, out of which comes what one did not know one knew.

It was a long play. It was several hours before they came to the final dance, the Riot and the scene of Reconciliation.

During the dance Jeff and Droyt and Lefty bathed the stage in red, in blue, in a weird nothing-color, expressing the tension of in-between.

six

I kept a close watch on Sophie, Mark, and Lawrence Dixon. So far they had not noticed the stolen spotlights.

The stage was blazing. Still no response. So Jeff had won the bet. He knew them better than I.

Yet—spotlights! How did one not notice spotlights, and turn and ask, "*Where* did the spotlights come from?" I was at a loss; I began to be angry.

The play was absorbing, but it was not absorbing in *that* way; it was not absorbing in that way for *us*; we had no right to be absorbed in that way. We were not people to be played on by effects; we created the effects, and were created by the effects. We gave ourselves to the activity and grew against the activity; we were not spectators.

What was wrong with Sophie, Mark, and Lawrence Dixon? How—finally one had to confront the question— how did Dixon dare to talk about sexuality and economics if he could not notice that there were these spotlights? He was a hypocrite.

The spots were stolen, it was well that they were not noticed. But it was disgusting that progressive teachers apparently did not recognize that that weird nothing-color, the color of the tension of in-between, came from a material means, and did not ask themselves, "*What* material means? *where* was it stolen from?"

I knew that this obtuseness of theirs boded ill for *me*.

seven

I looked up at the three fellows perched behind the backboard of the basketball-hoop. They were revelling in the color. It shone back on them. They were Indians. Whispering and gesticulating and arguing and putting their

155

fingers over their lips. They flickered in brilliant noon and black night, like Man, the domino. This sight—my three big ones up there, creating the effects—this was at least as absorbing as anything that could work on the stage.

The stage was entrancing. With Louise they had worked out a slow growth of vegetative life, stretching its muscles, and about to bloom like a flower. The lines of harmony rippling from Bernardine's fingers at the invisible piano were combining to a crashing wave.

There was a hiss of sparks and a bright flash. The place was plunged in darkness, house and stage.

"Shit!" said Droyt's voice.

There was a strong smell of burning rubber.

Mark made a sound like one wounded.

It was a pity, for the kids onstage, for the lights to blow five minutes before the curtain; everything else had gone perfectly.

Mark breathed badly like a man who is hurt.

The grown-ups laughed nervously; the small fry hooted and whistled. The house became noisy, but nobody hollered "Fire!"

"Shhh!"

Max came with a flashlight, climbing up the ladder.

"What in hell were you doing with those lights?" shouted Dixon angrily. He looked up the ladder. —"Where did you get those spotlights?" he asked in mild surprise.

Jake Landsberger softly appeared at the ladder. "Allow me, Max. I'm in the business."

He climbed up. He made a face and ripped out the connections.

To my rapture he drew a fuse from his pants-pocket. "I always carry one." They carried the ladder to the back wall and Jake climbed up and put a new fuse in the box. The house-lights came ablaze: Jake was on the ladder with his hand in the opened box; Max was holding the flashlight; Dixon was holding the ladder, flushed and hunched like an anxious mother. The audience burst into a roar of satirical applause, and Jake bowed and grinned and waved his hand.

Mark walked unsteadily out into the open air.

Quiet was restored. Lit only by the foots and borders, the

dancers resumed where they had left off, at the tension in-between, Bernardine took up again the rippling figures, where they had broken off. And as it was it was very beautiful, very well, in the circumstances, and also because of the circumstances.

eight

The last parents left before supper.

Dixon was shouting angrily in the temporary office. "*No!* No! I won't send them home. Not for a week. Not for two days. Just because Anders is nervous and upset? Whose fault is this? The boys did the best they could. Beautiful. Hm. The best intentions."

"Mark Anders is supposed to be the director," said a low voice.

"Then he mustn't be sick!" cried Lawrence Dixon. "Otherwise let him get out."

"That's a lovely way to talk—in such a loud voice. I enjoy it." It was the doctor. "And what about the spotlights?"

"God damn those spotlights! they'll hear from *me* about those spotlights. Don't let that worry you!"

nine

After the last parents left, Tony began to whine and wouldn't eat supper. So many faces strange were gone, and so much cake and candy as he roamed from one picnic lunch to another. Finally he began to wail and I took his temperature, but there was no fever, or only half a point of fever.

In the aftermath of Parents' Day the excitement, the let-down are not ordinary excitement and let-down that lead to hilarious misbehavior and deep sleep. But the repressed contents have been touched, releasing rage, fear, and grief— at boarding-schools where there is always in the background plenty of rage, fear, grief, and loss.

"He's that way because his mother didn't come," said Dolly.

157

I hadn't thought of asking Eliza to come; if she had known it was Parents' Day, she would perhaps have come.

"If she *had* come," said Dolly, "it wouldn't have been any different after she left. But she should have come."

Teddy was in a temper. He threw his shoes. "Make that bastard shut up!" he screamed.

"Shut up yourself," said Dolly. She picked my boy up and rocked him. This was not enough and he wailed on; but it was better than nothing.

"You're no help," Dolly said to me. "You can go out if you want to."

I did want to. I went my evening walk to the other school, my animation reviving with my desires.

ten

"Jeff Deegan, I want to talk to you." We went into the hall.

I sat on one of the chests of drawers. "What the devil did you mean by saying you were afraid to be alone with me in a room? Was that a decent thing to say?"

He hung his head.

"I know you're sore on account of Debbie Lowenstein. Is that my fault?" I assumed that he knew nothing of my instigation of it, but it made no difference.

"It's a lie!" he said. Then he said nothing.

"Well?"

"I'm sorry," he said.

"It's all right," I said.

We walked back into the big room. I did not put my arm round his shoulders.

— In the room, with perfect absent-mindedness, wearing a small smile as if he were sleep-walking, Lefty Duyvendak, who could masturbate to the count of a thousand but never come to the end, was chopping at the door-jamb with an axe. He had already cut a large chunk out of it.

I touched his arm. "I'm sorry," he said, as if awaking. He looked at what he was doing. "That's funny," he said and laughed. I shrugged.

Parents' Day

eleven

The Tridget of Greeva

— RING LARDNER

I heard Michael's voice downstairs and I knew that Davy would be alone. I walked in. He was sitting at the table working at problems in geometry.

"Here," I said. I laid a tin box of condoms on the table.

"What's that? Oh."

"I promised I'd get them, so I did. Dixon's against it, but it makes no difference."

(—It made no difference. No help for it. I'm sorry. I was no use. All right! There was nothing I could do . . . These were the expressions of the aftermath of Parents' Day. All right!)

"Thanks," said Davy. "You can keep 'em. I won't be needing 'em."

"No?"

. . .

"Well, I'm sorry," I said.

"It makes no difference."

"Do you want to work? I'll scram out of here."

"No," he said. "Don't."

"I'm sorry I didn't get a chance to say good-bye to your mother; she suddenly vanished."

"You and she got on thick as thieves, didn't you?" he said hostilely.

"She's a wonderful woman. I'm not sure I'd like to have her for a mother, but I'd be proud to have her for a mother."

"I know what you think; but it's not as bad as you think. When I write her I'll say you were sorry you didn't get a chance to say good-bye."

"It's not so important. Yes, do."

"She'll like that. That's how she is."

I sat at the table, pressing against him; I was cloudy with longing for him, but I was not amorous: neither holding myself back, nor in motion.

He drew away, which made me sad, but not hurt or combative.

159

"I got on badly with my mother," I said. "Awfully. We could not stay in the same house, not even in the same city, we riled each other so. She used to have attacks, and go away. She was fine, as soon as she got to the other end of the world from us, Miami or Los Angeles. I didn't admire her at all. Then one day I found that other people admired her tremendously, what they saw in her. They thought she was a kind of bourgeois gypsy. And she was. I saw it too and I began to like her too. But that was only two years before she died, in Florida."

"Oh?"

"She was a bourgeois gypsy, the way I'm a kind of bourgeois bohemian."

"What's that?"

"We can talk about that another time, not now."

It was hard for me to drag my eyes to look at him. And there was a little space, a quarter of an inch, between us.

"I love you, Davy Drood," I said thickly.

"I know you do. It can't be helped."

"Oh, I suppose it could be helped; it's not so bad as that," I said cheerfully. "Obviously I don't want to." My cloudy longing had vanished quite, but it would have given me intense pleasure to kiss and hold him in every possible way. ("Intense": I think keen rather than strong.)

With an apt generosity that would keep him forever pure—for, I must repeat it, he was noble so you will not find an equal, and he was the original of "The Knight"—he placed himself close to me, removing the quarter-inch of distance.

For a moment I held onto myself. But then I hugged him and sank my lips in his neck, and held him, too tight of course, so that I hurt him—only for a minute or two. This access being past, I said, "Thank you, boy. Such things—such as they are—are big to me," I said wryly. "What happened with Debbie? Why won't it turn out?"

He had paled, and for a moment he collected his forces so that he could talk flatly, in his thrill-less voice, and not be moved by whatever feelings. He said, "I don't know why; that's it . . . With you I can at least talk about it, and that's what use you are."

"Yes, you can. What happened exactly?"

"You know, we fooled around a lot, I told you that. I sucked her breasts. Both of them. First her right, then the left." He stopped. "Wasn't that a stupid thing to say?"

"No, you mean to say it that way."

"Then today—" He stopped.

"Yes, about twelve-thirty. I saw the two of you sneaked off."

"We really hugged. I mean—I held her something like you held me just now. Only I came off. In my pants. Wait. I'll show you the pants—"

"I believe you, Davy."

"Then—she didn't do anything; I could at least have been polite. I hated her like poison. I could have puked. I pushed her away. I couldn't even be polite. I didn't want to see her. And I still don't want to see her again, I mean ever." He stopped.

"What did you do?"

"I'm ashamed—I ran away."

"You came back here to change?"

"How did you know that? Did you follow us?" he cried in alarm.

"No. No, I didn't follow you . . . *Davor!*" I used his mother's name for him, and my voice came with a kind of stupid depth.

I acted badly. Being in the presence of the essential misery of these adolescents, if I didn't know what to do about it, and I didn't, I should have turned pale, for it is a grim presence. But a false well-being, a kind of flight from it, gripped me, and I took Davy's head in my hands and said, "Davor, you'll see. It's bad but it will be better."

"Not with her!" he sobbed. He was crying.

"Also with her. But we'll discuss it some other time. Tomorrow. Parents' Day is a bad day. Let me look at your face."

The swelling on his lip had subsided, but he had a blue bruise on the cheekbone.

"The day began badly. You had a fight before breakfast."

"Wasn't that a son of a bitch?" said Davy blankly.

161

twelve

Jeff Deegan was listening for me. He met me in the hall as soon as I reappeared and he said, "Here, would you like this?"

It was a coon-hat that he had made: hunted, skinned, and sewn together. There were claws beside the eyes and a tail behind. It was beautiful.

"Yes, I'd like it," I said slowly. "Who wouldn't?"

"Try it on."

I tried it on. It fit beautifully.

"How much—I mean, can I pay you for it?"

"No," he said, and ran away.

CHAPTER IX

THE STARE

Like the form of a dream but the matter-of-fact
of awakeness, wilful withholding
has formed again behind my eyes
one face indelible forever.

Withholding my hand and my will withholding
(only my fears forcibly forgotten),
a face (like the fading flush
of a fresco to a faded drawing).

I first myself hold back, and circle eyes
and heavy lips and a thrill-less voice
are carven on my rock-heart worn;
and when I hold also my hand

approaches me with friendly smiles
and perilous ideas (the while
elsewhere I hold my wishes also)
and widening stare for narrowing stare.

one

It seemed to me that because I gave myself more and more
to the love I felt for Davy Drood, I withdrew my feelings
and concern from the business of our school; partly because
there is not energy for everything, but especially because
it was not possible to have this love and still legitimately
regard myself as a member of our school. Rather, giving in
to these exceeding feelings, I defied our school.

Yet the truth was the other way. It was because I came
to feel a coldness in our school and was, as I was, useless

in our school, I withdrew from its ambience and *therefore* gave myself more unrestrainedly to my feelings for Davy Drood, for it is necessary somewhere to give in to concern. Yes, and in revenge I defied our school.

Withdrawing from these people, I was quitting my primary concern in this place: to make effective the children's creative spontaneity, especially their sexual love, as it arose. This concern was not practical, as I was, and as we were, and perhaps also as the children were (but I am not so sure about that). Yet it was the kind of impractical concern in which one could practically, that is hopefully altho foolishly, exhaust oneself. I was betraying it.

I allowed myself to believe that I was having a certain success at least with Davy (who was not one of the children), for he began to be forward with the girls. Having broken thru the first block, he quickly adjusted himself to his other difficulties. He found a mode of behavior in keeping with his picture of himself: he was pre-eminent, bound not to fail once he adventured, and always a gentleman. He became a Don Juan of half-measures, hid in a girl's closet, etc. Inspired by my affection and approval, he did not care about rebuffs. What pleasure he had for his efforts, I did not know; for we no longer discussed such matters.

two

One evening the girls dragged me into their big dormitory.

"Stay here," said Seraphia's daughter, gripping my hand tight, "you always sit with the boys."

She moved and made a place on her bed, but I sat on Joann's. "Are you jealous?" I asked.

"We're put out. We have nobody but Lawrence Dixon, and we've heard what he has to say."

"What shall we talk about?"

"About love, of course," said Claire. They wanted to talk about a new novel that they were all reading, successively, and even simultaneously, page by page. With a pang of envy I realized that books of mine would never be read by these dreamy audiences. We talked about the book and about love.

"Debbie says that you're for the Samoans, you're against love."

"I don't know what he's for or against," said Debbie coldly. She was angry with me because Davy had rejected her, and she was no longer talking to me directly.

There was an embarrassing silence. I played with Joann's ringlets. They were all lovely girls.

"When are you going to have our play?"

"The Group is going to have two plays," I said. "Beside the creative play I'm going to direct a regular written play, for graduation."

"What play?"

"Let's do a musical!"

"I've already chosen the play," I said carefully. "It's Euripides' *Trojan Women*. It's an old Greek play."

They were disappointed.

"Don't be so sure," said Debbie knowingly. "Some of these Greek plays are terrific. I once saw one."

"I chose this play partly because most of the parts in it are for girls, and I wanted to work with the girls."

"What's it about?"

"It's about War," I said.

"It's about War and most of the parts in it are for girls?"

"Yes." I got up.

"Kiss us good-night. Larry always kisses us good-night."

I went from bed to bed and kissed each girl. After I left they broke into titters.

three

The architect did not arrive till the middle of January. After lunch, I took him to look over the grounds.

Big snow was beginning to fall. It was cold and the snowflakes, full stars, shone on the architect's blue alpaca coat. He was a stout square man. The red flames leaped from the coal. He thumped about the foundations and twisted his lips. I pressed him about the chimney.

"Look, if you really intend to build a big building—I doubt it," he said—"this isn't the place. This is the wrong side of

165

the road. There, that's the place." He pointed to a rise behind the gym, where were some chicken-houses. "You can't have dormitories on the wrong side of the road. Can't you have the road closed?" A car screamed by.

"It's the post road."

"Let's go there." We went up to the other place. The snow was falling thick and fast, like the minutes and the days. He looked closely at the perfect flakes on his blue sleeves. If he had built this building, it would have come out in the form of a snowflake.

It was cold and windy; we were exposed. But I thought it was a good site—when the old wreck would be cleared away, and a terrace laid from the demolished blocks, down to the pond.

"No kidding. Will they really get the money?"

"How should I know?"

"Of course you know. What do you think?"

"No, they won't. Not nearly 100 thousand."

"Half? 50, 60 thousand?"

"Frankly, I couldn't say. I doubt it."

"What the hell do they want a big building for? What's that got to do with your school?"

"That's my opinion too."

"The whole place is ramshackle," said the architect. "So what? If you need more room you build a few more huts. But decent ones. Who put *that* thing up?" He pointed to the high dormitory that we called the Laundry, because they collected the laundry in the basement.

"I think they inherited that one."

"Don't be an ass. From whom? Do you think a farmer ever used a house like that? They built that four, five years ago. Somebody really figured it out and built it. You'd be surprised how everything is figured out and built by somebody or other. This one—" the gymnasium—"this one is the real firetrap. You ought to get the kids out of here right away."

"You tell them," I said.

"This fire business. What's—what's his name—Anders, what's Anders so green about? There's always likely to be a fire; people bet with the insurance companies about it."

"He's afraid for the kids. It's no joke."

166

"Certainly it's not a joke. Do something.

"You take the kids and you sleep them on the ground floor. You have the classrooms and offices upstairs. No? Then you take a pencil and figure it out: how many? You're 20 short, you're 30 short. Good. We build three more low wooden sheds, with green wood and without guillotine windows that stick. Look, one here—one here—one there. A flagpole. Down there you have the terrace. No, not here, there. What's wrong? It looks nice. You have something for your money."

"Don't sell it to me; I'm convinced. Sell it to them."

"Do *you* think there ought to be a big building? Maybe I'm missing the point."

"No, I don't. You're perfectly right. It's an idea in the mind."

"For God's sake, man," he cried. "If you have a limited amount of money, why do you want to put it into bricks? Spend it on the people."

"The salaries are good enough," I said loyally.

"I bet. The kids, the equipment—for instance that shop, the Arts and Crafts? And this gymnasium . . ."

I was offended. It was our school. "We do all right," I said; "equipment isn't everything either."

He laughed cheerfully. "I used to be a member of the C.P.," he said. "I went round the East Side selling *Daily Workers*. I was a smart young architect and that was my selling-point. 'Look at this place you live in? Huh? Look at this plaster.' I'd pick off a yard of it with my fingers. 'Is that right, to have the can in the hall? Phooey.' Next thing I'd pick myself up off the sidewalk.

"Let's get in out of this. I've looked enough." The snow was falling so thick one couldn't see anyway. The brook and the contour of the hills were gone.

He asked my advice, what tack to take.

"Tell them just what you told me. What's the sense of beating about the bush."

"Oh no. That's not how it works at all. These people all have what you call ideas in the mind. First you have to draw them a pretty picture, something vast, just to show that you can draw. Then you discuss it. This can't be done. That can't be done. Finally, after you sweat blood dropping hints, *they*

167

think up the right solution, and then you can begin to talk sense."

I grinned my best grin. It was a delicious version of Dixon's theory of the building planned by the ultimate users. Just at this moment we hurtled into Mark Anders, in the storm, and he caught me with the grin.

"It's you," he said. "No classes this afternoon?"

"I'm showing the architect around."

"*You're* showing the architect around. Did you test the foundations?"

"I thumped 'em," said the architect.

"What about the chimney?"

"I looked up the chimney, it's very dark."

"We'll talk about it and go over it again," said Mark and disappeared in the snow.

"What's biting him? Don't you two get on?"

I wanted to cry after Mark Anders, "I wasn't laughing at you, I wasn't grinning at you. I couldn't even see you in the snow. It was just something really funny—you'd laugh too. I'm not plotting against you. I'm not plotting at all. What this man says has a lot of sense. If we put the kids on the ground floor to sleep, there won't be any danger—" I wanted to cry this, because it was my fault that we had drifted so far apart. Of course it was also his fault, even more his fault; but in such a case it is the one who sees it who has the responsibility to take the steps. But obviously I didn't want to.

"I'm starved," said my stout friend.

—The lunch had been another little comedy. Knowing that my friend was coming, Bernardine had put herself out; she had made her specialty, a calf's liver paprikash, baked, with mushrooms and everything else. But of all the foods in the world, liver happened to be the one that my friend could not stomach. So he lavished compliments, while I stealthily finished his dish, and a second helping, as well as my own.

I was sick. This was another of Dixon's bright thoughts.

Parents' Day

four

I masturbated with the following image, and worked it
up into a boastful poem:

> Now is the dreadful midnight you
> have to do what you want to do,
>
> not by your will which is afraid
> but by my hand upon you laid.
>
> My hand withheld almost too long
> is loosed by love, its grip is strong
>
> is fearless, it has turned to fire
> the arpeggios of the lyre,
>
> and elsewhere we love carelessly
> who closely love Saint Harmony.
>
> Resist not, nor can you resist, those cries
> that in your heart arise,
>
> which I to song shall modify
> and both of us shall never die.

five

The snow was two foot deep. It was a Saturday sunny and
cool. Tony had the chance to coast on the wooden sled that
Liza gave him for Christmas. The two kids were tireless,
dragging their sleds up the rise of the chicken-houses, where
the architect would have put the New Building, if there had
been a new building.

Davy invited me to their party and loaned me the extra
pair of snowshoes: to climb up to his house, his mother's
house, on the hill beyond the gorge. The party were Davy,
Jeff Deegan, and I, and Ross and Corny Tate.

I had never gone in snowshoes, but I soon got the hang
of it: jump, keeping the heels high. From time to time we
tangled and tumbled in the feathery drifts, and almost
vanished from sight. One could lie there comfortably in the

softness, warmly dressed, if it were one's character.

A couple of hours we climbed, and then suddenly the view opened out. "In an instant!" as Parmenides says, for "there is this strange instantaneous nature, something lying between motion and rest, being in no time, and into this and out of this the moving changes to rest and the resting to motion." Far off was one last barrier of hills, beyond which lay the Hudson River. In the valley between, one could hardly see our little school; and seeing it from here, in the instant, one did not feel that it was, in the same way, our school at all.

In the heat of climbing, in the bright sun, so that eventually all of us were carrying our coats on our backs like knapsacks, one could lose, slough off, the concerns and fears of our school that were, after all, clinging to one only like damps of a swamp: in the skin, under the skin, but it was only the skin. (Speaking of it, it would be improper to say "I could slough it off," for the skin was I; but could say, "one" and also "one of *us*.") It was not a solitary height. We were happy. In our giant feet.

The Drood house was thru a thicket and up another little rise of its own. It was a very old house. We got into it, and the small living-room that had the big fireplace was all of dark polished oak. I kindled a fire. They went for water but the well was frozen solid and they brought back a bucket of snow. While they were gone, I stole a photograph of Davy in his ninth or tenth year.

We cooked some corn-meal and flavored it with a tang of quinces of last summer's canning. We brewed tea. All this was very good. Our damp clothes, hung on chairs, began to steam by the fire. I drew Jeffrey to sit down on my lap, since he was closest and without a doubt one loved them all. (But he held himself stiffly.)

In an instant, in the instant! — and is not the present the instant? — one could see that my fears down there, guilt, anxiety, and devices, and also my programs, my plans, were all foolishness. What difference did it make? (It was not so difficult as that to be happy.) 100 years from now! — if one said, "good Lord, man! it will be all the same 100 years from now!" this did *not* mean, it will be all the same because you, and these, will be dead and gone 100 years from now; for in the sense that we are members of one another, we would not be at all dead and gone; and most of our judgments of worth come from this sense of our community. But it meant just the contrary: it was a way, by thinking of a long time, 100 years, of considering these things, aspects of these things, as belonging to the eternal class of things.

Well! I—no, not "one" but *I*—I am an artist; I have the use, the habit, of considering my things immortally; this is what we do. (The relic of our thinking so, such and such an artwork, is the immortality for you.) We pride ourselves on it, tho I have not heard that it is a very happy activity for us—nor do we engage in it by choice. And what did one see if he looked at our things, artist-wise, in their immortal aspect? Yes! to get to the point! he saw that an artist was in love with a young man, in order to make himself, his things, more perfect, more ideal. To *un*make the loss. Then why these fears, this guilt? What else would one expect? In every group there would be one nearest, but what luck to come to know Davy Drood! One could have screamed with rage to see an artist timid to do and feel what belonged to him to do and feel as an artist, if he was an artist. Next such a man would foreswear the muse herself!

"For Pete Sake, Jeff Deegan," I cried, "don't sit on my lap if you don't want to! I won't eat you up." I shoved him away. —But Corny,

Corny was leaning his long self at the mantel—well-strung, now a little slack, but he could both tighten and also become unloosed: the nobility become unmanned, tho not quite humanized: and it was obvious that he was Talthybios in the play! the one who bears the bad news to each, and apologizes,

> Such things
> some other of us should herald,
> pitiless and shameless—

Looking from one to another, there were four of them, one could see that here, so high—no solitary height—they were all worthy of perfection; Davy Drood, in Davy Drood's house, did not stand out. I did not long for him, especially.

171

All right! I was an artist indeed. It brought me back to where I had started; there was something to be done with them one and all, and me myself; and if with them, then *for* them, and, perfectly, *by* them: that is, I was back at our school. There was no avoiding it, especially if one said "in 100 years!" But now where was gone the instant happiness? I was an artist scourged to it like a galley-slave.

Nevertheless, I did not intend again to succumb to such strong fears and guilt.

"What's about this architect?" said Ross. "Why is he against the New Building?"

"He thinks it's foolish to spend the money."

"I think that's shousy. The kind of building Larry said, the school could be proud of a place like that."

"Maybe. He thinks it's idiotic."

"Why does he?"

"He thinks there shouldn't be a school at all," I explained. "But a lot of shacks where you live together—the boys and the girls."

"No teachers?" said Corny.

"No, no teachers, not really," I said.

"The boys and girls together, in the same room?" said Ross.

"Away from home! that's all that counts!" cried Davy Drood. "Let's get out of here before we make more mess."

"Clean up first," I said, asserting my authority.

On the way down we had lively fun.

We split up and went different routes, and then waited up for the others. During the long pauses one fell in the snowbanks, or two or three fell in the snowbanks, couldn't tell who was doing what. It was lively fun so long as there was no question of preferences. The young fellows found it easy, easier than I, to disregard the fact that I was older. Nor did this offend me.

It got dark. I ran the last mile, altho the doctor had agreed to take over my Latin if I happened to be late.

I suffered, always, from the dread that I should pay for a little holiday with a disaster. As soon as I arrived I ran to look for Tony, but he was sound asleep.

"Take me up sailors, into your great ship
and I'll tell you a story to bring you peace"

High Seas

Sooner than not talk about my love
I have to blab what harms us both!
But ever-urgent love that will
be real and treat only with the real
day by day simplifies choices,
dispensing with all other errors
except its own darling illusion (this one
God sees for me).
              Ever is loving leading
to the disaster of following our bent!
at last out of the death of secondary choices,
disaster follows hard on death, to peace
all fear forgot. There *is* no safety anywhere
(where God's safety is, is not a place).
In the darling illusion of happiness
the High Seas of my modest daring
more safely for an hour than in the rocks:
"Take me up, sailors, into your great ship
and I'll tell you a story to bring you peace."

six

After the Staff-meeting, some of us were at Caroline's listening to phonograph-records. She lived across the bridge, in the Gorge. It was not our music but it was a relief, for a change, to hear the complicated music of the world played by people who knew how.

Harrison persisted in mimicking Mark Anders. "Playing in the haystack with matches!"—this had been Mark's theme. Harrison was trying to turn it into a song.

"What's so funny about it?" said Caroline. "The poor man is at his wits' end about fires, and they do play in the haystack and ruin the hay."

"But they don't play with matches there. That's not why they play in the haystack."

Veronica sat silent, as if she were concentrating on the music.

174

"If you thought it was sex, why didn't you say so?" I said.

"Why didn't *I* say so? Why didn't you say so? That's your dish of tea. Everybody was waiting for you. You're the defender of the little games of the young. '*And why*—' he began to mimic me, 'why *not* in the haystack? where *else*?'" He laughed.

"What's funny about *that*?" said Caroline.

"The way he twists it. He puts the question as if it had nothing to do with *whether* they should carry on or not—oh no, nobody could even be thinking of that question, it would be too stupid; but the question is whether or not they should screw each other *there*. Are haystacks functional for the purpose? They're soft, they smell sweet—but *what* about the prickles? Hm. After all. Why not the *haystack*? The very place. I'll ask my friend the architect."

"All right. So I twist it this way, and Mark Anders twists it with matches."

"But he can't help himself."

"Neither can I! neither can I! Let's talk about something else . . . Do you people know the place up on the hill, past the Corners, where suddenly it opens out and you can see the whole valley? But did you ever see it covered with snow? Harrison, it's extraordinary. You ought to go up. Drood will lend you a pair of snowshoes—if I say so."

Veronica said nothing and my guilt increased. I got up and passed her the dish of fudge.

"Dixon! there's the voice I was waiting for!" cried Harrison in glee. " 'We shall want fireproof dormitories. For what? for what?' Why didn't Dixon pipe up?" He roared so loud he began to choke. Caroline pounded him on the back. "It was his boys made all the noise," he gasped.

"Really? who? I didn't hear about it."

"You can guess who."

"Duyvendak? He comes over to see the Group III girls."

"No. Droyt O'Neil and your Drood."

"Those two? with Sophie's girls?"

"Sophie's girls!" said Caroline. "*My* girls!"

"Really!? Group II? . . . What was the noise about?"

"Nothing. I don't know what you're talking about. They were just horsing. I saw every minute of it. They did light

175

matches, to smoke. Why do you keep picking on Mark Anders? I don't say he's behaving like a rational animal, but he's not completely demented."

"*Isn't* he?" asked Dolly, from the corner behind my chair. I had quite forgotten she was there. I turned and pushed my chair, not to give her my back. She was knitting.

"Sorry," I said.

Veronica stood up. I stood up. "Really I must be going," said Veronica. "I'm worn out." She began to put on her coat.

"Can't I walk you back?" I said uneagerly. "I'd like to hear the Schubert and I hate to leave these lovely people, but—"

If she was maneuvering for us to go to bed so early in the evening—I used to sneak into her room in the Laundry—I did not want to.

"Please," she said firmly, "no! I'd prefer to go back by myself."—This made me anxious; I could not endure a breath of rejection.—"I'll see you tomorrow. Good-bye, you charming people; thank you for the coffee and the conversation."

Her footsteps could be heard in the crusty snow.

"What did you mean, Harrison, by saying 'your Drood'— my Drood?"

"Nothing. Just like that."

Dolly said, "If Mark is too nervous to navigate, then he ought to take a rest. Lawrence is right. All the same, *your* method of forcing him out is a bit thick."

"*My* method?!" I cried.

"Yes. Having the architect recommend that we keep the children in wooden buildings. You know Mark won't stay if there's not a fireproof building."

"Dolly Homers!" I shouted furiously. "Do you really believe what you're saying? Do you think I would do that?"

"What else am I to believe?"

The others were embarrassed. I was at a loss what to say first.

There was a wild cry of incredulity and fright, in the night. It seemed to be the voice of Veronica.

Seizing flashlights, we ran out toward the bridge, slipping in the snow. Faint moans could be heard and we recognized the quiet voice for Veronica's. We played the lights.

She was standing in the rocks of the shore, in a few inches

of water. I climbed down and fished her out, bedraggled and bruised. She began to laugh and said, "I thought I was jumping over the rail onto the bridge, and instead I jumped off the bridge into the brook." She could walk, supported, and we floundered our way to the Infirmary.

I tended to grimace. The action and her notion of it, apart from the motive, were just the kind of willed error—fixing the mind and compelling the action—that set my teeth on edge. It was a strain of her character that, threatening always a violent moment, made it impossible for me to be easy with her. The plausible motive of it, to punish herself and everybody else, did not irritate me, for it jibed well enough with some of my motives. But it was unfortunate for us both—or fortunate—that her manner of expression was grating to me, for what I could not abide was the sudden, the instant. (I preferred to be punished in the slow manner of punishment I preferred.)

I did not like to see, but saw, that my compulsive reference to Davy was grating to her. She refused to admit it but encouraged me, perhaps shrewdly, to talk on. All right!

There were no bones broken; the Doctor taped her up. I took her to her room, with the brandy and aspirins, and I kept her company. If *this* was what she had planned, she had achieved it.

seven

It is difficult to estimate what was the value of our sexual intercourse. I should at that time have said: "It is unsatisfactory but not unpleasant." Yet these bouts must have been somewhat satisfactory, "objectively satisfactory" so to speak, considering that they drew off the charge of my feelings for Davy Drood. Conversely, my feelings for the boy were the engaging interest, the fore-interest, that enabled me to have these sexual relations with the girl that were "objectively satisfactory," but I did not enjoy them.

I should have said, "They are not unpleasant but I do not enjoy them because—" and then found many things in Veronica, rather incompatibilites than defects, all of which added up to the fact that I did not love Veronica. But this lack of enjoyment—for why should a "merely physical" orgasm, whatever that might mean, not be at least enjoyable?—this lack of enjoyment was, I know, due to my own way of holding my body, my arms, the expression on my face: I cut off the feeling in the shoulders and neck, chin, lips, forehead, and then did not feel it. Then these tightnesses and holdings-back I interpreted as our incompatibilities. For instance, when I did not freely embrace her I thought, "She is afraid to lose me and clings to me." When I held my lips tight, I thought, "If she would see that I am lost and need a little mothering." And so forth, thru all the sorry category of ways of not giving in to simple pleasure with a pretty girl. Also, "These things are neither her fault nor mine."

But I should have insisted, "It is not *un*pleasant, there are no positive defects—" for if it had been painful or there had been faults that I could rationally pose to myself, I should have refused to take part. Nevertheless, it was part of my picture of myself that I should have a girl and thus I did not let myself feel the things that were positively painful; but then also I could not feel what was pleasurable. For instance, I held my head and lips away because of disgust, and I held back my shoulders and did not freely embrace because of murderous rage, and so forth, thru all the sorry category of ways in which the unfinished past grips us day by day.

I reproached myself for encouraging Veronica in a desire which I would never really satisfy, for what she, or anybody else, needed was love, and I did not, could not, love her. But on the other hand I felt, "What luck for her, to be able to have, even to this degree, the thing that she wants—*I* have never gotten this much!" This thought, of the disproportion between her luck and mine, buoyed me up in such occasions of callousness and almost cruelty as were inevitable; and I did not feel badly about making an even impersonal use of her, as occasion rose; for she was getting (not that I was giving) more than *I* had ever gotten. Also: "Since I can, I must give her pleasure, *noblesse oblige*," for I was always serviceable. Also: "What can she see, or want, in me of all people?" for I had both a low and high opinion of myself, and it was low with respect to Veronica.

When I would return to my room at two or three in the morning, I had the impression that Dolly Homers was listening for me and thinking her thoughts. This annoyed me.

LAKE TEAR

Clouded with love, will not a tear
drop from my spirit like that shining
Tear o' the Clouds out of which
the lordly River flows forever?

The weather in those misty hills
is weeping raindrops big as eyes
big as hearts, those muffled gorges
were cloven long ago; can they be brimmed?

—a featureless sea where blasts of dawn
unobstructed lighten the horizon
as if there were several suns. A wave is
trembling from the shoreless to the shoreless

and a rainbow of turbilous, pearl, and dizimal,
the colors of September brilliance,
stands across the sky like granite
and urges us to hope forever.

In dread I dared not touch the youth,

yet I touched him daily. How was this?

CHAPTER X

—FOR MEYER LIBEN

one

In dread I dared not touch the youth, yet I touched him daily. How was this?

Not that the desire was stronger than the fear and conquered it. Not even that present desire was stronger than absent fear, for one must explain why I daily put myself in the presence of desire. But the ones I feared no longer played in the immediate series of my feelings; the one I loved played in this intimate series.

When he was intimately present, it was less guilty to touch him, for one immediate act led to another. Intimate presence excluded the objects of fear (that apparently were not with me always, they were not inside me). Immediate acts bore their own warrant of innocence. The urgency to be more and more realized.

I desired to go on to the end—little by little, just in order to stand revealed among the ones I feared: presumably to be punished. Recreating an old episode that I do not recall.

To go on to the end and satisfy my innocent desire and brave the ones I feared and *not* be punished, but to justify myself. To put it up to *them* to relent of not playing in the series of my immediate feelings.

Thus, dreading to touch him I nevertheless touched him in order little by little to precipitate the perfect situation: that *the innocence of immediate actions would be the general social understanding.* (I felt that if I were in such a situation, I would unhesitatingly change my own immediate actions and comply to a general norm.)

181

I sought out the anxiety as a means of breaking down the barrier between myself and the ones I feared, partly hoping for approval of my pleasures, but hoping above all that *they* would reenter the series of my immediate feelings and actions.

two

From the youth, I concealed that I was afraid.

In his eyes I wished to be *already* in the perfect situation, a *member* of the society, of innocence justified. Only in this situation was easy love possible, would have been possible.

Not subject to judgment, but one immediate act leading to another.

Tacitly also I relied on his prudence and complicity; he was my accomplice in assuming a deceptive attitude of innocence and fearlessness. Then, as accomplices, we were isolated; and we already *formed* together the society for which I hoped at large — the society that would by a general deception conspire in immediate acts!

Apart from this one concealment, my fear — which I rightly assumed that he penetrated — I gave him my absolute confidence. Apart from the fear that colored everything, everything was innocent.

I felt both desire and fear; in any crisis fear would extinguish desire. But I was so determined to continue in his eyes to appear unafraid that this determination triumphed over fear. *The need to be consistent with my own words.*

Once the matter could be lifted to the realm of formulation and consistency of speech, I felt neither fear nor guilt.

I longed, freed from the fear connected with existent acts (yet needing to be inspired by immediate acts) to *challenge* them in the realm of formulation and consistency of speech. Here I had no master and nothing to fear.

three

Often in the realm of general formulation, I as if trustingly challenged those whom I feared.

Guilty but continually daring, confidently following the lines of argument.

Little by little I tried to add to generalities such specifications as would lead ultimately to a particular reference, my own acts. Then my color heightened and my words seemed not my own.

Pointing toward a particular reference now in order that when later I would be discovered I could say, "But I told you so all along!" Also, since I had no master in argument, to say: "Why did you not disprove the premises if you now balk at the conclusion?" Partly to confuse them, as a screen against danger. Partly to justify myself at least this much and not be completely destroyed.

Partly just still to have something to say, afterwards!

To bridge the gap between true speech and immediate acts—even tho afterwards.

To break down the barrier within me, between my poetic self, the unafraid master of consistent speech, and my cowering self of immediate acts. So my color heightened and my words seemed not my own.

The picture of myself unafraid that I maintained, and was determined to maintain, for the boy, was a deception considered as myself acting, but it was the essence of myself daring to speak.

I am not afraid to speak, I rely on the lines of argument. True arguments are not things feigned by me, but invented and discovered by me.

Then, having spoken them, I can always compel myself also to act in consistency with what I have triumphantly spoken. When it is a natural voice, not my sick self.

But such compelled action is without satisfaction and ease.

Little by little I specify the formulations towards the particular reference in order to be found out not completely by surprise. Not completely to their surprise, for they are led on by suspicions.

183

Hoping that my acts can transpire in an atmosphere *continuous* with the trusting conversations.

Hoping that the others too may be insensibly seduced into the series of immediate acts (not necessarily the same acts).

To break down the barrier between true speech and immediate acts.

Between my speaking self and my acting self.

To give ease and satisfaction to the self maintained consistent with my words.

To touch the boy.

four

I conclude that there was an episode (I do not remember it) in which I was surprised in an act.

There was a surprise, a sudden discontinuity between their assumptions and mine, the revelation of a previous discontinuity unguessed.

Vainly I tried to bridge this discontinuity by speech. Can one not recreate the scene? *the child is talking on even while he is being punished.* Primarily his speech is to bridge the discontinuity of feeling. But the next instant it is as if he were merely justifying himself in order to escape punishment; then, worst of all, simply justifying himself to himself, in order to preserve this much of himself from destruction.

When I speak as a poet, I speak primarily; I assume that I speak universally, relevantly for you also. I assume that the words are understood. (It is not so important to me that they be approved.) But between my acts and yours I do not assume such a continuity. Therefore the words seem abstract. Therefore they are perhaps not understood after all.

I speak without fear, before fear, before separation. Not to justify myself. The speaking justifies itself. (I am justified also in the innocence of immediate acts, but these are not in the same series as yours and there is no use in such a private justification.)

The blows were being struck: terrified, all the feeling of continuity was withdrawing into this mere thin line of speech, saying: "you see, it is simply this, don't you like it *too?*"

Yet the courageous little fellow did not, after all, stop talking! I will not stop.

To break *down* the barrier between true speech and immediate acts.

To include you also in the series of immediate acts.

CHAPTER XI

one

The winter was lasting a month too long. It seemed we people of the intemperate climate had only so much resistance in reserve, to fight off the winter and survive to the more hopeful weather. The children began to come down with the pneumonias, the agues, and the excruciating earaches. The Infirmary was never empty; after a while it was more than full, and the teachers had to spell the doctor as auxiliaries, they drawing on their not inexhaustible vitality. For the most part, the adults came down *after* the children were recovered, because they were recovered and we could afford ourselves the luxury. But if the children then relapsed, and parents and children were stricken at the same time, the generation was in a bad way.

Yet, getting sick—specifically, retreating to a good bed in bright rooms kept at an even temperature, and where the doctor's voice in the next room was paternally tyrannical— this also was a reserve of resistance. An organism designed for rough wear and tear necessarily has safety-devices to meet emergencies; our breakdowns are, beautifully, part of our resources. They are socially consecrated, they win respectful attention, no questions are asked if the thermometer reads above 101.

Tony was never out of the Infirmary more than a day at a time. Then the *other* ear would begin to ache—as if he were hungrily listening for something *else* that did not arrive to fill it with its welcome sound; and his feverish impatience read 102. He had no mother; he had me for a

187

father; but he had the Infirmary, where he could watch the others come and go.

Years later, when questioned, he could remember nothing about our school—not the brook, the barn, his Group, nor the Assembly—but he remembered three things: they were watching a fire and had to keep behind the rope; there was a brown horse named Texas that fell down and died; and he was sitting propped up in the Infirmary, watching a little girl leave.

The anxiety of 'phoning over to learn about Tony's condition—sometimes his fever was 103—this was just one more anxiety that colored my acquaintance with Davy Drood, that gave to my longing a piercing point. I was a morose bedside visitor. But Veronica, who was in love with me, used to bring Tony toys and sit with him an hour playing games.

two

Raised too strictly, in an inflexible institution with an absolute discipline—and therefore practiced in steeling herself against it with an absolute defiance and stubbornness—Veronica was able to suppress entirely her guiltiness and misgivings, and to give full sway to her feelings, such feelings as she felt. It was as if, at a given moment, she had *decided* she was in love with me and therefore she could systematically submit to this new feeling and, if possible, suffer it as much as possible. What she felt, and acted, was too simple for me to accept—for I moved in anxiety and half-lights; but its meaning was too devious and complicated for me to comprehend—for I was a simple soul. With her I was foolishly suspicious, but it was not foolishly that I was uneasy.

She acted as tho she had determined to be my wife. That is, she made herself indispensably convenient to me and was always on the verge of rejecting me. This method is infallible. What was difficult for me to decipher was whether she acted thus prudently by shrewd calculation or by the intuition that comes from inspired need. I hoped that it was

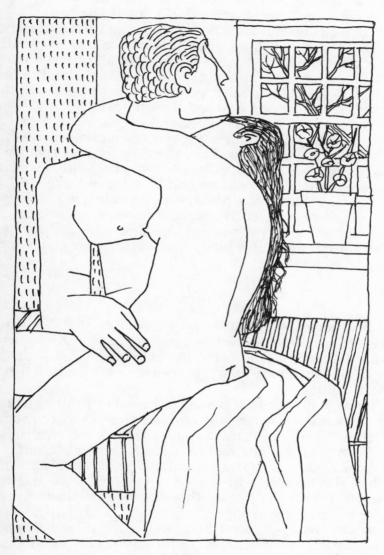

.. and perhaps one day we could be in Love.

by calculation, for I admired anyone who had the courage to want something, to strive for it, and to be clever.

Yet really no effort and no clever method was necessary in order to win me (to the extent that I could be won). All that it required was to need me, to seem to suffer without me. This appeal I could not afford to resist; afraid to be rejected, I could neither reject nor accept. I responded to it by surrendering myself and not my love.

Yet also, the kind of cold careful affection that I could muster held Veronica in terror and subjection; whereas if I had loved her, she would have become panicky and fled. As it was, *I* was now the inflexible institution within which it was possible to daydream and be fed (and be defiant).

So just as Eliza and I, perhaps not intending it, infallibly took the steps that led us apart, for we could not be in love, so Veronica and I, perhaps not intending it, took the steps that must indissolubly bind us, and perhaps we could one day be in love.

three

The doctor was rough and Prussian with his young patients. He hushed them with an iron voice. And when he was harried he did not spare them bursts of his anger.

The children were merry, hushed their voices, took their pain lightly.

One could hear him roaring, always in the other room (it did not seem so bad when he was present): "*Open* your mouth. Where do you think you are? This is the Infirmary!"

Everybody was afraid of him and nobody was afraid.

With the adults he was ironical, as if he did not like them. They also became a little more secure and were able to benefit from the illnesses they imposed on themselves. There was no use in hoping to get out of bed before he was good and ready—one might as well submit—and also he radiated an aura of irritation and disgust at one's continued presence. I came only as a visitor (I am not one to take sick). The doctor and I regarded each other with deep distrust and respect, for he was morally shocked that I had sexual relations with males; and this, curiously, made me too a little more secure. (With our doctor there was no question of hints and guesses, or apologies and rationalizations.)

Possibly the fact that he had silvery hair and a comically mobile face, and anecdotes and other funny noises, helped make his terror peaceful for the children. Mainly it was his firm hands.

He could interpret handwriting, and he imagined that he could read character by the conditions of the capillaries, and maybe he could.

four

"The explanation of the doctor is simple," said Veronica, "he is reliable"—as if to imply, "And you are not reliable."

"It's not so simple," I said. "For instance, do you think that I'm reliable?"

"Yes," she said surprisingly, "you're reliable too, in your way."

"In my way!" I exclaimed. "That was what Eliza said!"

"She was right."

"What's the good of it? she didn't rely on me."

"She'll bitterly regret it."

I was pleased; I was vengeful.

"Did you see her?" asked Veronica.

"See her? When?"

"I mean—when did she say that, that she could rely on you?"

"Long ago."—I did not seem to myself to be reliable; because I was anxious, I thought of myself as wavering. But since others saw that I was reliable, it must be so. It was that I imagined a picture of myself and I was consistent to the picture. Did they mean that I was honest? "She told me it," I said, "when she came to ask me whether she should have the baby or the abortion."

"Did she ask *you* that?" cried Veronica.

"Of course. Whom else could she ask?"

Veronica put her fingers in front of her mouth and stared at me in fright. "You fool," she said, "she did not ask for your *opinion*, she wanted you to make her decision for her, to

191

be her husband again. She had to have somebody to make her decision; but you refused her."

"*I* refused her?" I cried. "What are you talking about? Let us assume that you're projecting. What decision do *you* want me to make for you?"

"I knew you'd say that," she said.

She had unsettled me. "I *did* make a decision. I gave her money and told her to have the baby or not have it, to be free to choose; and in *either* case she could rely on me. That's why she said she could rely on me." I was misremembering; for it was not then that she said it, but before I went to New York. "I'm not boasting, but that was a hard decision for me to make, and I'm proud of it still!"

Tears came into Vonny's eyes. "I'm sorry for Eliza," she said.

"Why are you sorry for *her*?"

"Instead of making a decision for her, you made a decision for yourself. You're frightening. She said it *sarcastically* when she said she could rely on you, in your way. It's impossible that she meant it seriously. You misunderstood her, or you're lying and it never happened."

"It's impossible for me to lie," I said coldly.

—Even so! I cried to myself, from a long experience; if I was consistent with an imaginary picture of myself, it was the picture of a creative artist that I was consistent with; and such a picture has more of the self in it than there exists in the self; it is what the self will make of itself. It has always been that way. I picture myself and conform to it and feel that it is a bluff, and soon enough I discover that only this bluff is in me to become in reality. I was badly hurt by Veronica's revelation, for indeed I had refused Eliza when she needed me. (*But she had not seemed to suffer without me!*)

"You don't know anything at all about me and the way I behave!" I cried triumphantly. "For they thought, anybody would have thought, that I was *forced* to a decision, or to no decision, it came to the same thing. This event one could not postpone! because the blastula and then the gastrula keeps forming—endoderm, ectoderm, mesoderm. Even so I postponed it! I have postponed it! I've won the victory over myself and over Eliza, and best of all over the ongoing possibility of life. For they thought that in such a case the situation *must* be finished, and allow for something new; but *I* have been able to contrive that even so it remains unfinished, so that there will never be anything new."

I smiled—at myself. This smile—the doctor was right—had nothing in it of cruelty and malevolence; it was simply that sometimes the nature of the case was interesting, delicious.

But Veronica burst into tears and wailed. I was surprised.

"Why are you crying, Vonny? I'm not unhappy. Don't you see, it's interesting that that's how I am?"

Considering it, I realized that she was crying because the endless postponement I was describing did not allow for anything new.

She was not experienced enough to know that the fact that one can *say* anything of this kind means that it is already part of the past.

What was the fact? The fact was that it was to dissolve my suffering with Eliza, and find another recourse, that I first came to our school; and now it was no longer necessary for me to remain at that school.

Soon it would be spring.

CHAPTER XII

one

The doctor was now giving my Latin class, and now I had at last achieved the wish of my dream, to be in the class again and sit back, and silently criticize the teaching or make little nods of approval. He started the classes on time and now, again as in my dream, it was I who was always late; I was still far down the road when he rang the bell. The April air was raw, as the winter were about to come again, but it was not going to come again.

One of the big ones was walking towards me—away from our school—carrying a heavy satchel. It was Jeff Deegan. He was wearing a tie.

"Where are you going? is somebody sick?" I asked with concern.

"I'm going home for good," he said with dignity.

"What—going home?" Almost I said, "What home?" but I managed to bite it off. "Going home? Just like this?"

"No, I was going to stop and say good-bye to you—and thank you." He chose his words. "Now I don't have to. You're the only one."

"What the devil are you talking about?"

"He kicked me out. Told me to pack and go."

"Who? Dixon?—Do you want to go, Jeff?"

He hung his head. "I'd rather go than stay, *now!*" He said. He raised his head. "Good-bye." He held out his hand.

I disregarded the hand. "Put that bag down and don't be an ass. Why did he act up this time? Come on, quick; I have a class."

195

"Nothing."

"What do you mean nothing?"

—It was nothing, that is, the same as usual. Jeff was, as usual, fresh to him, fresh and overly frank. But Dixon understood, we all understood, that the boy was under pressure of resentment, of being unwanted, of being on charity, and therefore he had to be more than independent. Ideally, it was better for us to call his bluff and for him to assert his pride and leave; but in fact he had no place to go.

"Pick up that bag and trot back after me," I said in exasperation; I was exasperated because I was doing the best, but not the perfect, thing.

"No."

"You won't?"

"No, I won't."

"O.K. Sit there. Stand there. I don't care . . . *Take* that tie off, will you? How can I love a man who wears a tie? . . . if you budge I'll chase after you and brain you."

"I won't go back unless he apologizes," cried Jeff. His eyes were hot and dry. I did not have the courage to dare him to do the best thing and go on his way, and then we would fight it out and the bad blood would spill.

"If there's going to be any apologizing, Jeff Deegan, you'd better get ready to do it—the way you open your trap. You know what I mean. Now you sit there, if you have to sit all day."

He sat on his bag. His eyes did not become moist, but he took the tie off. I touched his head and went. I didn't look back.

The doctor was teaching our class; I was starving for my coffee; but I went upstairs and confronted Dixon.

two

"The boy is sitting on the road. You can see him out the window if you want. Please—inform me—what home? To exactly what home are you sending him home?"

"He'll have to go for at least two days!" cried Dixon. He was red, with shame rather than anger.

196

"All right, one two. Now the two days are up."

"Who is running this school?" said Dixon angrily.

"*They* are; you know the answer to that, Larry. You know as well as I that the others won't stand for it. Just think a minute. Droyt? Corny? Davy Drood? Duyvendak? Debbie? Seraphia's daughter? If Deegan goes for two days, they'll all go for two days. I wish I had such friends."

It was not the case that the fellow was unwanted or existed on charity; he was, of course, precisely at home. But he was unable to bask in the reality.

Dixon looked at him out the window, sitting on his satchel.

"Pass by any time you feel like it; let him sit there for an hour and a half and brood. Make up any damn yarn you want. Blame it on me. He'll apologize."

"No, I won't lie," said Dixon. "I'll tell him he doesn't have to go because *you* wouldn't stand for it." His voice was rich with hate.

"Good," I said. "If you wanted it to be otherwise, you should have broken our spirits long ago; but as an educator you elected not to do it."

three

We had tried to persuade the doctor to teach biology, but he would not. We took this to be some professional German nonsense. But to our surprise he offered to take over the Latin.

He took the Latin because he had a living interest in it, a present interest, changing himself. He taught the language — *amo, amas* — with the concern of a man who has lost his mother tongue. Not lost it, but immolated it. He taught Latin — *amamus, amatis* — as if he were shrieking, "Damn them, those fiendish butchers! I'll never go back *there*, no, not if they spring wide the gates of Paradise between the Rhine and the Elbe. Even so! we others, we human beings, we still communicate, for instance in this old tongue, *amabam, amabas.*"

Compared to the deadness with which German was dead

to him, Latin was young and green. (He could not speak it any more than I could.)

I sneaked into the Library with my coffee. The young people were sitting attentively round the table, and he was sitting, with his silvery hair, at the head of the table.

"But of course!" I thought, "if there has to be a director, let *him* be the director."

This idea did not burst on me, but it rose in me, finally with a flash, as the auroral sun flashes in the long-bright sky. And I sat in calm, order, and glory, all three: content with my idea for the future of our school, just as if I were going to remain at our school another year, or the year after that.

He did not teach them much Latin at all; in fact it is almost impossible to teach a foreign grammar to kids in a progressive school who cannot spell English and are quite unaware whether or not a particular letter is present or absent in a word. But he taught them linguistics and the philosophy of communication. He lectured them on the Indo-Aryan sister-tongues and taught them Grimm's first law; he entertained them with curious etymologies; he told them what he knew about Chinese. He brought in a great medical chart, a colored cross-section of the mouth and throat, and they worked out a table of clicks, grunts, and squeals that we do not use in our languages—but we use them to fascinate the very young.

Probably he didn't know very much about it, but he took the matter by a good handle; and he infused it with a strange passion. *Amabo, amabis.*

When he saw that they had no sense of English syntax either—how should they have a sense of English syntax?— he called on me, as a poet, the right authority. (For this I loved him.) So I brought into class contrasting passages of our authors, a paragraph of old Gibbon and a paragraph of our Anderson; and I showed that it was precisely by the subordination of clauses, or, so to speak, the insubordination of clauses, that each writer has expressed not only his rhythm and heart-feeling, but his dialectic and his metaphysics of the universal world.

He taught them a little logic and scientific method and

speculated in philosophical grammar. By contrasting the vocabularies of two primitive tribes, he demonstrated the social functioning of language.

Amabimus. Amabitis.

(If one came on him reading Rilke, he acted guilty.)

I sneaked away and rapped out our secret signal on the kitchen-door. As soon as Bernardine opened to me, I asked her if she thought the doctor wouldn't be a good director. "Why? is Mark Anders leaving?" she asked in surprise.

Then first it occurred to me that I was committing myself, I was committing myself again to take an interest in our school.

four

I went out into the watery sunlight. They were all sprawled on the porch, on the steps.

I was in the mood, the height of my euphoria, when I think that the classical curriculum, its songs, wisdom, and drama, is the basis of simple freedom.

I saw that we should use the porch for the Greek play. It had, as I have said, small, proportioned Ionic posts, painted ivory, the flutes grimy. Played on the porch, the play would be bound to reality. There were four fairly wide steps. Dancers could move up and down on them, allowing us another dimension. The whorls of the capitals were like high breasts, small, like the girls'.

In the shadows of the porch, there was a Middle Door — it is thru here that the bad secret, the "happening off the scene," reenters. The door could be thrown wide, revealing what was within; I tried it.

Jeff Deegan, who had come back, sat hunched and brooding at the end of the porch, not speaking with anyone. He had finally been crying; what thunder did Lawrence Dixon have, to make Jeff Deegan cry?

The Messenger from Without would come from that end, up the gravel path, past the garage. Suddenly he would disappear behind an orange curtain and re-appear transfigured, part of the play. (Like Jean, my ambition was to combine

199

the most quotidian and the most stagey.) But the Messenger from Within comes thru the middle door, and it is thrown wide. There is no longer a secret.

Euphoric, I darted my eyes from detail to detail, behind my dirty glasses. Now was the time to speak to Dixon about appointing the doctor as director. Now also—for when it is possible to do anything at all, it is possible to carry off everything at once—I would cross-examine Davy and take up what I had neglected. Davy was sitting on the steps looking at me (I had come thru the middle door). I sat on the steps.

five

Suddenly someone came from behind and snatched off my glasses and spirited them away. I clutched vainly for them and looked about in surprise.

They were in league.

They were formed in a circle to bait me. The scene was blurred to me.

"Please, kids. I can't see without my glasses. I'm blind as a bat."

They grinned malevolently. In the haze their grins were large.

"Give me back my glasses."

The glasses flashed somewhere. I unsuccessfully lunged for them.

"Be careful. You'll break them."

My eyes watered in the unaccustomed sunlight. The colors were clearer but the shapes were dim.

I sat down again and said, "All right, you win. I'm lost without them." I said to myself, in self-pity, "I'll get a headache without my glasses." But aloud I said sharply, "Come on, hand them back. Don't be stupid."

There was a pause. "Davy! . . . Jeff Deegan. Make them give me back my glasses."

"Why don't you leave them off?" said Joann. "You look handsome without them."

Next moment I struck out. It was Droyt O'Neil I punched

"Please kids. I can't see without my glasses. I'm blind as a bat."

because he was the biggest and stood tall above me.

But it was grinning Davy Drood that I was after. I grappled him close, from behind, my arm across his throat and shoulders, and I threw him down. I roared out. I lay on top of his body. There was sharp gravel in the road. I turned his face into it and pressed his chin and nose into the points.

He reddened and stiffened in fury and spat curses. Close to, I could see him very clear.

The others were too astonished to try to pull me away.

The hatred that I felt for him—the hatred that I felt, that I had in me to feel, not for him or anything in this present; certainly for this present, but not for him, who was dear; no, especially for him, for him—the hatred rushed upward into my shoulders and where I used to feel the pain between my shoulders. I was blinded.

At that time the hatred used to reach into my crooked fingers.—

I leaped to my feet in confusion. Mechanically I tried to help him from the ground, but he kicked me savagely in the shins. I dusted myself off, trying to regain composure. I strode in and slammed the doors.

six

There was nothing to do in the interim but sit down at the piano and touch the keys. I spread out my music.

Without my glasses, I could not see the music. But by squinting and bringing my head closer, hunching my shoulders, I could see it, and I touched a few keys.

My mind was solidly empty—nothing would be let enter there. I became interested in the noise of the music. It was the tiny prelude in C,

I had never yet played anything like this. At the small crescendo in the middle, against the repeated figure,

I became very interested, absorbed. I began to weep a little. (It was a tiny prelude, a small crescendo, and I wept a little.) I was absorbed in the sound of the music. So, squinting and weeping a little, without realizing either, I played the line over and over again, until I could play it. And then I played the crescendo more and more thunderously; it was a grand crescendo; and I let it spill over at last into the run. I went *back* to it, to play the crescendo again, starting with a still softer touch and reenforcing it to a still stronger thunder in the chord.—

I was absorbed in it. I did not see Davy Drood standing at my left.

"Here are your glasses," he said. "I can't bear to see you sitting there punishing yourself. You look so helpless."

"No! it's fine." I protested. "I'm interested in the music. I can read it all right." I realized that, patently, I was weeping.

I took the glasses but laid them on the piano.

"I'll never go near you again nor talk to you again," said Davy, as tho he had prepared the sentence beforehand. "I hate—I see we hate each other."

He went away. Did he go away? I kept staring at the music which I could read well enough, if I squinted but did not hunch my shoulders. I did not feel like touching the keys. I stole a glance to the left; he had gone.

I had been hitting the keys with more assurety, less fear to hurt them. I did not hold the keyboard so far from me.

It was not true what he said. I did not hate Davy Drood, tho he had rational grounds for hating me.

It seemed to me that my tie to this place no longer existed.

There was no longer a "real thing." Or, on the contrary, there was just that, a real thing, only a real thing. I could certainly pursue my duties here well enough, such as I saw them; so long as they lasted. If it were not *too* long! For I felt tired, a weakness in the shoulders.

I put the glasses in my pocket. In a certain sense I could see better, well enough, without their aid.

The time I could see Davy Drood's flushed head against the plaster wall, was the limit of what I freely desired of any of these boys. It was not true that I hated them.

But I resented their youth and excellence; and I wished that Davy would *drop* the ball.

"*Do you hate and love too much the one you happen to?*"

Bernardine came from the kitchen and said, "You're improving. You were playing this piece much better than I've heard you. Now you know the way to practice, patiently, slowly, over and over, and over and over again, the way I told you."

seven

I went upstairs to rehearse Debbie's long speech. She was Andromache.

"Come Debbie, there's no use still bearing me a grudge, we have to work together on this anyway. If you have a grudge I can't be so rough as I have to. I cut the play so that this is the longest speech because I know that you can make it carry. Read it thru again."

She obediently got her book. She read in her smooth emotional way.

"*Scream!*" I shouted; I could not scream.

She cowered. I closed the door.

"Scream! what are you afraid of?"

She screamed a word. "Like that?" she said timidly.

"No, scream on. Not one word. From here to here, the curses. '*Take him! dash him! dash him if you must. By Gods we're damned!*'—you see, I can't scream, but you can."

She screamed it and broke off. "That sounds terrible."

"No no, good. Once more."

204

She broke off. "I can't. It hurts my throat."

"Fine. I expect it would. Now bawl! Yes, weepy bawl—like a baby. But loud. No! no snivel. Wah! You see, I can't bawl."

She could still, a little.

"Good. Close the book. What is the speech about?"

"Well, she doesn't want him to take the baby away. Then she kisses him and gives him up, and curses them. That's what the speech is about."

"What has this speech got to do with your other long speech—what is it?—'*O mother, mother!*'"

"Oh, then she's talking about herself. Herself and her husband, and how to be a good wife, and—sexual pleasure."

"Well? why is this the second speech?"

"I don't see what you mean."

"No? then we can't get at it that way. Tell me, what's the play about? the whole play."

She frowned and was puzzled. It was a very simple play, there was nothing to explain; but I always looked for something subtle. The Greeks sacked Troy and killed all the men, and now they were taking the women away, each to a different fate. The contrasting fates, the contrasting reactions—that was the whole plot. Hecuba, the queen, would be an old slave; Polyxena was young, and now she was dead; Andromache was the model wife and—

"Oh," said Deborah suddenly, in surprise. "They're going to throw the baby off the cliff."

"Yes."

"But I can't say *that!*" She burst into tears. For a moment she bawled; she also smiled because she realized she was truly bawling, but she cried nevertheless.

"I'm sorry," she said. "My throat hurts. It really has nothing to do with the play. I'm upset today. I know it's just a play and I've read the speech thru twenty times before."

"Yes, it's just a play. Now, what is the relation between this speech and the previous long speech?"

She frowned, with concentration rather than puzzlement. She was a silly girl, but rather dear. "In the first speech," she said hesitantly, "she—she's boasting a little. Don't you think? She sets herself up as a model."

"Good for you! Yes, I think so. Well?"

"Well, that doesn't help. As it turns out."

"No."

"With the baby she really means it.—But her love for the baby doesn't help either!"

"Wonderful. Wonderful.—By the way, what does Hecuba say in-between?"

"*She* wants to use the baby to rebuild Troy; *that* doesn't help at all!"

"No, it doesn't. Then how does Andromache, how do you, end up?"

"With curses. Angry curses . . . That's funny. You'd think I'd end up with the bawling, with tears."

"The anger is deeper than those tears."

"But how does *that* help? I mean the angry curses."

"Yes, how does that help?"

She frowned. I said, "Don't think that I know the answer either. But what would *you* say, if you were Euripides. About the war; I mean after the war? Remember I told you that the Athenians were actually fighting a war—"

"The Peloponnesian War— What's the matter?"

I was desperately weak and tired, in the shoulders; I must have shown it.

"Let's run thru it again. Remember, the beginning, the middle, and the end, so it makes a whole animal! When I say Bawl! you bawl; don't be afraid. When I say, Scream! scream."

"Please. Not today. I can't any more today."

"No, not today."

"Are you ill?"

"No. As a matter of fact I feel unusually well and relaxed. That sometimes makes one look ill."

"I see it now," she moaned and the tears ran down her cheeks again. "They're going to throw the baby off the cliff. I never really saw it before."

"Look at it from their side, Debbie. They don't want him to grow up to be an avenging hero, another Hector."

eight

Mark Anders was coming in the door as I was stepping out. I backed up in confusion to let him pass. Now it was true that I was plotting against him, for I had thought that the Doctor could be the Director and I had mentioned it to Bernardine.

We nodded to each other. He was confused. He stepped back to let me thru, just as I had stepped back to let him enter. But it was he who had to come thru and I who stepped out of the way.

He believed, I knew, that I had turned the big ones against him, or had at least confirmed them in their opposition, for they were enemies by nature. But it was false, for in fact I had worked to keep the peace, especially when Lawrence Dixon was exasperated and was about to say something on behalf of his boys, that they could not be treated as tho they were ten and twelve. Yet it was not Dixon, either, who turned them against him; it was only himself.

Perhaps, also, it was themselves. They needed to have someone to turn against; obviously it would be the lower school, and best of all the father of the lower school. As if it were impossible to grow up and change without treading underfoot the memory of the past. Then if Dixon had not made the blunder of having two directors, it would have been necessary to invent some corresponding mistake. This particular thought cheered me up, for it applied equally well to myself. If *I* did not exist it would have been necessary to invent me.

Since before the fire, Mark had not stepped into this building. What brought him here? Part of my confusion was surprise.

I stepped back, and he had to come thru in front of me — while I was still in the building. We nodded shortly to each other. I thought that the doctor would make a good director instead of Mark Anders, and Mark was thinking whatever he was thinking. This was the state of the lovely sociality of our school.

He came thru the door and went directly upstairs. I knew that he was asking questions about me.

nine

When Seraphia, Dixon, and I drove downtown for our brandy, it was clear that we formed a triangle, and I was in an embarrassing and distasteful position. For Dixon needed, or clung to, both Seraphia and me; and Seraphia was jealous of me, and hostile. But I certainly had ceased to get pleasure from the company of Lawrence Dixon, he was not my type; yet I needed, and clung to, him, because he was the school.

But the school had become cold and indifferent to me, because my feeling for Davy Drood was frozen in my heart. At the same time I was, almost enthusiastically, committing myself to plans for the school, as if I intended, or would be allowed, to stay on there.

I had now finished writing the little book on communities that I had come here to write (pretending that it was for this reason that I came here). It seemed to me that my next task would be to write a book on education, collaborating with some educator of long experience who was sympathetic to me, namely Lawrence Dixon; but I knew with absolute certitude that I would never collaborate on such a book with Lawrence Dixon.

ten

I at once exposed my idea, that the doctor would make a good director, if, of course, Mark Anders could not stay on.

"Have you spoken about this with the doctor?" asked Dixon sharply.

"Of course not. Who am I to speak about it? I have mentioned it to nobody except Bernardine."

"Bernardine!" cried Seraphia. "Why Bernardine?"

"She feeds me cinnamon-buns," I said drily. "I don't think of anything without discussing it with Bernardine."

Dixon was silent and sipped his brandy.

A minute later he was enthusiastic. Certainly the doctor!

He began to praise the doctor's silvery hair. And of course exactly what we needed was a medical man, to inspire confidence in our sanitary arrangements—which, truthfully, were not so careless as they looked.

I was pleased at his enthusiasm. I myself truly believed in the idea. I drew for myself the picture of the doctor in the rough and ready school conceived by the architect. We had now gotten down to the simple fundamentals, the growing mind-body, I was fascinated by the doctor's graphs of weights and heights. The growing soul in the community of shelters. We should soon, in such circumstances, come to scrap the entire curriculum—*both* the classics and the sciences, and the social-sciences, and discover and invent something sensible and simple. I didn't know what, but the material circumstances themselves would spur the invention of a curriculum. What was bedrock at our school was the spirit, the intention. At this moment I was perfectly willing to collaborate on a book with Lawrence Dixon.—I spoke out.

I spoke as tho I were going to continue on, next year, the year after next, as a member of their school. Meantime, both with the staff and with Davy Drood, I had already lost my creative connection with their school. To me it was nothing but a real thing—I could see it clear-cut, "de-personalized." Next year, I told myself, Davy and those others would be gone, good! and the new top group would be the algebrists, with whom my relations, tho absurd, were not intolerably compromised. I would not get involved again, not in the same way. Nor would I spend all my waking hours with that gang, neglecting the interesting and the possible, the small ones, with whom, after all, something could be accomplished *before* the damage had been done. And no more Greek plays! but the words for "bread" and "water"; not the words! but *baking* bread, *drawing* water. Fetching wood, kindling a fire. Tending the baby. This sounded too simple—was it simple enough? Even so far, did we dare? to materialize it to this point? But if it was a spiritual effect we hoped for, we must cultivate precisely the material causes, for that is where the creative energy was to be found. When Davy and the others had at last gone away—the old school—and with them the fear and error that weighed my shoulders down: I told myself.

Dixon broke in on my reflections and said, "Your idea of

the doctor is magnificent. But those plans of your architect—"

"*My* architect?"

"Of course he's your architect," said Seraphia. "He's certainly not our architect."

"Frankly, we're disappointed, Seraphia and I. It's good that we didn't commit ourselves and cut off from the alternatives."

"What alternatives?" I asked. "The alternative was to get $100,000, and we can't get it. What he suggests, we can do. What alternative do we have?"

"We could move elsewhere," said Dixon.

I stared at him dumbly.

"There are always two alternatives: to stay or to go. We could rent another place for the money we'd have to throw away here . . . As a matter of fact, Seraphia has been looking into it."

I stared at her. I looked first at one, then at the other. I was able to see them, and the situation, with a clear-cut, "depersonalized" image.

"This weekend I saw a charming place. I've been going around. A Long Island mansion. Let me show you a picture of it."

"Is that where you went?" I said.

"As yet they want too much for it," said Seraphia.

"But the contour of the hills—" I said.

There was a pause. I looked instead at Dixon.

"You love the spot we've been at, don't you?" said Dixon.

"Yes, I—"

"There's not another spot like it, of course."

"It's my fault," I said. "I have no imagination. I can't think up anything without a material frame of reference. I don't know what to say. When I think up anything—the idea of the doctor—it's at our school. The brook."

"The place doesn't have any unpleasant associations for you, naturally."

"No."

"For Seraphia and me—"

She cut in. "To me it stands for poverty! I have to deal with the parents; you don't. You don't know. 'Explain *this*

210

away, excuse *that*—if you can?' Frankly, the idea of your architect gives me the creeps. *It gives me the creeps!*" she shrieked. As usual she was drunk by the second brandy.

I looked at her.

"It's about time," said Dixon—I looked at him—"about time I got out from under my father's wing. The place was my father's . . . I don't like this Long Island place much myself, either—"

"Either? How could *I* have anything against it?" I protested.

"There are two other interesting possibilities. One is in the Berkshires."

"That sounds attractive," I said dully.

" 'What's this?' " mimicked Seraphia. " 'My daughter says that she lives in the Laundry!' . . . 'Oh that's perfectly all right, we are planning three new shacks. We have a world-famous architect!' "

"Is this decided?" I asked.

"No! nothing is decided!" said Dixon firmly, before Seraphia could say anything. "We haven't even had a staff-meeting on it, have we? How can you ask such a question?" he said angrily.

"I've lost track."

I looked at Seraphia; she was licking the inside of the glass with her tongue.

"I'll talk to the doctor first thing in the morning," said Dixon.

"But if the new place has a fireproof building," I cried, I looked at the photographs, "Mark Anders won't object to remaining. It was only my friend's plans he objected to, like Seraphia, as it turns out."

"What's it to me if he objects or doesn't object? Are we to make everything depend on whether Mark Anders objects or doesn't object? Obviously if the doctor is going to be the director, he ought to visit these three places himself."

"But you don't even know if the doctor will accept!" I pointed out merrily. (The brandy was good for me too.) "My prediction is that he will tell us one of his anecdotes."

We began to laugh gaily.

Before we left, I 'phoned a telegram to the architect: "Forget it. A thousand apologies."

I left Lawrence and Seraphia in the car and climbed unsteadily to my room.

A large boy was curled on a quilt on the floor alongside my narrow bed. As soon as I entered, Jeff Deegan started awake, as tho he had been listening for me.

"What are you doing here? I'm sorry, I'm a little drunk." I was at once sober. "What's wrong now?"

"Nothing's wrong. I want to sleep here tonight, on the floor. Let me. Anyway I won't go away."

"Aren't you in enough trouble? Now you're sneaking out."

"Don't worry. I'll get back before it's light."

"Why do you want to sleep here on the floor? You can't sleep in my bed, it's too narrow."

"I don't want to sleep in your bed. But—*Near* you."

"O.K. Go to sleep." I kissed him on the cheek, bending over. My head reeled. I undressed. I threw a coat over him, and put out the light, and crawled between my blankets.

I could not sleep. After a while I would have a headache and tomorrow I would be beat. The thought of the boy was persistent. He was pretending to sleep, but was holding his breath. I presumed—since always I presumed to the surface a motive that was perhaps unconscious and perhaps not existing; but he had denied it, and we uniformly interpreted this to mean that he wished it—I presumed that he meant me to make love to him. But there was no sense or pleasure in it for me, now.

It was the situation that we pleasure-starved ones dream of, that the love comes to us in the night, especially the one we didn't think of, but we unwittingly laid up treasures of benevolence; and this situation does not fail to come to pass always when it is senseless and distasteful. (The reason for this disproportion is in the nature of the universe.)

The only feeling I could feel—such was the measure of my character—was the wish not to do the cold, the disappointing thing; because another time I would want him, and I had to take care, now, not to jeopardize the situation then. With no lust, rigid myself, I reached down and touched Jeff's face and neck. But he held himself rigid, holding his breath, and did not respond. I drew back my hand. Too much was required of me. It was not I, not tonight, not today, not this year, not at our school, not in this life, who would be the prince to this rigidly sleeping beauty.

The headache was now close to appear there, and split my head. I wondered why the car below had not driven away; I had been listening for it to start. Were they embracing, or quarreling? Seraphia was badly drunk. I felt sorry for Lawrence, in the humiliating dilemma that I had often experienced. There was a dull crash of glass and I leaped up on the bed and looked out the window.

"What is it?" whispered Jeff Deegan.

"Seraphia. She's broken a window in the Laundry."

"Why?" He jumped up beside me, to look.

"She's drunk, and she hates it because it's mean and poor. Come. It can't be helped. Go to sleep. Get off my bed."

I kissed him warmly on the mouth and lay down and turned over on my side and fell asleep—no headache at all.

CHAPTER XIII

*Here again can be seen the unwisdom of put-
ting new wine in old bottles, of trying to alter
a detail without upsetting the foundations of
the whole system.*

— FREUD

one

Soldiers in training were encamped in the village. A
number of the adventurous and intelligent among them
gravitated toward our company. The proximity of so many
young strangers was exciting to us. They came to our parties. Tho I had sexual bouts with a few, there was little
pleasure in it, for the death confronting them made their
flesh eerie and taboo. They sought out the young women,
Caroline, Jessie, and Veronica. But their especial favorite
was Dolly Homers.

Dolly was the only one of our school who had an active
sympathy with the fighting and read the news as a strong
partisan. She wanted not just the end of the war, but victory. She sought out the soldiers. Frequently she could be
seen with the same couple, in the town or flying by in a car.

Between these cheerful soldiers, subordinated and harried towards death, and our school where most of us were
working to make our young ones never subordinated and
never soldiers, the relations were cordial, interested, and
evasive. We freely discussed everything except the thing uppermost in mind.

Early in the morning the couple came in their car and
told us that Dolly had been taken in an ambulance to the
Asylum.

She had been wandering naked in the wet field; when they

approached she fled provocatively, or bruised herself on the stones. They were frightened, and so forth.

We roused up Dixon. I went back to manage with Teddy and Tony. I 'phoned Eliza to come out on the noon train.

two

—I must explain that it was this incident (an analogue of this incident) that has put me in the way of writing this history.

One knew—some had said aloud—it was obvious—that we were not up to the task of our school, not by character, knowledge, or available energy. (I do *not* mean that others were more able to it than we; for where were they? who was doing it? Nor do I mean, on the other hand, that in the absence of more knowledge, character, etc. it would be better to wait for a change; for the task was indispensable. And it was *only* our school, in a broad sense, that would ever make the change and release the energy. I mean simply that we are in a bad strait.)

One knew—it was obvious—but one did not like to think that some of us were "really" crazy.

We say, speaking of our friends, "Oh, that one, she's mad. *They're* quite demented. He's off his hooks. I blew my top ten years ago. But W.? he's *really* crazy, no joke." No joke.

It occurred to me to take notes of these things and see how they look on a page.

Or again: our friend is in a bad way, takes flight in drink, is driven to pleasures that give no pleasure. We say, "Why doesn't he take hold of himself, take up regular habits, and get himself a nice girl?" To be sure these are just what he can't do. Then let him come to our school! But, in fact, he's *really* crazy.

Or again!—for why should we individually reproach ourselves for succumbing to the universal necessity?—people say, "Let's reform this institution and reelect XYZ and consolidate the gains"—and in fact, they are *really* fighting the war and inventing other bombs.

But W.? he's <u>really</u> crazy, no joke".

three

One was not allowed to visit the Asylum. According to the rules of our peaceable society—in our country there was peace—all but experts were protected from the experience of "extreme situations," births, strong pain, and insanity. For instance, I have never seen a childbirth tho I am a father.

(One could sometimes experience his own extreme situations, without anesthesia, with as much knowledge, objectivity, and available energy as one then happened to have.)

Within these rules, hemmed round by darkness, and every visible maw of darkness armed with teeth, we were supposed to teach the harmony of the soul, to educate the feelings and convey the facts of life.

four

Mark Anders spoke to me kindly, but I took his words in bad part.

He advised me not to return the next year because, in his opinion, the set-up without Dolly was impossible for Tony. Even with Dolly it had not been of the best. He recalled to me how Tony used to run wailing after me on the road. Because of my duties, I was always at the other school. It seemed to me that Mark's voice had a menacing edge.

"Veronica will take care of Tony!" I said angrily, committing myself to Veronica in a way that I would not have suspected in myself; but my helplessness was always at work in the depths. "If my work here is unsatisfactory, that's another matter," I said. "I suppose I am *still* on trial?"

"Do as you see fit," said Mark. "This is only my opinion of how such a child should be provided for. I'll discuss it with the others."

"I dislike the imputation," I said heatedly, "that I'm not as concerned as the next one about what's good for Tony. Where else do you expect me to go? I've made mistakes, I have to admit it. But I can learn; I'm not a fool."

"I didn't mean to hurt your feelings," said Mark kindly.

I had not lied to them the other night; I was devoid of

imagination or invention except in the place where I was. And yet—likely it is the same thing—I was helpless to struggle to maintain myself in the place where I was, to cling to it.

My mind was fixed in its scene. My fingers could no longer cling, they were numb. In them there was the tension only to claw and rip.

But I clung with my lips and my beseeching eyes.

What Mark said opened beneath me a kind of gulf. I became dizzy.

"I don't think I'll be here next year either," said Mark.

"I'm sorry to hear that," I said sincerely. But I would not stay to talk with him.

"The son of a bitch!" I knew, with an hallucinatory clarity, that he was asking questions about me. I was indignant that an educator should question children. But my suffocating fear was even stronger than my indignation.

five

I paced the building in terror.

For more than an hour Dixon was closeted with Davy Drood.

I could not take my ears from the expected opening of that door. I ran icy shivers—all this for an outcome, a disclosure that I also even consciously connived at; a disclosure that to Dixon would not be a disclosure; and for which I had so laid my plans that I could say, "But I told you so all along." But I was suffocating with anxiety. Was it because of the hatred of Davy Drood—his hatred for me, that would bring him to betray me? my hatred of him, that at last could reproach him with betraying me?

I was possessed with the fear, rising from my own bubbling turmoil, that the boy was now betraying me. Obviously, that he should do so was the root of my fascination in him. Yet I was indignant, for whatever had passed between us was his inviting. And what had passed? Not very much! (I cried to myself in self-pity).

Day by day for weeks and months my longing had been turned towards something. But the outlet was closed, a door slammed between us. It was *this* energy, turned back on me, that was boiling and bubbling and suffocating me.

Dixon's door opened, and I came down the corridor toward them. Davy hurried past me without a word, and I turned pale.

"Well, I asked Davy," said Dixon. But his face showed nothing.

"What did you ask him?"

"Whether we should move or not. I showed him the photographs." He rubbed his hands in excitement.

He never betrayed me, and I gave my trust entire. I gasped and could have vomited.

"Don't you think I should have taken him into our confidence?" said Dixon, surprised.

"No! why did you? why is it his business?"

"What are you thinking of?" cried Dixon. "Davy has been here eleven years, in this place. It's his *school*. This is the school he must come back to as an alumnus. How could I possibly *not* ask Davy Drood?"

"You're right. I'm at the end of my wits—about Dolly. What did he say?"

"He said it was all right with him," said Dixon pleased, "whatever Seraphia and I thought best."

"How did he like the photographs?"

"He thought it was a good-looking building!" cried Dixon, rubbing his hands joyously.

"That's just fine."

"Does he know about Dolly?"

"No."

Lawrence became thoughtful. It occurred to me, a vagrant idea, that I had never heard him laugh when sober; I realized with a shock that he was without a sense of humor.

"Come in here, I want to talk to you a moment," he said.

The tears started into my eyes and I went in. He closed the door.

He was calm, for him, without his jumpy tics. He spoke from deep in the throat. He looked tired; relaxed from our usual tight alertness we seem to sag and be tired (we who are tired). He faced me squarely, gripping the table and bending his tallness towards me, and said, "I am going to tell you something that nobody here knows, in fact nobody in the whole world. Not even Mae knew it. Davy does not know it, and he must not be told, yet."

If the secret was so esoteric as that, I did not need to be afraid, I listened with a more objective interest.

"I am Davy's father. His name is really David Dixon."

"*Really?*"

"You're surprised. Couldn't you have guessed it?"

"No. I don't think I could."

He rubbed his hands.

"I'm puzzled," I said. "You say nobody in the whole world knows it; you mean nobody but Ann, Mrs. Drood."

"No. She doesn't know it either. Only you and I."

"Oh."

"That's why I was a little hurt—at first—when it seemed—when you came—it seemed you were taking away Davy's trust in me. He stopped coming to me, as he used. I admit it, I was jealous. It was all foolishness. The way he sees eye to eye with us about the moving, with Seraphia and me, he's closer to us than ever."

"No no, you were right! you were absolutely right. I behaved badly myself. Lawrence, in a sense you're the father of them all, aren't you, of Corny, and Naomi, and Debbie, and Jeff Deegan, the whole school."

"No," he said positively, "I'm their teacher. I'm Davy's father."

"I see. I understand . . . why do you tell me this? Why me? why just now?"

"I knew you'd ask that! I'm not sure why. An impulse. The moving! Yes, I'm sure of that. Going away from this spot, where my father— You're against it! *You're* the one I have to persuade. You mustn't disapprove of it. You must approve of it."

"I *don't* disapprove of it, Lawrence Dixon. I told you that before. You just took me by surprise. I wasn't ready for the idea."

"Have you seen the *new* photographs?" he said. He pulled them out of his pocket and I looked at them. I looked out the window.

The April had turned warm.

221

Tho the ground was soft and wet, they were lobbing the ball to each other, and they were oiling their bats. On the porch the girls were reading in the sun, on their bellies, heels in the air. I watched them. I could not stay, for I had to return to Tony and Teddy. Which was Davy Drood?

There he was. One could see, even lobbing the ball, that he was easily the best.

With revulsion I turned against my desire.

six

When she heard of Dolly, Veronica wept. Then she said to me, "You needn't rush back here after every class, just to look to Tony. I'll keep an eye on him, I'm always here. I know you like to stay over there and work, and see Davy Drood."

"Thank you, Vonny. It doesn't matter. It's not important for me to be over there. I might as well be here, or going back and forth. In-between. No place in particular. I ought to spend more time with Tony. Do you know that they are going to move the school?"

"Is Eliza coming?" she asked, with a sure intuition.

She would have liked me to say one small word, even pretending, or even gallantly, that I preferred to be here because she was here. This word I could not say. I could embrace her, copulate with her, kiss her (this with less satisfaction), but I could not bring to my lips a word of affection. I imagined that this was for the honesty; nothing about me was honest but the speech, but the speech was scrupulously honest. Yet actions speak truer than words; if I acted a measure of affection, why was I unable to speak at least that measure?

—Years ago, when I was eleven or twelve, I used to stammer miserably. I could not get a word out and I blazed with anger at myself. I do not know why I did nor how I stopped. But if I did know, I think I could have uttered a small word of affection and said, "I love you," even if I felt it was a lie.

"I appreciate your offering to look after Tony. But I can't

let you do it because I know you don't like it, you don't like children."

"I shouldn't offer to do it if I didn't want to!" she said spiritedly. The tears started into her eyes and she blinked them angrily away.

With much brooding, and some suffering, she had invented a picture of our relations in the present and future. For all I knew, or could say, or hoped or feared, it might be the true one.

It was not that year at our school, nor the year before that in another place, that I had first slipped into the way of non-commitment, of non-committal commitment (for not to commit oneself and to go on is equivalent to committing oneself to go on). But it was at that time, during those few weeks, that this mania grew in me into a monstrous growth, and even flowered in the philosophical conviction that such a way was wise, noble, profitable.

Secretly, I felt that if I held back and sufficiently distracted my attention by giving in to non-commitments, then one day life would sneak up on me from behind and deal me such and such a blow.

seven

When the doctor heard about Dolly, he made up his mind not to be the director of our school. He declined the beautiful offer. Our school, just on that day, did not look at its best.

He had taken a long time for his decision. At first he had been too astonished to say Yes. His picture of himself at our school had not been of the man who becomes the director. Dixon pressed him, he had first to prove that the offer was bona fide and perfectly reasonable. But then, as the doctor was brought to understand that he was not a liability nor a beneficiary of our school but an ornament and a likely director of it, he inevitably became insecure about the status of the school itself. If *he* was fit to direct it, what was wrong with the school? He began to back-track. He insisted that he was no longer young enough; a few years

223

ago this would have been just the opportunity; but now he had to make sure of the future, make money, see his children thru college. The war was ending and he had a chance to set up a private practice in a small town.

I climbed up to the Infirmary to confront him. "Is it true that you have said No?" I asked him point-blank.

"Yes. No."

"All right," I agreed, "no. I'm sorry for the school. I think you're right."

"Sit down," he said and gave me one of the precious Turkish cigarettes. Just now we respected and did not distrust each other.

"I'm sorry that they're moving away," I said.

He waved it away. "Why do you bother your head? . . . Let me tell you a Jewish anecdote. There was a loafer in the town named Mendele. Mendele was a beggar, a disgrace to the town. The authorities held a meeting to decide what to do about Mendele. The only thing was to give him a job on the town payroll, a sinecure. Then he wouldn't have to work and he also wouldn't be a loafer. But what job? Every job, every sinecure, requires some little effort, just to sign your name, and Mendele wouldn't make any effort what-soever. He excused himself. Finally, 'Let's make him the Messiah-blower! Every town needs a Messiah-blower. When the Messiah comes, somebody must be ready to blow the horn.' But Mendele cried, 'Messiah-blower! With *my* lungs? How can I blow a horn? The weak I am I couldn't even hold up the horn.' 'Mendele, you don't understand. Who needs to blow a horn? It's now the year 5434 and the Messiah hasn't come yet.' 'With *my* luck,' said Mendele, 'the Messiah will come next week!' "

It was a good joke. We laughed. "It means—" said the doctor.

"I know what it means!" I cried. "*You're* Mendele! And *I'm* a Messiah-blower! . . . 'Have *you* seen the photograph?' " I mimicked.

"Idealistic? Photographs you can't have! Utopian? Photographs you can't have!" The doctor grinned his sly and happy grin.

"I won't be here either," I said; and we two Jews roared

224

in mutual appreciation.

I pointed to his sampler: *Humor ist wenn man trotzdem lacht.* "Doctor! why have you got this dead language hanging on the wall!"

"That's just it!" he cried.

eight

I waited impatiently for the noon train, but Eliza was not on it.

Late in the afternoon, when one no longer expected her, she appeared. And this very fact, that I had ceased being impatient and did not care whether she came or not, made our meeting amiable. I was at the end of my tether. I had no plan, and it was agreeable to see her.

"But I told you that Dolly was cuckoo. Why don't you ever believe me! *Cuckoo! Cuckoo!*" she sang.

Her attitude seemed to me fresh and remarkable, as if it proved that we two were sane. As the safety of my place here began to founder—for I had come here to take refuge and find safety—then my former state seemed to me a kind of safety, the very state from which I had fled here for safety.

Eliza was six or seven months pregnant. She was one of those women who in this later stage are placid and self-justified. She was on good terms with McWilliams and sometimes chose to call herself Mrs. McWilliams. And all this was, surprisingly, agreeable to me; it was stable and convenient. It hardly roused my resentment—so far had I grown away from her and grown toward what was possible.

Since Eliza was contented and friendly, I was able to explain to her, in resentment and also because it was so, that I too had found a possibility of some contentment.

"Do you mean Angelica?" Her tone was unbelieving and satirical.

"Veronica," I corrected her.

Liza did not have a high opinion of Veronica; but it was not necessary to defend one of my wives to another. Indeed, it seemed to me that instead of having no home, Tony (myself) was in the way of having two almost cordial homes.

—I did not attempt to conceive in any material detail my future cordiality to McWilliams. —It was necessary for me to entertain this illusion in order to endure the hopelessness that was eating at my heart.

nine

Since I noticed nothing, I did not notice that Veronica was jealous of Eliza, and hated her. She had no cause to be jealous, for I did not intend ever again to live with Eliza, not even if there were no obstacles. But she was jealous because Eliza was an artist and a woman of spirited intellect, whereas she was deficient, she felt herself deficient, in these things. It seemed to her that these were grounds of love; that is, if she had been homosexual, they would have been grounds of love to her; but as it was, they were grounds of hate and fear.

"You love her, you will always love her," she said, to my astonishment; her face was swollen.

"No, I don't love her—if I ever did," I said.

It was painfully consoling to her to blame my non-committal affection for her on my attachment to Eliza. She was frustrated and therefore anxious and therefore afraid and therefore jealous. But alas! I had been non-committal long before I ever met Eliza.

"Why are you lying? you are jealous of Davy Drood," I insisted. "You need not be; I don't get any satisfaction with Davy Drood."

"No! he's not my rival," she insisted.

Nevertheless, she was jealous of Davy Drood, and of all those boys of mine, but she could not allow herself to feel this jealousy, for then there would be no having me at all. They had penises and gave such and such pleasures, that she could not rival. She made the rationalization that no woman could be an artist; but Eliza was an artist and therefore terrifying.

More obviously, the truth was that *not* to have me, except just in the peculiar circumstances that I loved Davy Drood and that she did not feel jealous of it, *this* was the possibility for her to love at all—such as it was. This was sad, and this sadness was the state in which we lived. A terrible wrong had been done, somewhen, perhaps from the beginning; and we had to turn ourselves to the undoing, if we were to live on at all—it came finally to a matter of life and death. Even tho we, who were supposed to turn ourselves, did not have the knowledge, the available energy, etc. How were we to be expected to have them?

Her face was swollen and she had been hiding, at the age of thirteen, for no other reason than that she had seen Eliza and myself taking each other for granted.

"I thought we had this out long ago," I said in anger.

"I realize you're irrational about her and it can't be helped," she said. "So am I. Let me alone." She tried to go away. But I seized her brutally by the arm.

"You could at least be civil to her. You make it hard for me. What am I to do with Tony?"

"She's not civil to me. You don't notice *anything*."

"It's about time we got out of it!" I shouted. "I've had enough. Now I have to watch her *and* you, and myself." I returned to my old thought: "It's like a cage of tigers! How can I trust you with Tony if you hate Tony's mother?"

She was frightened and again put her fingers in front of her mouth.

I took Eliza and Tony to the train, and I boarded the train with them and went away to the city for the night.

CHAPTER XIV

one

As soon as I arrived in the morning, I knew I was found out. Knew it before I could see it, for there was no one in the downstairs hall on whose face I could read the news. Just so; why was there not? a face on which to read the assurance that there was nothing to fear. Like those who are deluded that they are hunted, I looked for small signs and interpreted no-sign as a sign; except that I was not deluded, but in fact I was found out. Found out in my misdeeds that were no secret anyway; misdeeds that I did not know for sure to be misdeeds (this was just what I did not know). But I was guilty because I was not approved. I came into the downstairs hall that was empty and my heart was pounding.

Then I saw two of them, Ross and the fuzzy-haired girl, and I saw at once that I was found out. My breast-muscles tightened and my heart stopped pounding. At once there was a little space between myself and the surrounding. This space was the withdrawal of feeling from the surface of my skin. If not for this withdrawal, a flush of shame, disgrace, would have passed over me from the soles of the feet to the roots of the hair. I was not willing to feel this feeling.

On the table was a note for me to expect Mark at about eleven.

At the foot of the stairs appeared Michael who had been waiting for me to come. His voice was obscured by the thin void it had to cross to reach me, that blurred my sight and hearing (I could taste or smell nothing at all). He said, "I told you so! Don't think I'm mean to say it. I can't help it and it doesn't give me any satisfaction."

"I didn't say you were wrong, did I?" I said almost cheerfully. My voice, everything that began from within me, was quite, not quite, under control.

"Yesterday Anders questioned every one of us. One by one."

"Did he really allow himself? One by one?"

"Boys and girls."

"What did he find out? I'm interested."

"Not much," said Michael. "Enough. Naturally nobody would tell him anything. Nobody likes him anyway. But one of the boys betrayed you."

"Betrayed? isn't that a strong word? was there a dark secret?"

"Betrayed! betrayed!" cried Michael.

"What did Davy say to him?"

"*He* didn't do it!"

"Of course not, you idiot. I know who did it. But what did Davy say?"

"He wouldn't talk. He just said and repeated that you were the best teacher the place ever had."

"Oh? . . . What do you think?"

"What do you mean what do I think?"

"Do you think I'm a good teacher?"

"Frankly, no. You're insecure. If you settle down—some day—you might be a good teacher. What do you think about me?"

"I think you're a conceited ass. You love yourself more than any boy I ever knew."

He turned pale, and blushed, as I could not.

"What did Corny say?"

"Corny wouldn't talk, so he began to cry."

"And what did you say, Michael?"

"I told jokes, of course. I pulled his leg and got him mad."

"Yes, I can imagine that."

"What will they do? will they kick you out?"

"They? Was Dixon in it too?"

"No! Can you picture Dixon questioning us, one by one? Are you demented? I just mean, they, they."

"How should I know what he'll do?"

"Will you have to leave right away? today?" His cruelty
rose.

"Michael!" I said warningly.

"Aren't you going to ask me who the one was who told?"

"I told you I know who."

"Who?"

"Jeff Deegan."

"How did you know?" He was disappointed that I knew.
"Yes. It was Jeff Deegan. I told you he hates you like poison."

"He doesn't hate me." That is, I refused to believe that he
might hate me, for reasons of his own.

"I told you to watch out for him long ago, last fall,"
persisted Michael.

"All right!" I cried sharply. "You *win* the medal for being
damn smart."

The touch of anger made a rift in the transparent wall.
Now woe welled in me.

two

Agitated, I had no appetite for the breakfast that Bernardine kept for me, yet I had to go to it nevertheless, in
order that everything might be as if nothing were wrong.
But when I tapped our signal, I felt a searing pain in my
fingertips and had to dig nails into my palm. Holding back
the need to claw and rend: the ends of the crooked fingers
with which I had grasped Davy on the gravel. But I did not
rend, nor utter an unusual sound, nor flee.

I left the coffee half-swallowed and fled out into the
springtime and walked hastily up and down the road and
around the building. Impatient for Mark's arrival. The kind
of thought with which I tried to burn up the feelings that
could not be expressed in behavior that had to be as if
nothing were wrong, was that I was about to be criminally
prosecuted and jailed. I should also have imagined, and
endured, other torments and punishments, rather than give
way and burn with shame.

But by the time Mark came, I had fixed, transfixed, myself
to a narrow chair in the hall and was lost in a quite different

231

dream (I cannot recall what dream). When he came in the door I was jarred out of my daydream; I leapt to my feet and a spasm of nausea made me spit thru my nose the half-cup of coffee that I had not wished to down. He was astonished. "Wait," I said, "I'll get a rag and clean this up." I ran for the rag and on hands and knees dried the floor. I was embarrassed to dispose of the rag and stuffed it in my pocket.

"Aren't you feeling well?" said Mark Anders.

"It's nothing at all. I just gobbled down my breakfast too fast."

. . . "Sorry," I said. We sat down at a cleared table in the dining-room. "Now what's eating you?" I said lightly.

Mark said bluntly, "Did you or did you not ever have overt sexual relations with any of the boys here?" He had prepared the question beforehand and spoke it out at once, as if to make sure he would not be confused or sidetracked and that it was just this question that he asked.

"Yes," I said, "I did. That exists."

three

I had toyed with the idea of baiting him a little, for sport and instruction. I could have asked a question or two: "What are sexual relations? What are not sexual relations?! Are we, now, Mark Anders, having a sexual relation? And what are overt sexual relations? Where do *you* draw the line? Is it overt if the persons rub together? or must the parts rub together? or suppose they touch and, say, both know what they are doing but avert their eyes and talk on as if they did not know? Must the parts be exposed? For instance, sometimes at night, sitting on Davy's bed and entertaining him with the habits of the world, I masturbated him thru the blankets and then, sick with longing, fell on him and came in my pants. Was this an overt sexual relation? Other times—"

The purpose of this would have been to tease him and to force him to mention certain words and confront the material facts of life. I thought also of what I might say that would sound interesting and be profitable to my students.

But I had no heart for small victories, and I said, "Yes, I did."

He was taken aback by the direct answer. "I am glad you admit it right off," he said. "I won't have to pursue it further. I have plenty of information."

"So they tell me," I said drily.

He flushed. "They tell you everything."

"Of course they do. They trust me." I meant it as a sentimental self-justification, not as a rebuke to him, but he took it otherwise.

"You will have to resign at once," he said angrily.

"And what if I won't?"

"Then I'll take it to the trustees."

I considered this a moment. I was not in a position, just now, to thrash this out. "I'll resign," I said.

"You can stay out the term, because of the play."

"That's only sensible. They've worked very hard."

"You've plotted with them against me," he said angrily.

"I did not!" I said angrily. "You're your own worst enemy!"—But I held my peace. I was pleased and secure because I was not going to be put in jail; it was as simple as that. "Is that all?" I asked.

"No, one more thing. You are not to take a job in any other school. If you do, I'll see that you're dismissed. I'll—I'll hound you. And worse. I realize it's not your fault, but the children must be protected."

I trembled, with fear, with anger, it is hard to say. I trembled with excitement. I gripped the table between us as tho I would tear it in two and confront him. I chose my words:

"I do not intend to go back into these schools, now. Not just now. Not for three, four, five years. First I must find out something. I shall come back. Depend on it. Then we'll see."

He stood up. "That will do. I prefer not to discuss it."

"Sit down a minute, Mark," I said. "You've won."

He sat down.

"Tell me, Mark, do you really have such a strong fear of homosexuality? It's not very Balinese."

"Between an older man and a child!" he cried with horror.
—There was evidently a memory he had that served him
as a screen for something else. Yet also—I scrutinized
him—he was partly lying; it was I he hated and feared, some
idea he had of me.

"I should think that that depends on the person involved,"
I began to say—but I realized suddenly that also this situation, in which I interrogated him, would be interpreted by
him as a sexual attack.

I stood up. "I'm sorry," I said. "I was thinking of something
else. Maybe we'll discuss it some other time."

I held out my hand and he awkwardly shook it.

If he had held out his hand first, recreating a scene that
I had often lived thru, the punishing authority that finally
offers me its consolation, my eyes would perhaps again, as
often before, have flooded with tears. But this time it did
not happen that way.

four

I was hamstrung by not knowing. (When I can always
force myself to affirm it, and finally I act it with vindictive
joy.) I knew that it was not homosexuality but sexuality
they were afraid of; but I did not know what in my own
behavior was love and what was spite and the need to
destroy excellence. I was able to tell over to myself the
reasons that justified me; but I did not know which of these
reasons were rationalizations.

Because I was unhappy, I did not trust my desires, and
I felt enough to feel that I was unhappy.

It was I who was afraid or I should have found out. *What*
was I afraid of?

five

The devil with it! Let me describe again the excellences
of our school. There were, to repeat it, four groups, and each
had its own style. In Group I, the following occurred:

234

Parents' Day

Group I (ages 6-8)

The butcher came at an unusual time to slaughter and dress a calf. The teacher of the youngest group was unwarned, and the kids were roaming in the field. They hastened in fascination to the spot. They did not see the killing but they watched the flaying, they could not be torn away. They were sick with fright and feasted their eyes.

Their teacher came and saw that they could not be removed without commands and threats. Tho she was herself a squeamish little woman, she put up a brave front and said, "How interesting! and isn't it interesting what he's doing now!" She pointed out which was the heart and which the lungs, and where the round steak came from and where the rib roast, while the poor dead beast hung with its hide dangling over its ears.

At meal time the children were nauseous. There was meat on the platter. They were not encouraged to eat; but their teacher thought—she herself, to her surprise, ate voraciously—that they should experience enough of the dining-room to make them vomit, and not hold back their vomiting. For several weeks they would not touch the meat.

She watched for some spontaneous motion from them. They began to indulge in an apparently pointless horseplay of tearing off each other's overcoats and jackets. They were mutely reliving the flaying.

She heightened it to a game, a dance, a ceremonial. One of the number would be the calf, dressed in two, three, or four coats: it was comic if under the brown coat suddenly appeared a white coat. But the red sweater was the underflesh. The butchers wailed in woe, but the victim was dead and supposed to be silent; often he laughed boisterously.

In this totemic sacrifice, different children preferred different rôles: the Victim, the One who Holds, the One who Cuts the Throat, the One who Flays. The little teacher screwed up her courage and said, "How interesting! and isn't *this* interesting?"

After a time, they were all beasts of the field, going on all fours and bellowing. And the game turned into the more amiable play of animal-masks.

Group II (9-11)

When the language of her group became stupidly dirty, obsessively returning to a few words, as if they were soldiers or sailors, Caroline could not hope to teach them articulate composition. They did not learn new words.

She stood at the blackboard and carefully printed the words most frequently heard:

FUCK　　　　BASTARD　　　　COCKSUCKER　　　　SHIT

She asked them for contributions; their vocabulary in this kind was somewhat greater than her own. The words were accurately defined.

Suddenly it struck her that the classroom itself was in a mess; papers and crushed chalk underfoot, the blackboard dusty gray; the condition of the books was shameful.

"Shoot!" she cried. "I can't stand it any more. Let's clean it up here."

—We had recently been mentioning an amusing passage in Fourier, where he says that since children have a passion for filth, the garbage-collecting of society should be given into their hands.

They brought pails, rags, and soap and went to work on hands and knees with much slopping, and much thoroness. With continuing enthusiasm (I saw it so I believe it), they proceeded thru every classroom in the school, driving us others out of the way. This took all day and recurred sporadically for months.

Group III (12-14)

From the city they sent us a desperate and "probably hopeless" case. We were the last resort; if we could not manage with him, Norman would have no social schooling whatever. Norman was large and fat, intelligent, malcoordinated; he was a complete baby, given to wailing and full-dress tantrums.

We warned Sophie's gang, since by age and knowledge he would go in with them. They set themselves to cooperate, with their beautiful tact and fraternity.

But so far as we could help, Norman was hopeless. Taken in by his brightness, a teacher would encourage him to speak up in class. But whether one agreed with him or disagreed, or kept silent, he would at once go on to reproaches, anger, tears of self-pity, rage in which he would tear up books; whether one restrained him or not, it ended with a tantrum. Every class hour was spoiled. If one of the kids threw Norman's soap into the brook, then Norman, bawling with self-vindication, would throw the other's camera into the brook. This was his idea of justice. A week of this experiment was enough for the staff.

The boys were exasperated with the fat boy and pitied him; away from him they burst into fits of ridicule and endless discussions. (He was not dangerous except to property.) But when we tried to call it off and admit failure, they became indignant with us for not really trying. We relented for a few more days.

"We try to be brotherly!" they said. "We are brotherly! This doesn't work. *What do we do wrong?*"

—Once they had admitted it to themselves, that there was such a thing as a brute fact, unamenable to discussion, our algebrists were remarkably transformed. They became motherly. Their feminine feelings rose to the surface, accompanied by a softening, and deepening, of their hitherto metallic voices. Their affection for one another rapidly changed. Too rapidly and strongly: we did not dare allow it, allow these alert conformists to grow independently into the condition of being willing to confront brute facts.

The Staff was not ready for it. We were willing to admit the fact of failure: the disproportion between our general task and aims and this particular burden; but we were not willing to go so far as to make our school a true sampling of the nature of the entire world. It was we, not Sophie's gang, who violently brought the situation to an end and sent Norman back home.

None too soon. In a few more days Group III would have fought us, for their fact, with fists and claws.

"All very well!" said Schuman bitterly, "but what will become of him now? No other school will take him, we were the last resort. *No* one takes the responsibility? Is this supposed to make *us* feel secure and happy, the way you boast?"

Group IV (15-17)

For a couple of months the big ones had a new counsellor, a tall homely fellow, the son of a country pastor, but himself not religious. (He was a pacifist and our local conscription judged that the interests of the people were best served by putting him in a prison.)

As best he could by reasoning and cajolery, he tried to get the girls and boys to be more prompt and orderly in cleaning the rooms and making the beds.

Finally he resorted to satyagraha; he took it upon himself to make the unmade beds and to do the sweeping; he ostentatiously spent several hours a day at this work. He hoped to shame them.

He did not understand them at all. With a few jests, but no twinges of either guilt or compassion, they let him do their duties for them. Indeed, one or two who had used to make their own beds, now left it for the counsellor. All were glad to slip into this new convenient convention. "If he thinks it's so important," said Seraphia's daughter, "he has the mental set to do it. I don't and I haven't."

Not like a good satyagrahi, he became angry and said, "You all think you're making a fool of me"—indeed nobody thought this—"but in the long run I'll win out. The same thing happened to me. My father said, 'The important thing is to get used to its being clean and neat, not matter how it gets that way. After a while one will make the effort himself, because it's too disgusting when it's dirty.' You'll see. After I'm gone and it goes back to filth you won't be able to stand it and I'll have my revenge!"

"Ho!" cried Michael. "You have a father, a conscience! That's what's wrong with you. Long as your father did it you didn't notice; but after he was gone he began to talk out inside of you. That's called the Super-ego. Now we don't have any consciences. It won't work!"

—It worked. His conscience, or father's voice, or common

238

The wall thickened about me.

reason, or whatever it was, led him to being dragged off to prison. And now he was gone. And the girls and boys could not bear to see the place disorderly, too disorderly; for they loved him, and they were not unwilling to have him win the victory.

These were four episodes of our school, one from each group.

six

In the hall, Jeff Deegan had glared at me with hatred; this I could not deny to myself.

I sat in the kitchen with Veronica and Tony, where I was loved and wanted.

"You betrayed your trust as a teacher!" Dixon had said, in his ringing voice of arriving at a remarkable formula. No, I did not.

"No, I didn't," I said quietly to Dixon. "I kept that always in mind. But I don't know what it involves; that's what one must find out as he goes along."

I avoided brushing against anyone, as if the contact would be scorching. But I was able to talk in a friendly way with Davy, Michael, and Corny.

The wall thickened about me.

Bernardine was indignant with Mark. She said, "Bourgeois hypocrites! You're an artist, a gentleman. If you did your children any harm, I would see it the first. They are afraid of words; in Europe we don't even have these words."

She was baking, and she let Tony make a small pie in the top of a baking-powder can.

I defended Mark and said he must consider the customs that our children were used to. But as I said it, I was ashamed before Bernardine, for it was stupid.

Yet I could not deny that Jeff Deegan had glared at me with hatred.

But Vonny was angry with Lawrence Dixon, because she thought that it was his duty to rescue me. I was astounded at her thought, for it had never occurred to me otherwise than that Dixon would be no support in any emergency whatsoever.

"Dixon!" cried Bernardine, echoing my very thoughts, "what could you expect from *him*?" Yet I defended Dixon.

"He did try to rescue me," I said. "The first thing he said when he saw me was, 'We must put you in the hands of an internationally-famous psychoanalyst. This will satisfy the trustees.'"

"Yes, and what came of that?"

"He 'phoned her right off!—"

—I floated and bobbed on the swells of being cared for, in the hands of Higher Powers—

"My impression was that he woke her out of bed and she said it wasn't worth the trouble. So he told me I betrayed my trust as a teacher."

"You're *joking!*" cried Bernardine.

"No! no!" I cried happily. "That's what happened!"

I felt that Vonny showed the flushed anger, the spirit, that I should have shown and felt. I did not show enough spirit. Clearly I was reconciled to having such things happen to me, I delivered the verdict beforehand.

But all of this was speculation and sentiment. Jeff Deegan's eyes were a fact.

I did not feel ashamed before Tony; he was the only one.

Dixon pounced on me like a tiger. I could experience at last the pounce that I had guessed at during our very first interview in Greenwich Village, when he sat so twisted that I thought he was paralyzed. But now I was less concerned.

"Excuse me," I said, "I am not used to being abused. Only praised."

"You will have to get used to it!" he shouted.

"We'll see about that."

He rubbed his hands and giggled.

Lefty began to play *Chopsticks* in the next room.

Tony's pie came out perfectly and he ate it piping hot. We were pleased.

"Why do you waste yourself in a place like this?" said Bernardine. "You're an artist, a poet. You must try, make a career."

I saw that I could not explain to her that just because I was an artist it was here that I had to try. What else was worth trying? For she held our school away, there, in its place.

241

Droyt joined Lefty at the piano.

"How can I bake a torte where there is such bourgeois hypocrisy!" cried Bernardine.

Vonny burst into tears.

"What's the matter?" I asked.

"Afterwards I won't see you," she said.

"No, I love you, a little," I said . . . I snapped my fingers in excitement—

"Of course! Bernardine! Don't you see?" I cried. "*Chopsticks! Coteletten Waltz!* The Chops are Cutlets!"

"What do you mean?"

"I kept thinking of the Chopsticks that the Chinese eat with. Because it sounded Chinese. But it means chop! chop the piano! chop the meat!"

At this moment I chanced to see my face in the small framed mirror where Bernardine used to make herself up. I was blushing deep red. Partly warmed by the heat of the oven, I was blazing with shame and disgrace. I was not protected by any wall, that *I* could see thru and still not be seen. They were looking at me. Altho there was no one but Bernardine, Veronica, and Tony, and they bore me no ill-will, the wave of shame passed over me, I was powerless to stem it.

It was Droyt and Lefty, the two masturbators, the successful one and the unsuccessful one, who were playing *Chopsticks*. This was why, until now, I had failed to make the simple verbal connection (for I am apt at verbal connections).

As the blush receded, I began to tremble with anger.

seven

"What's about Vonny?" said Michael knowingly. "When you leave will she go with you?"

"None of your damned business," I said; but I did not turn on my heel. "I don't know. You know about everything. How the hell should I know?"

"You don't like her, do you?" said Michael.

"No."

"Why do you torture her, then? Why do you stick around?"

"*She* sticks around." I didn't see any reason not to say whatever I thought; it was no longer the time to be deliberate.

"Bullshit!" said Michael deVries.

"Maybe I love her, but I don't like her. Did you ever think of that?"

"If you love her, why don't you love her? instead of acting like a non."

" 'Fraid."

He was, touchingly, surprised. "But you *said* you weren't afraid of anything. It was the first thing you said to me. You lied to me!" —He cried it out, betrayed, just as I had cried, "Jeff Deegan, you lied to me!"

"I'm not afraid of anything." I said it quietly, as previously, for I was not afraid of anything. I had moments when I was neither active nor passive, but grew into the next moment. Also I mumbled " 'fraid," like a comical shut-mouthed fifteen-year-old, as if I were the boy and Michael were I.

"She sticks around and I stick for her to stick around. I've got to have somebody to love me!" I bawled, but of course, being as I was, I did not bawl it out.

"You'll see," said Michael knowingly, "you'll drive her away in the end just like you did the other one."

"We'll see about that," I said sharply.

. . . Why did I say it sharply, when I did not feel the courage that should go with that sharpness, if a man is prepared to put up his best fight, win or lose? I did not feel the courage because I was continually apprehensive that my mother would go away and re-marry (and this also was what I wanted). Nevertheless! we *would* see about it; that was sure.

eight

I, stripped unto the naked pride,
ride rapidly

I dressed carefully, not as usually. Of my three, I chose the tie that was not bright but not funereal. I left so much of my mustache, a fringe across the lip a little fuller at the

243

corners, as might suggest that it was the first mustache I ever was growing. If they were going to look at me, ought I not to determine what she saw? With polished shoes (but they were torn) I boarded the train.

Ann Drood said she had an engagement but could see me for twenty minutes. I said it must be that evening, tho it was likely not so important, no, certainly, it was not a matter of life and death.

The death was not yet established in my heart; it was necessary to me that she should say so, in order that it might be established there. Meantime, when I saw, from the windows of a hurrying train, how the springtime evening darkened in the thin trees, my eyes still started tears. I had invented for myself the fancy that I was a Knight, a man of ease and even gaiety, who could invent something and had an idea: *Noblesse oblige!*—

"What on earth do *you* want?" cried Ann Drood.

I did not look at *her*, but I noticed that she was dressing to go out and soon putting on her hat.

"I stole a photograph of Davy, about age 10, from your house on the hill. We went up there by snowshoe."

She looked at me, and I looked down. "Is *that* what you came here to tell me? . . . Are you well?" she asked in a more kindly tone.

"No, I mean—I was in love with your boy and now I have to leave the school."

"Are you leaving? Are you going to leave the school? That's too bad. Do you have a better offer?"

"I mean, they're making me leave because I fell in love with Davy. I am not supposed to fall in love with the boys; especially being a teacher."

"Fall in love? What are you talking about?" She interrupted putting on her hat.

"Sexual love. I had sexual relations with him."

"Oh. I see."

I looked at her with one hard glance. She was cold to me.

"I'll tell you something he says about you!" I said. "When he was eight or nine he used to sit in front of the clock on the desk and grasp the clock with both hands and stare into it; but you didn't return on time—not at the time *he* expected, tho maybe *he* misunderstood. You must bear that kind of thing in mind!"

"You mean homosexual love," she said, "like—" She named a well-known French writer, as if to show me that she understood these things in an urbane way. Despite myself, the remark made me feel contempt for her.

She became angry. "No! what right do you have to give me advice? I *don't* approve. I don't approve at all. I'm a tolerant person but that's not the way for a teacher to act. No, not at all. Not with a boy with David's background."

"I'm sorry—you think so," I said slowly. "I hoped you—" I didn't know what I hoped.

She gripped onto herself, to the sensible attitude that was the rudder of her life. "Thank you," she said. "Thank you for coming to tell me, so I can know what steps to take. I realize that it's hard for you to come to me with such a story. I appreciate it."

"On the contrary! It's what I want most—to talk to you seriously."

"What time is it?" she asked. "Oh!" she cried in alarm. But her absorbing curiosity came to the surface. "You say you had—sexual—sexual relations with Davor? Does he—can he—does he have an orgasm?" ("Did he play a manly role?")

"Why don't you discuss it frankly with him sometime?" I said sharply. "Maybe it would bring you closer together. How long can this evasion go on, year after year? until you're dead. No, I won't answer the question *for* you!"

"What good are you to me then!" she cried in exasperation. "I must be going." She gathered up her purse.

"Just one moment," I pleaded. "Here is a poem I wrote for Davy I'd like to show you." I fumbled for the copy that I had neatly typed.

She took it and glanced at it impatiently.

> Lord bless Davy Drood and gently heal
> · the sharpened corners of his smile.
> Thou canst, from no matter what,
> by life new strength of life create
>
> and sweet ease. Tho boy-horrifying
> memories are ever crying,
> Thou makest them the riches of
> victory and quiet love.

245

She read it impatiently; but she seemed surprised that she could understand it, and she paused, and said, "Boy-horrifying memories. How did you guess that? ... Ever crying, ever crying ... May I please keep this?"

"Yes, I typed the copy for you. I have another copy."

She folded the paper and put it in her purse. She looked at me, one glance; our eyes met; her eyes were wet. "I doubt that you do much harm," she said lightly.

She held out her hand. "Thank you again. Good-bye."

"Good-bye," I said mechanically. "No, I'll go down with you."

"No, be a good boy. You go ahead."

"Ann!" I wailed, "You won't speak to me again." But I hurried out.

I waited in the shadows across the street, till she emerged. I followed her for several blocks at a half-block's distance; she moved along fast.

> I, stripped unto the naked pride,
> ride rapidly, I lend you aid
>> *noblesse oblige* along the way.
>> My pride aspires to beauty, I
>
> have no peace among this folk
> I cannot serve and will not strike.
>> Lord, give me peace at last, as surely
>> as Thou hast given me vain glory.

CHAPTER XV

A PROBLEM OF ART AND
A PROBLEM OF ECONOMICS

— FOR JEAN

one

As Talthybios, as Corny Tate—one did not see them as two, the youth acting the herald, but as the herald strangely young and familiar, or the youth surprisingly clad and about to say unusual words—as he came up the gravel drive from the direction where the ships were parked, he bore on his extended wrist amazingly a black bird: the left wrist imperiously high, fist not quite clenched.

One was astonished, did not expect him to appear with this menacing bird that was a crow five months old. His sandals were bound with golden bands about his legs. Was it a falcon, that black bird? Corny's tunic was rose.

The curtain blowing before the left wing of the porch was dawn-smoke, but the herald did not appear from behind it but up the gravel drive from where the ships were busy to depart. But Corny halted against the sheet: black bird, golden leg-bands. And the young New Yorker had on, surprisingly, a rose tunic.

He could not say his first words, tho he half-opened his mouth. Like everyone, he was entranced by the black bird perched on his imperious wrist; the bird dug its claws into his flesh as if about to take flight. What was portended by this silence, for the weeping girls on the steps? By the mouth

247

half-opened and the bird stretching to hop away—one did not distinguish between the mouth half-opened and the stretching bird.

"Wife of Hector," whispered the prompter behind the sheet. Was this the portentous suggestion of the unconscious? one shivered with fright for the cowering queen on the top step. But it was not this thought that could touch the forethought of the entranced Messenger whose lips moved drily. The whisper suggested, *"Abhor me not."*

From that violet air, from that pale cloud, had sounded the music of the pipe, from nowhere. The music had past, and the women lay as if dead, while Debbie rose from cowering and stood high in woe. *"Wife of Hector! Wife of Hector, once Troy's best!"*

The bird sprang among the first rows. The Messenger stepped forward reaching as if to retrieve the speech. —

> "Wife of Hector, once Troy's best,
> abhor me not!"

Corny proclaimed; and one cringed with terror and melted with pity for them all, the young girls on the wooden steps and the rosy Dawn that had moved up the gravel drive and halted. The voice behind the curtain was dumb, for now he *spoke* his thought:

> "Not willingly am I the Messenger
> of these agreed messages."

It was too late to recover the words, because the black bird had scurried among the seats. The bird was not out of character, because one did not distinguish the reality and the illusion. Standing high—the Herald stood below the steps—Andromache prepared her moan.

(Too late. I now wished I could restrain her. I had feared that these outcries as we schemed them would sound mechanical and contrived; but now I knew that they would be too harrowing to be bearable.)

The Director had introduced the action briefly and well, saying that in this wartime, the time of the ending of the war, we had a duty to perform such an action as this, tho it was hard to do and watch. (But Dixon too had imagined

"Abhor me not!
I am not willingly the Messenger".

that one could distinguish between the play and the reality.)

The sixteen-year-old New Yorker proclaimed:

"Not willingly am I the Messenger."

There was not one present among us who did not have a son, a father, a best-friend, and a lover in the war that they were fighting again, that they were *still* fighting. How had one imagined that one could distinguish between the illusion and the reality?

Out of character, the black bird flurried and scurried among the feet among the seats. It was too late to recapture the fleeting words. The Herald stood below; Debbie drew herself high in her woe. She was carrying a doll at her breast; the doll wept.

She screamed—twice, the second time mezzo-forte. (So we had planned it, in order that one would expect still a third, fortissimo, scream.) Luckily! for it was the fact that the third scream had not yet come, and was expected, that kept one's skull from cracking at the sutures.

Up the gravel drive from among the parked cars, he bore amazingly on his wrist a five-months-old crow that he had found as an abandoned fledgling.

The pipe-music had died away. One yearned for it to sound on, in order to hinder the portent of the silence.

The framework, the porch, was solid. The play was bound to a good reality. The Ionic whorls of the little columns were high breasts, like the girls'. But could this structure outlast the third cry?

The horns of the parked cars began to hoot and call: *hurry!* the ships were busy to start out. No time for this delay and palaver.

No! No!

The auto-horns sounded and shocked the entranced; some of us found our voices and called out, "No! No!"

There was not one present who did not have a son, a father, a lover, a best-friend in the war. How could one imagine that we could distinguish between the play and the reality?

The truth was that they were going to dash the baby from the cliff.

Parents' Day

"But I can't say *that!*" wailed Debbie and burst into tears.
"You can say it."
No! No!
If the youth halted, and the bird dug its claws in his flesh,
about to flutter away; and he was too fascinated and stood
with his mouth half-open—do you think it was an actor
playing a rôle and could not remember his lines?
But the bird *sprang* into the front rows, and Talthybios
proclaimed:

> "Abhor me not!
> I am not willingly the Messenger."

The horns were crying out: no time! the ships. But some
of us found our voices and said, "No!"
She was clutching a doll to her breast. The doll wept.
Nevertheless, Andromache spoke the third scream.

two

FOR ERICA KLEIN

Now am I homeless quite; not only I
but the small boy, my loved and earnest charge
—without a chamber, and the world is large,
our clothes in boxes open to the sky.

Yet just today, tho I could bitterly cry
(secretly from the child, to whom I smile)
and blame the lust and the muse and the lack of guile
that have betrayed me every when I try

—instead! my eyes are wet with glory
for the courage of my and your and every human heart
that hopeful and cheerfully again and again
loves each new home, roots there, takes part,
decorates the place and celebrates its story,
and is not tired, and longs to remain.

Our clothes were in boxes by the road. While we waited
for the taxi, Tony sat on a box and kicked his heels. Moving
was exciting to him.

Persons who calculate whether or not to have children most often wrongly estimate the disadvantages and advantages. What they think of as important would in the event prove to be unimportant; and the things that will eventually cause pain or perhaps give some comfort will never have occurred to them at all. Money, space, liberty; health and temperament and the ability to assume responsibility: these are important factors; but what surprises is the way these factors work out, not as foreseen. The presence of the child produces such an alteration in the way of life that the calculations of former experience are irrelevant. When a new absolute value is working—that is, something existent that one must put up with—the weight of every other value, especially relative values like convenience or mobility, is radically diminished. And from the depths rise, unsuspected, both new strengths and antagonisms that make one weak.

It is a personal trial; one can learn little from other people's experience. (From one's own experience nothing, and from others' very little.) To mention a single point: a man becoming a father might find that he identifies himself with the child, himself as child, or with his father, himself the father; both of these, of course, but *one* rises to the surface, and the balance of the entire personality is altered. No man can foresee how this will work itself out; yet it makes a profound difference to everything else, to career, income, love, courage.

I have not seen, on the whole, that the pleasures or other advantages that people promise themselves from children ever come to be; but plenty of surprising pain and heartache.

With Tony, so far, I had discovered only one strong compensation, a very strong one, and one that without him I should never have learned. It was this: that here was something for which one could do much work and undergo much hardship, *and not need to look for a return.* (The compensation I had discovered was that one did not need to expect a compensation.) There was no return, could be no return. Therefore there was no question of justice or injustice, of exploitation, of hurt pride or hurt feelings. Of being wanted or not being wanted; but instead, simple necessity. If Tony was cheerful and affectionate, as for the most part he was, that was sweet and comforting, but it was not a reward. For whether he was or not, one had to give one's effort to the best of one's ability.

The consequence of this effort, not the purpose of it but simply the inevitable result, was that I was important to someone; I was deeply, inevitably, essentially important to Tony.

One other thing I learned with Tony, that I ought however to have learned previously. Patience. By patience I do not mean holding oneself back in longsuffering, but relying on the underlying forces that move slowly, and less visibly, and beyond our control. These forces are strong; by drawing on them one discovers a truth, recovers health, produces a work, and so forth. With Tony I did not learn to *be* patient; I am impatient; but I learned that that exists and is necessary.

I was bitter, thinking of that school, over there, across the road, thinking of the plan I had dreamed up. The plan of fetching water, sawing wood, picking fruit, kindling a fire. Baking bread. Tending the baby. And the free sexuality of the children.

I shrugged my shoulders—the gesture by which one does not express the anger against them and oneself. My bitterness was impatience. Since I was fundamentally right—I have gotten more and more confirmation of it—since my thought was in keeping with the underlying nature, I might as well be patient; that is, I should find ecstasy and glory in being patient, if I could be patient.

But waiting there in the road for the taxi to come, I was in a bad fix. I could not make a living, to support myself and Tony. The inability to make a living was the occasion, if not the cause, of all my trouble and folly; it drove me to stupid expedients that could not work out, in inappropriate situations.

Yet superficially considered, this inability was an absurdity. I was healthy and not really very indolent; I was clever and well educated. What was wrong with me?

Of course many things were wrong. Yet I could not help but feel that there was one thing that was right that also prevented me from making a living. (I am speaking here for all my artist friends, and it is worth saying.) I was creative, I could invent something, an idea, I could shape something. Obviously this was not done by my own doing, hardly by my own effort. In honesty, then, I could not sell these inventions; they were not worth money; they came to me for nothing—at most a little effort. I had to give them for nothing, or at least offer them, for I had not found that people were eager to take them.

It was hard and bitter that I could not be paid at least for the little effort, but effort as such is not a commodity.

It is true that people did pay money for creations, ideas, inventions. But this was by a dishonest convention. We knew, we temporarily endowed, that what we did was worth no money (worth more than money, of course, for you cannot buy it with all the money). Therefore we had a sense of personal uselessness, of guilt, of worthlessness—related no doubt to every underlying sense of guilt and worthlessness. This put us in an intolerable position on the market; we could not bargain for a price for our worthless, priceless things, not even ours. Rather we cringed, we begged, longing for someone to say, "Freely give what is freely given to you; and here, we love you and here is bread."

Yes! as I loved Tony and gave him bread, and wanted him only to grow and be happy. And if some one among you thinks, if some one should say, "This is an infantile and dependent and servile state," then that person is a false liar. For the truth is that we ought all, all creative and visited by the creator spirit, to love and nourish one another, prior to any questions of dependency, superiority, servility. It is those who have forgotten how to create anything who speak that way. But we give ourselves to it.

Meantime, as the world was, everyone else could, dearly or cheaply, sell his time and things; only I not. This confirmed my sense of being worthless and unwanted. Naturally I reacted with pride and withdrawal, a pride proved rational by the obvious, even famous value of my time and things; and so I confirmed myself in reactive pride. Proud of my poor clothes. Less and less able to make a living.

And where else should I live and work and hope to be visited by the creator spirit except just in our school? If I was an artist, *there* was the subject, and medium, and goal of art, the growth of life. And if I needed to love and be loved, there was the act of love. If I longed for the peace and liberty of mankind, it was only there that I could do something to forward it, for it is only there that it can be forwarded.

I had made many stupid errors. The thought of them did not cheer me. I could not keep the tears from streaming down my cheeks, but I hid them from Tony.

The coal fire was still burning! eight months later thru snow and rain, it was amazing. Max was still hovering near! to keep the flames from spreading. Tony jumped around in the sun and pee'd on the fire and talked to Max.

A horn sounded. "Daddy! here it comes!" cried Tony.

the end

New York City
Winter, 1947–1948

AFTERWORD

Goodman wrote this book in the winter of 1947–1948, when he was thirty-six. It was soon rejected by Madison Avenue. One editor told him that it was the best novel to come across his desk that year . . . but of course we can't publish it. Finally in 1951 an old friend with a press printed up an edition of 500. It got one review. A little book club took it on, but few copies were sold before the firm went out of business. On the best-seller list that year were *The Caine Mutiny, From Here to Eternity,* and *Catcher in the Rye.*

The book is set during the war years, when—like society in general—Goodman hit bottom. His wife had left him and for a while he was literally homeless. Editors and publishers were boycotting his work, which to some seemed seditious, to others simply obscene. And of course his insistence on sexual freedom in life as well as in stories made it difficult to earn a living as a teacher, his other calling.

Adversity did not silence him. On the contrary, some of his liveliest writing—like *Communitas* or *The State of Nature*—came in the wake of black-listing and dismissal. But he realized that there was something wrong with the way he addressed himself to life; it was not merely the world that was full of misery and fury. Therefore in 1946 he had undertaken a systematic self-analysis, using the "practical

257

yoga" techniques he found in the teachings of Wilhelm Reich. *Parents' Day* may be regarded as a second stage in that self-analysis, a literary anatomy of his own motives and morals, performed on the living conscience. Goodman said as much in the brief preface that he wrote for it but then discarded at the last minute:

> . . . the nature of the subject has laid on me, as an author, a painful necessity: to account for myself, for my relations to the children and to the child I am. For if I did not try in good faith to show myself in the action, the subject would be seen thru my dirty glasses without its being shown that I had on, have on, dirty glasses. Therefore the character in this narrative named "I" is drawn as biographically as the author has been able. The other characters are, of course, fictional combinations adapted to the plot.

A similar note is struck in the application he made earlier, and as usual fruitlessly, to the Guggenheim Foundation. From the outset he saw his book as a kind of case-history, taking himself simultaneously as patient and therapist:

> In manner this book marks a change from my fictions of the past ten years. The delineation is naturalistic, rather than expressionist or symbolist. I attempt to dispense altogether with the pervasive irony of my other novels. I try to muster the courage to make absolute judgments of value, after (and by means of) analyzing the motives prompting me.

The challenge of such a conception would be to prevent the novel from becoming merely an exercise in self-justification. Indeed, the fact that he speaks of it as if already complete in the imagination, though little can yet have been on paper, shows how great that danger was. On the one hand he knew that he must avoid irony—the earnestness of his voice depended on there being not a jot of difference between himself and his narrator—and yet on the other hand it was essential that in spite of foreknowledge he should somehow arrive at new discoveries as a result of what happens to him in the course of the novel. His solution was to find these insights in the telling itself, that is, in author's-time or reader's-time, even though they seem to take place in novel-time.

From the opening pages we know that the events are leading to a catastrophe, when the narrator will be unmasked as a pederast who seduces his favorite student. He begins by admitting this, both to the reader and to the other characters:

> Harrison was laying down the dictum that a teacher would not have sexual relations with a student because his position gave him an unfair advantage. . . . I thought that his dictum was correct, but I said, "Yes, it is an unequal advantage; but what if the teacher falls in love—and he can't help himself—or herself?"
>
> I said it as a confession before the fact, to call attention; as a threat; an alibi, whereby I could later say, "But I *told* you so all along."

Even foreshadowing serves as self-revelation when one is writing one's own case-history. As he relates his story Goodman is scrutinizing it for clues, relentlessly dogging his own tracks with second-guesses and dubieties. The story unfolds as both the report of what happened to him and as the psychoanalysis of that report, like the telling and interpretation of a dream.

Goodman spoke of *Parents' Day* as one of his "community novels." He thought of himself as well-suited to communal life, and in truth he thrived whenever he lived or worked in common with others—until they threw him out.

Community is the subject of *Parents' Day* in much the same way that it is at the center of Nathaniel Hawthorne's *Blithedale Romance*, a book that Goodman surely had in mind while writing his own ambivalent tale of utopian longing subverted by love. "Blithedale" was the historic Brook Farm community, of which Hawthorne had been a founding member. His hope was to settle down with his fiancée in an Edenic life of art and agriculture—but this was naive. For one thing, the colony never really paid its way, and Hawthorne would have trouble getting his investment back.

259

Still more significant, among the younger folk there was much flirtation but little matrimony, exclusive love between individuals and loyalty to the group mixing like oil and water. There would be no honeymoon cottages built in West Roxbury, for the atmosphere was not domestic. Hawthorne left before the year was out, and he and Sophia began married life like other people, in rented premises with strangers for neighbors. Ten years later he wrote *The Blithedale Romance* about the incompatibility of love and fellow-feeling.

In somewhat different terms this was also the theme of *Parents' Day*, though unlike Hawthorne Goodman initially views his utopia as an asylum *from* marriage, not *for* it. This communal alternative to the domestic life that has gone sour on him succeeds only so long as he can maintain his social balance. "It seemed to me," he says at the end of Chapter IV, "if I could stay at this distance and this nearness, as I had all day, with no blundering step of fright, I would become progressively happier. It fitted me well, this distance and this nearness. What happened to me, and what I made to happen, would regularize itself if I could stay here."

The assistant director of the school Mark Anders has already warned the narrator that "it's hard to keep the proper distance"—from the students, he means. The reply—that there are enough differences of age and experience to guarantee "natural distance without having to set up conventional barriers"—might make sense in the ordinary course of things, but for a character like Goodman's, still obsessed with the dilemmas of his own early adolescence, it is beside the point. Just as he has predicted, he falls in love, and soon he is admitting, "It seemed to me that because I gave myself more and more to the love I felt for Davy Drood, I withdrew my feeling and concern from the business of our school; partly because there is not enough energy for everything, but especially because it was not possible to have this love and still legitimately regard myself as a member of our school. Rather, giving in to these exceeding feelings, I defied our school."

The first half of the novel, roughly speaking, tells the story of how Goodman is drawn into the healing community; the second half how he is expelled from it. Just as in *The Blithedale Romance,* the conflict is built into the very bones of the novel by the choice of a first-person narrator, whose interactions with other characters are so heavily imbued with consciousness that a reader cannot always tell where observation leaves off and projection begins. Once Goodman gives in to romantic love, his sense of community grows dim, and in its place there appears the vivid paranoid conceit that the authorities are on his trail—as they will be soon enough. Scenes begin to lose their dramatic dimension; they shrivel to the *tête à tête* dynamics of fantasy, the fevered imagination confronting its object.

Even before he falls in love with one of his students, Goodman has chosen his role as provocateur:

> I resolved to do battle according to common sense for the sexual opportunity of these dear young people, disregarding my own twinges of guilt and despite the fact that my own desires and behavior (too blinding for me to distinguish what in them was love and what was fright and what was envy and what was hatred), despite the fact that my own desires must compromise my efforts.

His very first step in this crusade brings him into conflict with the authorities. Having encouraged seventeen-year-old Davy Drood, the late-blooming object of his affections, to approach the girl who has been flirting with him, Goodman makes it a question of policy by requesting permission to provide the pair with contraceptives—adding that he intends to do so regardless of the official decision.

Like any other headmaster Lawrence Dixon refuses, unwilling to risk the consequences for his school. "Who is the girl?" he immediately wants to know. Balked there, he shifts the focus to Goodman's motives, quick to spot the bad faith:

> "This is just why you have homosexual tendencies, in order to have sexual relations with women by proxy, thru other men. Exactly. Now you want to use Davy Drood."

Himself a master of such casuistry, the narrator hastens to agree, all the more since he has brought the matter up in public:

> I was pleased; I was only too eager to air my guilty secrets, and I exclaimed, "Right! this time you hit the nail on the head. Why do you think I have been forced into this stupid way? Not thru *my* doing—but just because when I was at the age of the boys in Lawrence Dixon's group, instead of their encouraging me to love my girls honestly and honorably and gladly, they frightened me, and shamed me, and thwarted me, and made me guilty. It happens that I can remember the exact incidents that did the work! Very banal! But that was not at a so-called progressive school."

Goodman is remembering—though he does not tell us so—the humiliations he suffered in junior high school when he was caught kissing a girl in the hall and sent to sit all day with a class of younger children, his knees pressing the bottom of a third-grader's desk. There were other incidents as well, freshly rankling after his self-analysis, so that it was easy for him to feel the justice of his cause, and not so absurd to offer his perverse motives as a clinching argument. His frankness is disarming; even Dixon is convinced, in principle, and by the end of the scene Goodman has not only managed to have the last word, but to put it in Dixon's mouth: "Probably we are trying to prevent their pleasures simply out of resentment," the director gloomily admits. "Maybe all of it is a rationalization."

Too true! but not merely as a characterization of Dixon's bureaucratic stand. After all, if Goodman were really concerned with his young friend's happiness and sexual freedom, why make such a public issue of it? Why not just buy the contraceptives for the boy, as he means to anyway? To no avail has Davy Drood begged him not to give his secret away. The truth is that Goodman's behavior is calculated to belittle his friend's desire, to embarrass and humiliate him. Ultimately he even manages to thwart his satisfaction, since by the time he produces the condoms Davy has passed into a new stage in his awkward and luckless development, and missed his chance. Dixon says it bluntly, in response to Goodman's tirade: "You think you're a friend to Davy Drood . . . but in fact—you're saying it out of your own mouth—your motives are envy and hatred!"

Later, in a characteristic hairpin-turn of analysis, Goodman admits that Dixon was right; his love for Davy is tainted by envy and resentment of his youth and excellence, and beneath it all lies a layer of anger—for the humiliations he suffered as a child, and will suffer again when the authorities find him out.

The plot contains every element necessary to repeat the catastrophe of his youth. The punishing authority is played by the assistant director Mark Anders, an antagonist as obsessively devoted to sniffing out secrets as Goodman himself. For Anders the dangerous sexuality that must be stamped out is symbolized by Fire. Halfway through the story one of the old school-buildings burns down— spontaneous combustion in the coal cellar—and this event immediately spreads into the system of meanings of the novel. First off, the children are counted and re-counted in a paroxysm of bed-checks that betrays more than normal concern for their well-being. Anders posts round-the-clock guards near the smouldering ruin, its phallic chimney still dangerously erect. Puns like *fire: firing*, rhymes like *desire*, metaphors like *licking* and *contagion*, lurk everywhere. A man who loves to make the sparks fly by beating the fireplace log with a poker, Anders is revealed as a fanatic, while Goodman himself is excused by analogy: "spontaneous combustion" means "but what if I fall in love?" The title itself, throughout the period of composition, was not *Parents' Day* but *The Fire*.

There is something terribly contrived about this aspect of the novel, as I suspect Goodman realized before he was finished; yet he persists in drawing out the allegory, even to the last pages, as if he believed that hidden in it somewhere was the key to his own fiery nature. In his elaboration of this leitmotiv he has much in common with his beloved Davy Drood, who sits in his room day after day playing imaginary baseball, throwing dice and marking down the score in careful record-books. The ritual holds life at a distance, waiting in dread for the moment when suddenly . . . what?

A little episode with his four-year-old child at the very beginning of the novel perfectly illustrates this clinging of the ego to its constructs:

> In the big block-room, we built a bridge together, and each built a building of his own. My character was to build a structure of unbalanced cantilevers, kept firm by adding always more weight on the shorter arm, and so the whole grew more intricate and inter-dependent. Before I could see what he had made, Tony demolished his building with loud joy; but I did not want to knock down mine, and we left it.

Goodman's carefully engineered novel called *The Fire*, a system of tensions and ambivalence held in place by continual efforts of judgment and interpretation, never comes tumbling down. But at a certain point it becomes clear that there is another novel growing in the interstices, a deeper truth about himself forcing its way into the light. Of course this too was planned, expected. Although he does not have the courage of the child, simply to wreak his impulse — *which* impulse? — he does have the faith that if only he keeps laying block on block, higher and higher, at some point a hand will be thrust into the impasse. As he says in Chapter XIII, "Secretly, I felt that if I held back and sufficiently distracted my attention . . . then one day life would sneak up on me from behind and deal me such and such a blow."

To a degree this expectation is fulfilled, in a sequence of plot eruptions that changes the novel from *The Fire* to *Parents' Day*, yet even this revolution does not bring with it the heart's ease he longs for. The discovery is another disappointment.

I have already described how the narrator cannot resist flaunting his secret, longing for the catastrophe that will demolish everything — "with loud joy." The plot is regularly punctuated with such moments, and when the final crisis comes there are few who do not know the truth already, though no one but Mark Anders seems to suspect him of *acting* on his sexual preferences (where there's smoke . . .).

In Chapter I he tells a fellow teacher that because he is homosexual he cannot give good advice about her absent husband; in Chapter III he reveals himself to Davy, the first step toward seduction; by Chapter V Mark Anders knows about his "homosexual tendencies"; and in Chapter VI the director himself can speak of "your homosexual attachment to Davy," though still unwilling to surmise the whole truth. The old Doctor who is the narrator's favorite—a cultivated man and himself a refugee—is the last of the patriarchs to be in on the secret, and he knows by Chapter XI, still three chapters before the confrontation scene.

There is much private meaning in this sequence. Goodman's own father abandoned the family—"ran off with an actress"—just before Paul was born, and this loss accounted for a good deal of his ambivalence toward authority, both his impulse to defy and his yearning for acceptance.

I will have more to say about fathers in a moment; however, even at the climax there is still one person who hasn't been told the truth. After the punishing authorities have dealt with him, and he has made his answer, the narrator immediately boards a train for Manhattan, not to escape but to dive deeper into humiliation. He goes to reveal himself to the most threatening figure of all, Davy Drood's mother, in a scene toward which we now see the whole novel has been inexorably moving.

The significance of Davy's mother is not something that dawns on the narrator at the last moment; on the contrary, he has his theory ready at their first meeting, on Parents' Day at the school:

> Always it was not these boys that I was bent for but in the end the mothers of these boys. *This* was the respectability, the regularity, the due process leading to acknowledged power, that I, who was unkempt, rebellious, and begrudged, was fantasying when I fathered myself on Davy Drood and the others—to be the cause of their perfection, to unmake the damage in myself.

265

At their final encounter Goodman brings nothing further to light, but the scene between them serves as a kind of re-enactment of a childhood memory, with what release of feeling every reader must judge. The unkempt narrator carefully cleans himself up before going to face her. He tells her the truth about his seduction of her son; then he bitterly accuses her of neglecting Davy and of demanding an impossible manliness from him. Ann Drood does not want to hear these things. She waves Goodman's confession aside in distaste. She has another appointment and asks him to leave; he offers to accompany her to the street, but she refuses—"No, be a good boy. You go ahead." These are her last words to him, "be a good boy."

In spite of all preparation, there is something unexpected about this scene, something out of control. The point is not that Goodman learns anything new, but rather, that for once he allows what he does not know to exist, dramatically, instead of smothering it with analysis.

In the next scene—the final one—we see the fantasy played out once again, this time ritualistically, in the student production of *The Trojan Women*. Talthybios the herald steps forth, a raven clutching his upraised wrist, to speak the fatal words to Andromache:

> "Abhor me not!
> I am not willingly the messenger."

This time the mother will not have another engagement.

Now, for a second glimpse of expectations overthrown with less "loud joy" than hoped for, let us return to the father figures. Dixon is the most appealing of them; his views are closest to the narrator's, and his commitment to the students is most complete and trustworthy. It is not their final confrontation that contains the clue to Dixon's significance, but an earlier scene between them, in which the dialogue suddenly gets out of hand, quite beyond the bounds of ordinary verisimilitude. The narrator is expecting the worst, the long-awaited accusation, but instead he is amazed to hear the director confessing to him that he,

Lawrence Dixon, is Davy Drood's father. No one knows the truth, says Dixon, not Davy, not even Davy's mother. How can this be?

The narrator tries valiantly to find the handle on Dixon's revelation—"in a sense you're the father of them all, aren't you?"—but this is not what he has in mind. "I'm their teacher. I'm Davy's father." To this the narrator replies, "I see. I understand," but in fact he does not see at all, nor is it possible for the reader to comprehend this confession. One might guess that Dixon, always a bit balmy, has gone mad; as the book nears its climax one after another of the characters is revealed to be at wit's end. The world is crazy. But such an explanation explains nothing. Goodman offers no commentary, and we are left to absorb the revelation as best we can. No further reference is made to it.

Some readers will take this as a flaw, an unraveled thread in the novel. I regard it as one of its truest moments, though I cannot say precisely what it means, aside from reiterating the possibility of "fathering oneself" on someone else, as Goodman says he too has done with Davy. The important thing is that here with Dixon, as later with Ann Drood, Goodman renounces analysis. He dares to let his characters step beyond their bounds, no longer oversees their acts; they take charge.

Goodman finally realized that the fulcrum of his novel had shifted, though not till after he had finished it did he rename it. It was no longer the account of how he fell in love, seduced his student, and was unmasked and punished. *The Fire* might be an adequate symbol of that plot, but not of the new meanings that had found their way into his book. And so the title was changed to one that hinted murkily at the truth: *Parents' Day*.

To understand parents one must understand children. Insofar as there is any solution to the problem of parents in *Parents' Day*, it lies in the children—in their collective presence as the given, the task—and especially in the narrator's four-year-old Tony, who at the end of the book comes into prominence. As he sits by the road waiting for the taxi to come and take them away, the narrator sees that the child is all he has left, and considers the meaning of being a parent:

> It is a personal trial; one can learn little from other people's experience. (From one's own experience nothing, and from others' very little.) To mention a single point: a man becoming a father might find that he identifies himself with the child, himself as child, or with his father, himself the father; both of these, of course, but *one* rises to the surface, and the balance of the entire personality is altered. No man can foresee how this will work itself out; yet it makes a profound difference to everything else, to career, income, love, courage.
>
> I have not seen, on the whole, that the pleasures or other advantages that people promise themselves from children ever come to be; but plenty of surprising pain and heartache.
>
> With Tony, so far, I had discovered only one strong compensation, a very strong one, and one that without him I should never have learned. It was this: that here was something for which one could do much work and undergo much hardship, *and not need to look for a return.* (The compensation I had discovered was that one did not need to expect a compensation.) There was no return, could be no return. Therefore there was no question of justice or injustice, of exploitation, of hurt pride or hurt feelings. Of being wanted or not being wanted; but instead, simple necessity. If Tony was cheerful and affectionate, as for the most part he was, that was sweet and comforting, but it was not a reward. For whether he was or not, one had to give one's effort to the best of one's ability.
>
> The consequence of this effort, not the purpose of it but simply the inevitable result, was that I was important to some one; I was deeply, inevitably, essentially important to Tony.

Tony is his justification. The school authorities won't have him but Tony needs him. It does little good for the fathers and mothers of the book to tell the narrator he must grow up, and indeed, up to the last moment in his narrative he has refused to be on the parents' side: he spends Parents' Day, for instance, with Davy's mother, not Tony, and other appearances of the little boy have often been occasions for flight on the part of the narrator, accompanied by wails from the child and guilt in his father's heart. Yet there have also been songs and play, loving attention and dutiful concern. Now, at the end, it is apparent that however much the narrator has resisted being a father, has tried instead to be one of the children (refusing to keep "the proper distance"), he nonetheless *is* a father and must accept his place in the world of adults.

He has resisted because he is unwilling to take on the burdens of fatherhood—for example, the tics and knots of character that plague even so shrewd and good-hearted a man as Lawrence Dixon, who has "fathered himself" on Davy and the others, and thereby achieved "the respectability, the regularity, the due process leading to acknowledged power" that Goodman envies in him.

Davy's mother is not the only one who tells him to "grow up"—all of society insists on it. He has fled from that world to a utopia of children, believing that here at least they do not make war or sell their lives as commodities; but there is no escape into Never-Never Land for this Peter Pan. That is the meaning of the gloomy sentiment he puts in the mouth of Dixon:

"Hm. But there is a fatal conflict between our characters with our persistent pasts and our growth in the living present. This flaw is pervasive, in the staff, in the children. I have it, you have it, they have it.

"Hm. There is another conflict, between our good educational practice and the crazy mores of the world. I shouldn't be surprised, I shouldn't be surprised at all, if there were a close relation between our damaged characters and the crazy mores of the world.

"Do you want the truth? I am not afraid of the truth—I will drink to the truth—" He filled another cup. "The truth is that we are engaged in a job really beyond our wisdom and available energy. The results are dubious."

Goodman meant this to apply to Dixon and all the others, including himself, as is demonstrated by his repeating it in the preface, in his own voice, where he also gives the reply of Dixon's drunken girlfriend, perhaps the most "damaged" character of them all:

> "Do not drink to that!" cried Seraphia, to my astonishment, and she knocked the cup out of his hands. "Apart from people like us, nobody is doing anything about it at all."

It is half the lesson of growing up—that apart from the world of damaged characters, doing their best *and* their worst, there is no society, no community. Life is what it is. This was an important recognition for the social philosopher of the Sixties, the future author of *Growing Up Absurd.*

The other half of the lesson of growing up is that, just as there is no ideal community apart from the society we all inhabit, so too there is no key, no solution, to the problem of one's own nature and fate. Goodman liked to quote the saying of Adler, that as a child one believes there is some secret which only the adults know, and that growing up means discovering that there is no such secret. Goodman began his book as an attempt to solve the enigma of his own behavior, trusting that even if self-analysis failed, still, having given himself over so completely to the search, life would sneak up behind and, Zen-like, deal him such and such a blow of enlightenment. This too was a miscalculation. Yes, there are surprises—that is why he has to change the title of his book—but in the end he finds that he has misunderstood the kind of insight possible. His insight is that there will be no insight.

At the crisis Lawrence Dixon's first response is to try to rescue the narrator: "We must put you in the hands of an internationally-famous psychoanalyst. This will satisfy the trustees." After a whole book of barren self-analysis, the narrator finds this hilarious: "No! no!" he tells us gleefully. "That's what happened."

The resources of analysis have been exhausted, and Goodman is left with the unwelcome truth that society is what

270

it is, that he is who he is. Yet by this very fact of exhaustion he is a changed man. Analysis has after all brought him to the moment, in the final pages, when he turns away in exasperation and disgust: "The devil with it! Let me describe again the excellences of our school. . . ."

None of this makes him happy or brings him peace, nor is he now satisfied to renounce the child in himself and assume adult obligations and rewards. To be sure, he agrees to the fathering of his own small son, which he regards as necessity, the bedrock of existence, but he also demands the right to preserve the child in himself, the artist. This is his final word in the novel, that an artist *must* live as a child, and that society ought to care for him, for all its artists, as a parent does a child:

> Yes! as I loved Tony and gave him bread, and wanted him to grow and be happy. And if some one among you thinks, if some one should say, "This is an infantile and dependent and servile state," then that person is a false liar. For the truth is that we ought all, all creative and visited by the creator spirit, to love and nourish one another, prior to any questions of dependency, superiority, servility. It is those who have forgotten how to create anything who speak that way. But we give ourselves to it. . . .
>
> And where else should I live and work and hope to be visited by the creator spirit except just in our school?

But his community will not have him, not on these terms, and he will accept no others.

—*Taylor Stoehr*

271

Printed May 1985 in Santa Barbara & Ann Arbor
for the Black Sparrow Press by Graham Mackintosh
& Edwards Brothers Inc. Design by Barbara
Martin. This edition is published in paper
wrappers; there are 300 cloth trade copies;
& 150 numbered deluxe copies have been hand-
bound in boards by Earle Gray.

Photo credit: Ruth Staudinger

Paul Goodman (1911–1972) the well-known social critic (*Growing Up Absurd, Communitas*, and many other books) had several careers before his fame in the Sixties as the philosopher of the New Left. He was trained in philosophy at CCNY and the University of Chicago, taught literature in various colleges, became an expert on community planning with his architect brother Percival Goodman, taught in a progressive school, founded with Fritz Perls the Gestalt Therapy Institute and practiced psychotherapy, married and raised three children — all while living on an average income about that of a Southern sharecropper (when he started doing therapy in the early Fifties, his income jumped to $2,000 for the first time in his life). But these were just his sidelines, and the reason that he lived in voluntary poverty rather than following one of the more lucrative callings open to him was that he regarded his work as a creative artist as his true vocation. Among his thirty-odd books his novels, plays, short stories, and poems would fill a shelf by themselves. His masterpiece is *The Empire City*, a comic epic written in the tradition and with the zest of *Don Quixote*. His *Collected Poems* contain, among hundreds of fine poems, the extraordinary sequence he wrote in mourning for his son Mathew, *North Percy*, probably the most moving elegy in American letters. His short stories, collected in four volumes by Black Sparrow, contain such anthology pieces as "The Facts of Life." Published in a tiny edition in 1951, *Parents' Day* has been out of print for several decades, during which time it has become an underground classic.